The Canine in All of Us

The Canine in All of Us

To Dan

Happy Birthday!
Best wishes!

Daniel Desjardin

Daniel Desjardin

Library of Congress Control Number:		2010910842
ISBN:	Hardcover	978-1-4535-4331-3
	Softcover	978-1-4535-4330-6
	Ebook	978-1-4535-4329-0

This book was printed in the United States of America.

To order additional copies of this book, contact:
Xlibris Corporation
1-888-795-4274
www.Xlibris.com
Orders@Xlibris.com
84294

Dedication

To my very special friend, Tamela, who inspired me with her sense of humor and friendship. To the other girls in my life Marianne, and Nancy who inspire me day to day with treasured memories. To my coworkers, and dear friends that gave me the inspiration to write with laughter from the heart. To my sister Debbie, for her love and miss very much. To my parents, who made me the person I am, And finally to the one who stood by me for twenty two years with love and support in my life's decisions. I love you!

CHAPTER ONE

Donald Freeman is a thirty-five-year-old single man who stands 5'8" with an average build and weighs 175 lbs with short brown hair parted down the middle, who wore contact lenses that showed off the true color of his hazel green eyes. Everyone who knew Donald would say he had an outgoing personality and was very charming and polite. For his upbringing, he grew up in Sutton Falls, Massachusetts, where the Douglas and Fraser firs covered the hills, which are known for making the area smell like Christmas year-round. His parents, William and Sharon, owned and operated a seventy-five-acre campground for seasonal campers there. The campground was known for its historic covered bridge, which separated a small pond by a waterfall that emptied into a winding stream of ice-cold clear water, which flowed downstream into a huge lake a few miles down the road. The chirping of the crickets and the sounds of the croaking bullfrogs lying along the banks of the stream could be heard throughout the campground as the sunset faded into darkness. It was as if they were talking to one another. Donald remembered once while he was walking along the bank of the stream, picking up debris that littered the flow of the ice-cold water, when the croaking sounds had stopped, it was as if he had interrupted a long-distance call between friends by the sudden fall of phone lines by human contact.

The summertime was so busy with the campers coming from all over New England; some seasonal campers started arriving as early as the Memorial weekend. Some of them stayed for weeks at a time while other families stayed until Labor Day weekend, when the park officially closed for the winter months.

The city folks came to get away from the hustle and bustle of their workweek to relax and have fun. There was swimming, fishing, canoeing, horseshoes and volleyball, and plenty of hills around the campsites for hiking.

The campers got in touch with nature and the wildlife that roamed throughout the campgrounds looking for food. There were deer, ducks, raccoons, fox, and a variety of birds.

The smell of the hamburgers and hot dogs sizzling on the open fires like miniature firecrackers over open flames drove them out of the woods into the campsites looking for their next meal. There was always something going on throughout the campgrounds; some of the seasonal campers sat around playing cards and drinking until the wee hours of the morning, while the teenagers and their friends hung out at the covered bridge or down by the swing sets that was at the entrance of the campgrounds and across from the country store that sold ice cream sandwiches and cones and other supplies that the campers may need. The store carried a variety of things that would get the campers through until they drove for miles to the nearest supermarket to get what they really needed. The teenagers and kids would hang out in these two areas until their parents came down from their campsite with flashlights in hand telling them that they needed to head back to the campsite for the evening and it was getting late. These were Donald's fondest memories of Sutton Falls that he will always carry with him. It was his time to move on and get on with his life and out of the harsh cold winters at the age of thirty and leave home.

He relocated to Coral Springs, Florida, and purchased a very spacious two-bedroom, two-bath townhome along with the bank for the asking price of an unbelievable price of sixty-five thousand dollars at the time of purchase while he was relocating from Sutton Falls. Donald lived with his dog Freeway, which he rescued while driving along a stretch of Highway 75—an expressway in Broward County—one Saturday afternoon when he came upon him just walking in the gulley along the side of the road. Freeway was a border collie, black-and-white with two white front paws. He was wearing a bright red dog collar from what he could tell. By his appearance, he looked frightened, scared, and very hungry. Being concerned for the safety of this dog, he pulled over to the side of the road to try to help him. Donald stepped out of his 2001 candy apple red BMW, with a few sticks of beef jerky that he had with him in his car. Donald loved to chew on beef jerky while driving. It was his only substitute for smoking since he gave up cigarettes four weeks ago. He called out to this dog, "Here, boy! Here, boy!" several times; then the dog had stopped in his tracks as he heard Donald's voice calling out to him. Now Freeway turned around and looked back to see who was calling him. Donald was waving some of the beef jerky with his hands to try to get his attention and to keep him from walking any farther along this busy stretch of road, which was just east of the everglades. Donald was successful in completing this dangerous task, as the cars drove by with onlookers. He was successful by luring him into his BMW and took him to his town house where he was going to take care of him and keep him from getting hurt or cause danger to anyone else by dashing out in front of a car, trying to cross the expressway.

Upon reaching home, Donald lured the dog once again out of the car and into the town house with the rest of the beef jerky that he had left. Donald then proceeded to talk to him to let him know that it was going to be all right, that he was safe, that he was going to take care of him, that he didn't have to be scared, that he was only trying to help him, and that everything was going to be okay. Donald then proceeded to the main bathroom, which was on the first floor, and drew a bathtub full of warm water while he gathered several beach towels and shampoo from the bathroom closet, which he was going to use to bath and dry the dog off with.

Donald then walked back into the hallway where he saw Freeway sitting on the tile floor in the entryway of the town house just staring up at the door as if to say, "Let me out. I know I came in through this door so this must be the same way out." Donald then proceeded to pick up the dog from his underbelly, carried him into the bathroom, and then gently lowered him into the warm bath with no resistance whatsoever from the dog. Freeway attempted to jump out of the tub and to escape as Donald splashed water all over him before the shampoo treatment came next. Freeway shook and shook from left to right several times to get the water off his black-and-white coat, like dogs normally do after getting wet. He was just being a dog, and Donald did not mind; anything was better than the smell he was carrying around with him when he found him. Donald then proceeded to lather him up from head to toe and then rinsed him off and gently took him by the front paws to help him climb out of the tub and on to the towels so he could be dried off, when he made his escape to freedom from Donald's arms and made a dash for it. Which being in a town house limited his places to go.

He ran into the kitchen area of the town house where he sat on the floor, waiting for Donald to come around the corner. Donald then followed him to the kitchen and wondered if the dog was still hungry. Instead of going back to the bathroom and cleaning up the mess, he just made his way to the kitchen to get Freeway settled in.

Donald opened up his refrigerator door to see what he had to feed him. There were a few leftovers from a few nights ago that he could feed him until he could get to the store for dog food. He had leftover chicken tenders from the night before, which Freeway devoured in seconds. Then came a couple of slices of meat loaf from two nights ago, which went down quicker than the chicken tenders did. This dog must have still been hungry because he nudged Donald's hand with his cold nose as if to say, "You have any more?"

Donald spoke to the dog and told him, "I have no more food. I will have to go out and get some more food for you in the morning." Donald tried to calm the dog down, but all he did was whine and cry. The dog was still shaking tremendously; was it from the bath? On the other hand, was it the ordeal of being out there on the expressway?

Donald then spoke down to the dog and said, "We now have to find a place for you to sleep!" Donald then walked over to the hall closet and pulled out an old quilt that was given to him from his grandmother years ago before she passed away, which was his favorite. It was handmade with love, from the stitching right down to the fine details of vibrant colors that was put into making it. Its colors reminded him of the foliage in the fall in Sutton from the maple trees in the area and around the campground.

There were shades of oranges, corals, beiges, greens, and yellows. and other colors you might see in the fall if you lived in New England. Donald only brought this out on those too few cold nights of cold weather, which South Florida only experienced once or twice a year if at all.

The quilt was rather torn and tattered from all the wash and dry cycles that it had gone through. Donald placed this on the floor next to his queen-size bed so that he could keep an eye on the dog and yet make him comfortable as possible while being in his care. Donald then walked over to his computer, which was on the other side of the bedroom, sitting up on the antique oak desk that was handed down to him from his dad, which was handed down from his father, Donald's grandfather. He then proceeded to work on the flyers to pass around the neighborhood the next several days, hoping that someone would come forward to claim this dog. He then took out his digital camera from one of the side draws, took several photos of the dog as he lay on the quilt on the floor, and then proceeded to transfer them to his computer; he was going to add them to the flyers for more of a visual effect.

It was a Sunday morning, so Donald headed out to the local convenience store around the corner from his town house to get some dog food and a leash before Freeway woke up, who was sound asleep on the quilt, making strange sounds as if he was dreaming. He left one of the flyers with the young man working behind the counter and asked if he could tape it to the front door so other customers coming in might recognize this found dog.

Donald was going to pass out the rest of the flyers on the way to work on Monday to other convenience stores and gas stations on his route to work, hoping that someone would recognize this dog as they stopped off for coffee or gas. He thanked the young man for his willingness to place his flyer on the glass door as he paid for his few groceries and canned dog food and a new bright red leash since the other collar that Freeway was wearing was rather torn and dirty. Donald headed home before Freeway woke up, and he was able to feed him and take him out for some playtime to the local dog park in hopes that someone there might recognize him. They spent the entire day outdoors, and before they knew it, sunset was approaching, and darkness was not far around the corner. They had fun walking, running, and interacting with the other dogs at the park that Freeway was so exhausted from a full day of exercise he fell asleep on the front seat of the BMW on the way back to the town house. It was going to be an early night for the both of them; after a little television and food, they both fell sound asleep. On the floor on Grandma's quilt was Freeway dreaming away from the sounds he was making and Donald up on the sofa, snoring loudly away.

Monday morning was finally here before Donald knew it. He was up, showered, and ready for work. He had already taken Freeway out for his morning tinkle on the fire hydrant around the corner and then continued on with his morning jog around the block with Freeway in tow. Then back to the town house where he had showered and dressed, ready to head out to work. However, not before he stopped along the way to pass out a few flyers, which he did for the remainder of the week. Donald was hoping to pass out all fifty flyers that he had printed up by the time the weekend arrived.

In the mean time, the dog that he named Freeway was sound asleep on Grandma's quilt at the town house behind a closed bedroom door. Donald wasn't going to take the chance of coming home to a huge mess or something destroyed in the town house, so he closed him off in the bedroom, the only room that he could deal with if a mess was to be found upon arriving home from work.

Freeway remained there for most of the week except for his daily walk to the fire hydrant and during mealtime when Donald came home from work in the evening.

Several weeks have passed by and yet no luck or response from the flyers. Donald then made an appointment with a vet from the yellow pages and took the dog that he named Freeway to the vet for a wellness exam and had him checked over to make sure there were no signs of any kind of canine diseases, and at the same time just maybe some kind of identification from a possible microchip might be implanted under his thick black fur coat. This would tell him whom he belonged to. Those days of manually tattooing some kind of identification usually with numbers is no more. It has now been replaced with new technology, using the microchips. After a rabies shot, several vials of blood samples were taken from Freeway among the rest of the other shots, which were required by the county in which he lived in. Donald and Freeway then left the veterinarian's office with a clean bill of health along with his rabies tag and license.

Freeway was good for an entire year before having to go back to the vets. Donald was now able to call him his very own. Donald was pleased with the results that Freeway was in good health but yet somewhat disappointed that there was no identification whatsoever to be found on Freeway to find out who his rightful owners might be or anyone who might have the rights to him.

Donald was shocked over the amount of the vet's bill, which had amounted to a few hundred dollars, which he didn't expect to be paying so much for when he wasn't sure he would be able to keep the dog, unless the rightful owners did not come forward to claim him. Donald was happy though that he had done a good thing and saved this dog's life from any harm to himself by being out there on the expressway.

Donald now had a companion to keep him company and to take to the park and exercise with by throwing a Frisbee around. Freeway and Donald spent the next month bonding and getting to know each other's habits. Donald would get up at eight o'clock in the morning to get ready for work, and Freeway would get up at five o'clock in the morning to want to go outside and pee on the fire hydrant. They had come to a compromise, and they both would get up around six thirty in the morning. This way Donald would be able to jog around the block to get his morning exercise, and Freeway could then pee on the fire hydrant and join him in his jog before he gets ready for work. Freeway now had the privilege of sleeping on the foot of the bed at night, rather than on the floor on Grandma's quilt.

Donald had the right to the sofa, which Freeway had to give up and was off-limits when he came home from work. Freeway was rather contented lying on Grandma's quilt, chewing on his rawhide bones. They both seemed to like the new living arrangements and were more tolerant with one another. Donald just kept on reporting to work at 9:00 a.m. as he had done for the past four years, but this day, September 5, was about to change everything for him, as the months had gone by for him and Freeway since they have grown to know one another.

Donald was in for a shock of his life once he arrived at work where he was greeted by Lisa, the sister of the owner of the shoe store that Donald was manager of. Donald was also a close friend of her brother, and he was just informed that her brother had just passed away in the middle of the night from a heart attack and that his position was going to be let go in four weeks. Saddened and upset over the news, Lisa had no option but to close the doors to her brother's business, which was in women's shoes and accessories. She was going to close the doors after her brother was to be laid to rest in his hometown in San Francisco where he grew up most of his life near her home. Donald was in awe of the loss of his longtime friend and boss and, on top of this news, also losing his job. He would be getting six weeks' pay as compensation for his service to her brother's business since she had no choice but to sell the store or close it down. The economy was not so great, so the sale of the business was the only option. She asked if he could stay on for four more weeks until she could find a buyer or sell off what she could at bargain prices and donate the rest of the inventory to a homeless shelter downtown. Donald was okay with that but deep down was not. So that same evening on the way home from work, from being saddened and depressed by the loss of his job and good friend, Donald decided to stop at the local hangout in the neighborhood for a few drinks before heading home.

He needed to let this bad news settle in, which was just about the time happy hour started, and his drink of choice was Jack and Coke, which had a special three for the price of one for the next two hours.

As Donald sat and drank at the bar, he watched the customers come and go; when the two hours special was just ending, it was now approaching the eight o'clock hour. Donald was already falling off his bar stool after putting down six of his favorite cocktail, which were more Jack than Coke. He needed to get his drunken ass home to walk Freeway and to feed him as well as his self. The snacks on the bar were not enough to absorb the liquor consumption he had just taken in. He was only a few blocks away from the town house, so he drove carefully down the backstreets, trying to avoid any police cars or tickets or even an arrest. Therefore, he paid his tab and stumbled to the door and across the parking lot to his car. He fumbled with his keys to unlock the car door and climbed in to the driver's seat and put the car keys into the ignition and started the car. In addition, he proceeded to back out of his parking space very slowly and headed for home. While he was sitting at the bar drinking, reality was finally sinking in. He was about to be unemployed in four weeks and terrified of what might become of his home and Freeway. Could he end up losing his home? How was he going to take care of his bills? Would he possibly lose everything, and would all he had worked so hard for be gone in an instant?

Upon arriving home, he found Freeway chewing and tearing up his favorite video collection of *I love Lucy* tapes, which you could no longer purchase, which was an entire collection like no other; it had every episode released on television as well as the outtakes and bloopers during the making of the television show. It was a thank-you gift from one of the seasonal campers back in Sutton falls for saving his dog that had fallen out of a rowboat in the pond while he was fishing, and the dog did not know how to swim because he only had three legs. His right hind leg was gone due to a birth defect.

So the owners turned him over to a local animal shelter to be adopted out. They did not want him. It was his way of saying thank-you for saving the dog. Donald was only a few yards away on the pond in his own canoe, when he dove into the water as he watched this nightmare come alive before his eyes. He felt the need to assist this person in rescuing his dog. He had compassion for living creatures and wanted to be helpful in any way possible to rescue this dog,

He was so mad and furious at this very moment and not thinking clearly and under the influence of several Jack and Coke's, and maybe Freeway was looking for some attention and that this was just his way of reaching out, or was it retaliation for him not being home on time? Donald grabbed Freeway by the bright red collar, scolded him, and then walked him down to his car, where he threw him into the front seat and drove off in the direction of the expressway. Where was he heading with him? Freeway was just being a dog and by the yelling from Donald, which made him more nervous, couldn't help it and just relieved himself on the front leather seat of Donald's BMW. This made matters worse for Freeway. Donald pulled off to the side of the road just around the area where he had first found Freeway wondering months ago and rescued him from traffic.

What could possibly happen now to make Donald's day seem like a piece of cake? Donald's day was about to change for him in the worst possible way. He was about to be arrested by a highway patrol officer named

Mario Perez who was approaching the BMW from the rear just a few feet away as he was pulling Freeway out of the car and got caught doing the most heinous thing that any human being could do!

Donald was going to leave Freeway out on the side of the road where they first met. Officer Mario Perez was a highway patrol officer, male, who was thirty-eight years old, muscular build, black hair, blue eyes, at an early age Erik Estrada. Some of his fellow female officers would say that "his ego precedes him twenty seconds before he entered the room." But that was the female officers who thought he was too cocky. He has worked traffic patrol duty in the Broward County sheriff's office for the past four years. His position with the sheriff's office was with the traffic department. His assignments were to the major expressways, looking for careless drivers who were driving recklessly and ticketing them and sometimes making an arrest depending on the situation at hand.

Officer Perez pulled up behind Donald's car with his flashing lights on. He stepped out of his patrol car and walked over to Donald and Freeway and proceeded to ask him what he was doing "out here this time of night with this dog?" Once the officer got a whiff of the Jack and Coke on Donald's breath, Office Perez read him his rights and ordered him to turn around with his hands behind his back and handcuffed and arrested Donald on the spot for animal cruelty and driving under the influence of alcohol.

Freeway ran up the incline and headed for the woods just a few feet away from Donald and the officer on the side of the road of the expressway. For just one brief moment, Freeway stopped in his tracks and turned around to see what was happing with Donald and then ran off into the brush.

Donald was now handcuffed and placed in the backseat of the police cruiser as Officer Perez placed a call on the police radio to dispatch and asked that they send a tow truck to come and impound the BMW.

When vehicles are usually towed by the sheriff's office, they are usually taken to an unknown location until the suspect is released from jail. That is when the owners have to pay for the towing and additional fifty dollars per day while the automobile is in storage at the tow yard. Donald was now going to have to pay some hefty fines.

Officer Perez and Donald now were going for a little drive downtown to the sheriff's office once the BMW was removed off the expressway and booked for the charges he was just arrested for.

CHAPTER TWO

LaVonda Georgia was a forty-five-year-old female who stands 5'7, medium build, and with black shoulder-length hair with salt-and-pepper highlights that show the real beauty in her blue eyes. She was born and raised in a small town named Hickory Cove in southern Georgia, but she moved around a lot between Tennessee and North Carolina, then eventually back to Hickory Cove. She was a widow with three children—two boys, one named Matthew who was ten years old and the other son named Scott who was twelve years old, along with a daughter named Savannah, eight years old. She struggled to make ends meet to keep her family together after the loss of her husband, Earl, who died of a heart attack while on a weekend hunting trip with his friends. She eventually found a job working with the Internal Revenue Service for fifteen years, until her termination for accessing restricted information from their database. The IRS filed criminal charges against her. However, the lack of evidence against her was not enough to send her away to prison. A trial lasted a week, and her trial ended up in a hung jury verdict. This lasted over a four-day period of deliberations. LaVonda was finally released from the local jail where she was incarcerated for two months, to go back into society and pick up where she left off in her life. A fresh new start somewhere else was what she needed to forget the nightmare she had been through and wished had never happened.

Now LaVonda's three children are all grown-up and living on their own. She had two sons and a daughter. Matthew who moved back to Hickory Cove was twenty-five years old, single, very handsome, with black hair and blue eyes that just makes your heart melt, and had a way with women. He had a reputation that would put a dog to sleep if any of the women with boyfriends or husbands who flirted ever caught him while tending bar. He was just one of those men that you had to spend at least one night with to say you conquered Mt. Everest. His looks along with his Southern charm was very pleasing to any women as well as a few of the male patrons who he made drinks for while bartending. Women would just throw themselves at him. He worked part-time as a bartender, making good tips on an average night, three to five hundred dollars per night, while he went to the community college part-time to become a veterinarian. It was his dream ever since he was kid when he recalls taking the family pets to the veterinarian's with his father, growing up and seeing just how many animals needed attention and how cute and adorable they were and yet helpless due to an illness or injury, and he wanted to help them get better. He once told his father on the way home one day from the vet's office that he wanted to grow up and become one of those doctors who helped god's creatures, and with a smile on his father's face, he said to him, "You can be whatever you want to be as long as you set your mind at it." It was a dream that was only six months away until he had to take his final exam with the hope of passing and his father looking down at him as his guardian angel, and he would receive his degree and become a veterinarian. His father would have been proud if he was only around to see him as he struggled to get to this point in his life with working long hours and going to school days, becoming the caring young man that he grew up to be and making his dream come true.

His brother Scott on the other hand was living the simple life in the mountains of North Carolina, in a log cabin that he built himself with the help of a few friends.

Scott was now a park forest ranger who rode through the mountains and hills looking for any danger of forest fires left behind by campers and tourists who like to visit and set up camp along the trails that overlooked the majestic mountains and streams of North Carolina. His favorite time of year was when the seasons changed, the trees had turned to autumn colors, and the air was crisp and cool. The shades from deep oranges to the dark greens reminded him of why he chose to become a park ranger. The deer and wildlife that just roamed the hills were just breathtaking. From time to time, he would spot a buck or a doe just drinking from the cold spring waters that flowed throughout his area that he was in charge of watching and protecting. He had a dog that was always by his side. He was a golden retriever that he called Scout because he reminded him of the time he was a Boy Scout and the camping trips and weekends hiking as a young boy. He found Scout at a rescue center that was about to close down due to financial needs, and he was one of the remaining few dogs left behind that needed to go to a good home before it closed its doors. Scout was about three years old at the time when Scott took him in to keep him company at the log cabin up there in the mountains. After all, Scott could only go so long without having someone or something to keep him company in the cabin up in those hills.

Single and loving it, the outdoors and Scout were the only interests in his life, and he was very much content with that.

Savannah, their sister, was now twenty-three years old and living in Nashville, Tennessee, where she and her husband, Dusty, who was thirty, had set up home. Dusty had come into some money from a settlement due to a bus accident on the way home from work one evening when the bus he was riding in slipped off the icy road.

The bus driver had a mild seizure while driving the bus. The bus driver and several of its passengers had suffered some injuries. Dusty then was awarded a large amount of money in the settlement from the bus company due to the accident where he lost his feelings from the waist down and was now wheelchair bound. Savannah did not care about the money; it was her love for Dusty that kept them together. After all, they were childhood sweethearts and had spent a lot of time together. He was the love of her life; now that he could no longer be intimate with Savannah, she always had her trusty old friend that she had stashed away in the cookie jar if she wanted pleasure. They built a home on a five-acre piece of land with a small pond where Dusty would sit in his wheelchair, trying to catch the catfish that he stocked in the pond. He would then carry them up to the house in a basket that sat on his lap for Savannah to cook when she felt the need for her fried catfish and green bean casserole and corn bread surprise, along with her mother's favorite peach cobbler that she loved so very much for dessert. Savannah would send Dusty off to catch fish while she did a little fishing of her own "from the cookie jar." Children were not an issue for them. He could not give her any, and she did not really want any.

She was so busy taking care of Dusty that whatever time she had left for herself, she would spend it horseback riding at the neighbor's property next door or getting her hair done at Tanya's House of Beauty and then off shopping for nice, pretty clothes that she only had the chance to wear while attending church on Sundays as she wheeled Dusty down the aisle of the church to the front pew. This way the women in the church could see how pretty she really was while hiding the sadness that really was inside. Savannah would then invite some of the church ladies over after service for refreshments of iced tea and mint juleps and homemade cookies, which was in another cookie jar next to the one where she had stored her trusty friend, which incidentally was now uncovered by one of the women from church as she was helping set up a tray of cookies to take out to the men who were gathered outside the house, talking about the catfish in the pond and the upcoming fishing tournament that was going to be in town next week. Juanita, who found the pleasure toy in the wrong cookie jar, had just lost her partial teeth as she opened her mouth as she gasped and was horrified. Juanita then carried the pleasure toy wrapped in a paper towel and waved it around into the living room where the ladies were all sitting and just talking. Savannah turned beet red of embarrassment in front of the other church ladies, grabbed the towel, and dashed off to the bedroom where she slammed the door and did not come out. The church ladies busted into laughter. A couple of them got up and walked over to the bedroom door and knocked on it, and one said, "It's okay, honey, we all have one. It's just that we don't hide it in the cookie jar." Then, in a split second, the bedroom door opened up, and there was Savannah standing there with a big smile on her face.

LaVonda decided to relocate to South Florida to start a new beginning in her own life. She now owns and operates a homeless shelter from her six-bedroom, three-bath Victorian home built around the late eighteen hundreds, which she purchased for a mere two hundred and thirty thousand dollars. The square footage alone was around 3,800 square feet. There were some major renovations needed before she could move in. An absolute beauty, it reminded her of the homes in Georgia. Renovations took about several months with the help of numerous hunky broad-shouldered carpenters and plumbers as well as electricians that she hired. "Child pleases!" This was one of her favorite sayings every time she saw a good-looking man. Well, the house was full of "child pleases" just crawling all over this large home five days a week and sometimes on weekends to bring the house up to code before she could take up occupancy by county requirements. Each floor had its own air-conditioning unit that controlled the temperature of the three floors; there were hardwood pine floors that covered the modern and updated kitchen with stainless steel appliances—from the two side-by-side refrigerators, freezers, double ovens, and a microwave oven, to the glass stove top that has six burners and the dishwasher that was actually in a drawer. A small wine refrigerator was in the walk-in pantry. The cabinets were all maple with matching crown molding, and granite tops were her choice for the countertops. The breakfast area alone sat at least eight, which overlooked the backyard that was fenced in with black wrought iron fence that was six feet high lined with boxwoods all around the inside perimeter.

The living room had sixteen-foot ceilings with crown molding throughout, which flowed into a parlor area that was going to be her office. A large dining room sat fourteen people, with a fireplace adorned in white marble. The master suite had its very own fireplace, two oversized closets, and its own private bathroom with a white claw-foot tub and a separate shower. From a stairway to the third level was an attic that was unfinished. Gingerbread trim work was on the outside, where the wraparound porch stood, and a storage building was in the back of the house, which she wanted to turn into a garden shed eventually. LaVonda used money that she had stashed away while working for the IRS; the house was located in the downtown district of Fort Lauderdale, which she now called Dixie Arms, because it reminded her of her Southern roots. She lived on a side street not far from the riverfront, which was an up-and-coming tourist spot under construction with stores and boutiques and cafes and restaurants and antique shops with the Southern charm she left behind.

Southern women were very hospitable toward one another; if you were in need of support or someone to talk to in confidence, they would be there for you. And by word of mouth, your business would eventually spread through the community.

Even though her home was furnished and updated with modern appliances, she mixed the furnishings with goods she found while dumpster diving or on trash days once a week. She would get up at three o'clock in the morning and ready to hit the streets, looking for stuff that she could turn from trash to treasure left on the side of the road before the garbage truck picked them up. Among the mixture of antiques that she cherished was a part of her husband's belongings, which he called a hobby of his.

Earl liked shopping at consignment shops and estate sales in the South for merchandise of value that he recognized that would make him some money after he purchased these goods to only turn around and sell them for more money, which he then invested into stock so they could live comfortably when he was alive. She had no worries in the world; she was a well-kept woman.

There was not a thing Earl would not do for her and the kids. She hauled a few of the pieces that she loved, which Earl had found, and kept them in the back of a trailer she pulled behind her 2001 black SUV. She was very strong willed with a heart of gold, a woman who would give her last kidney if she knew it would make a difference.

The Dixie Arms was there to help the misfortunate and those people who were having hard times and no place to live, whether they had any job skills or not. She found them a job so they could earn their own money. She took them into her home and bathed them, gave them a place to sleep, and put clothes on their backs and food in their stomachs. Money was one thing she did not give them; she was afraid they would spend it on liquor or drugs and end up back on the streets where they would end up sleeping on the park benches or in cardboard boxes behind buildings downtown. If you proved to her that you were trying to make a difference in your life, she would help you out with a little cash from time to time to get you back and forth to work by either taking the local bus or metro rail; then you finally earned her trust. You had to earn her respect before she gave you a dime. She no longer trusted people with her money because of Earl's poor judgment in choosing his stockbroker who had taken all his money unknown to her and invested it in bad stock when she went to cash in the stock certificates after Earl's passing.

She has a little bit of money put away in savings but not what she was used to having and spending on her and the kids when they lived together as a family. Over the next several months, all her donations for the shelter came from the people in the community who wanted to help with the shelter by clearing out their closets and cabinets and used these donations as a tax write-off. They donated everything from food to clothing along with household items, which she stored in the storage shed in the backyard, which was eventually going to be her garden shed for when the time came and the houseguests graduated out from the shelter to be on their own. LaVonda would then let them rummage through the things out there in the shed and let them take whatever they thought they could use with them, which helped them with a head start with some household goods such as pots and pans, towels, bookcases, kitchen appliances, bowls, and cooking and eating utensils when they were on their own. The food helped feed them, and there were clothing, which she had stored on racks and racks in two separate bedrooms on the second floor of her home. One bedroom had things for the men, and then in another bedroom was for women's things. Everything from shoes to handbags, coats, hats, and accessories were stored for people who would end up eventually having a full wardrobe of clothes to wear when they were released from her shelter into society.

She was not shy at all with her opinions and vocally told you so. She would tell you as she saw it. She'd say, "Either you shit or get off the pot." Some of the people who knew her loved it when she would tell them that they were "too cool for colored TV," a phrase she used a lot when she liked someone. She told you the way it was going to be whether you like it or not. She wanted to be the one who made a difference in those people's lives as she was paving a path for a better life for them. In her own way, she was trying to compensate for her own mistakes that she had made in her life in the past. LaVonda was well respected and liked throughout the community for her charities and food drives that she helped organize. She was particularly fond of the holiday events where she made Easter baskets with hams and all the fixings for an Easter dinner. Fourth of July, she threw a cookout in the backyard and served hot dogs and hamburgers with beans and potato salad and soft drinks. She would make her own homemade ice cream or lemon sorbet, which was for dessert.

Thanksgiving time was with turkeys and all the fixings, and the first Christmas at the Dixie Arms, she opened up her home with the help of a few local friends that she had made and a few volunteers and threw a holiday dinner in her backyard with the Christmas music and lights and thanked those who helped her out at the time she was moving into the shelter between all the renovations and moving into the Dixie Arms in March. After all, it was warmer in Florida at Christmas time compared to other parts of the country where it was much colder and had whiter Christmases.

She remembered the time when she was planning the official grand opening of the Dixie Arms. She was just sitting down in the backyard, looking up at Dixie Arms, her home and shelter, drinking a glass of sweet tea, reminiscing on how nervous she was because she still needed to have a few things done around the shelter. The shelter was open, but she never got around to having the official grand opening that was supposed to have happened after she had most of the renovations done. Any excuse to have a party was also on top of her list for things she liked to do. She was waiting for the new sprinkler system that was replacing the old ones up on the third floor to be finished. At the same time, the new hurricane shutters were being installed to replace eight of the existing wooden shutters that were old and dilapidated and practically falling off the house. She was optimistic. She was on constant overdrive, starting from the third floor working her way down to the first floor, getting everything in order for the grand opening. She finally finished the third-floor railings and installed new floorings to match the rest of the house by taking out the black-and-white checkered vinyl tiles that covered the floor.

She turned the third floor into a game room with a built-in stereo system with speakers and the forty-two-inch flat-screen television for her houseguest that will stay with her until they were ready to go out on their own. Therefore, they could watch the forty-two-inch flat-screen television together as they hang out on a new sectional piece that would sit eight comfortably instead of placing separate televisions in each of the bedrooms, which was part of her own rehab on helping the homeless houseguest break down any barriers or walls that they might have put up around themselves to open up and interact with other people they now had to face in the real world after they left her shelter. The five bedrooms on the second floor now have a fresh coat of paint in various shades of green, yellow, and blues. This would make her houseguest feel warm and comfortable with the security of them knowing they had a roof over their head instead of being on the streets sleeping under a bridge or on a park bench where it's not safe for them in these times. She did, however, purchase brand-new double-size beds and mattresses for each of the bedrooms; she slept in each bed a different night just to make sure they were comfortable. She had also purchased dressers and mirrors from a local consignment shop that had estate furniture for sale at good prices. Her houseguest would have to share the two bathrooms on the second floor, which was not going to be an issue any longer by turning one bathroom into the women's room for the women houseguest and the other as the men's room for the male houseguest. Both bathrooms had walk-in showers with frosted glass doors; a white claw-foot tub was installed as well as double sinks and vanities in both bathrooms. There was also a large storage closet in both for towels and accessories of the houseguest that they could store on their very own shelf. The other two vacant bedrooms also on the second floor were now transformed into his and hers shopping boutiques. One was for the male houseguest and the other for the women. All these items were donated by local stores that were rotating out their inventory for newer merchandise, so they donated their goods to the Dixie Arms, and they could use it as a tax write-off at the end of the year. These clothes were then separated into both bedrooms onto the racks but not before she put on a fashion show with some of the outfits and danced to the music blaring down from the third-floor stereo system. These clothes were going to help the people coming into Dixie Arms build their self-esteem as well as give them something to look good in when the time came to send them out into the working world when they had to go for job interviews. Some she kept and moved to her closet first. The first floor was already updated with the new kitchen and eating area.

Her office was set up with file cabinets and office equipment, which was once the parlor area, that could be closed off by the double pocket doors that separated the living area from the parlor now her office. A local office supply dealer donated everything for her office. She did have to start taking interviews for a cook and housekeeper that could freshen the bedrooms daily and clean the bathrooms, and then she needed to have a cook come in to do breakfast and meals for those houseguests that would be staying with her. She was thinking of having a housecleaning service come in three times a week for the housekeeping duties but decided not to hire anyone at the moment.

She decided to make her houseguests get used to making beds and picking up after themselves since they were eventually going to have to do that on their own one day. She would first show them how to make a bed since they were not used to that, since they slept on benches or cardboard boxes, with newspapers or trash bags as blankets. Then they would be on their own after that each day. The houseguests would not receive any food until they were made. It just happened to work out great, and the houseguests that did decide to stay with her did make the beds and then came looking for her to check so that they could get something to eat. It got to the point after a dozen trips up and down the stairs that she caved in and believed them and never had to check again. Her method did work, and it taught them how to be more responsible in taking pride in their belongings and care of their material things because in a moment it could all be gone. She did do most of the cooking when it came to the meals, in between running the administration part of the shelter, but when it came down to having to meet with her donators and anything else that required her from being away from the shelter, she would have to hire an assistant. This was her first priority, getting some decent help to assist her in running the shelter. The cook for the shelter would have to come later; she would juggle this for a short time with her other responsibilities until she could find someone later down the road. LaVonda had called on her friend Officer Mario Perez and asked him if he knew of anyone looking for a part-time job that would eventually lead to full time in a matter of months. They needed to have experience in doing clerical duties as well as handling the phones and watching over the shelter when she needed to step out to conduct business for the shelter and have to meet potential employers who she could send her houseguest to when they were ready to go out and find employment. Sort of like a wonder woman or a superman, until she figured out the rest of the staff she would have to bring on to assist her in running the Dixie Arms. Officer Perez was at home since it was about ten o'clock in the morning, and he probably would have been home since he worked the night shift for the Broward sheriff's office.

The phone rang about four times when she heard his voice on the other side say, "Hello?"

"Hey, you," LaVonda said in her Southern charm.

"How are you?" Mario replied. "Well, darling, to tell you the truth I'm just getting in from a busy night and getting ready to take a shower and crawl into bed to get at least five to six hours' sleep before work tonight.

"Oh, I'm sorry if I interrupted you."

"No problem," Mario replied. "How are you doing?" he asked.

"I am just as happy as a pig on the farm rolling around in the mud," she replied.

"Glad to hear you're that happy," he replied. "To what do I owe this honor of this call? Besides catching me half naked," he said it with a chuckle in his voice, and LaVonda giggled back to him.

"You have not changed a bit, still ornery as ever. I was wondering if you knew of anyone who might be interested in a part-time position doing some clerical duties, answering the phone, and just be here when I need to step off the premises for a while," she told him.

"What are the hours?" Mario asked.

"Well, I thought they could work from around ten o'clock in the morning till about two or three o'clock in the afternoon."

"Those sound like great hours. Let me see what I can do. Can I get back to you later tonight while I'm on duty?"

"Sure," she replied back. "Just don't be calling me at midnight, okay?"

"I wouldn't want to wake you up from your beauty sleep. I know that is what makes you look so damn good!" Mario chuckled back.

"I am looking forward to that call tonight!" LaVonda replied back as she told him to get some rest and that they'll chat later. "Sweet dreams."

"Only of you," Mario said as he hung up the phone.

Mario always put a smile on her face, she thought as she was sipping her sweet tea. It was a shame on how nothing ever became of that relationship besides them just being good friends. She reminisced on how she made the Three Juanitas party planners grow with their business with the help of her hiring them for her grand opening. She had called on a Saturday morning to go over the plans for the grand opening and the menu on the food as well as the music. It was just one more thing checked off her list at the time of all the madness going on with her. She wanted to make the opening of the Dixie Arms a reality, which she was so proud of owning, and hoped it would make a difference in all those who walk through the doors as they seek her assistance on getting back on the road to recovery.

The party planners went over the list of things that she wanted for the opening. There would be a jazz band staged at the bottom of the staircase, which leads upstairs to the bedrooms on the second floor and third floor levels. Therefore, as the guest arrived and entered the Dixie Arms, they could hear the music, as well as enjoy the view of the living room area. She wanted fresh flower arrangements all throughout the shelter as well as adorn the fireplaces' mantels. Helium balloons would be scattered along the stair railings, which will serve as a backdrop for the band, in shades of purple, green, and gold, giving the look of a Mardi Gras effect. Their buffet would be set up on the main dining room table with a menu of cocktail shrimp and sauce, crab cakes, fresh fruit platters, and assorted cheeses and crackers as the appetizers.

The main course consisted of spicy fried catfish fillets, fried okra, macaroni with three cheeses, creamy coleslaw, smoked beef brisket, Creole chicken on steamed rice as well as chicken salad on croissants, assorted dinner rolls and corn bread, and chef salad with an assortment of dressings. The kitchen area served as the dessert area where there was red velvet cake, butter pecan cake, banana pudding, assorted cheesecake slices, pecan pie, and Mississippi mud cake. The bar area was set up in the walk-in pantry area just off the kitchen where there was a built-in wine cooler for the assorted wines. For some of her friends, she also had in the pantry Jack Daniel's, Johnnie Walker, vodka, and assorted mixes, with a punch bowl filled with a Bacardi confetti punch consisting of fruit cocktail and lemonade, grapefruit juice, and white rum and club soda. Coffee and tea were available in the dessert area if anyone chose to have that after dinner. The guests could enjoy their dinners on one of the ten round tables that were set up to seat twelve per table out on the back lawn, covered with white tablecloths and colored napkins in purple, gold, and green. Each table had matching floral arrangements in the same colors with a couple of helium balloons tied in some way. Here the guests would be able to sit and enjoy the evening and mingle and dine at the same time after they toured the shelter and saw what they were helping to contribute to the city with their charitable donations that they gave her that evening. She prayed that it would not rain. Just in case it did, the tables would then have to be moved up onto the covered front porch. The party planners, the Three Juanitas, were so excited to take on this event, knowing this would bring them more business after this evening was over.

Once the word of mouth spread throughout town that they were the party planners for the grand opening of the Dixie Arms, it would surely drum up more business for them. They, too, had just moved into the area a few months ago blocks from the shelter. LaVonda had driven by the Three Juanitas numerous times since it was just blocks from her place. She wondered what the place was with a name like that. She found out the day she made the call to them, after calling information to get the number first. They were a new party planning business in the area that was run by three women who happened to be best friends, and all their names were Juanita.

She could not wait to see this house come to life once again, filled with people and laughter all for a good cause. This was one of the benefits of living in the warmer climate, to be able to do many outdoor activities. When it was time to start bringing in funds to keep the shelter open, she would go to the local markets and speak with the owners or managers and introduce herself to them. She would explain her cause and place of business in which they had no problem checking her out first to make sure she was legit, and then they donated the meats and supplies she needed. Some made checks out to her shelter if they could not donate any goods she needed, along with the assistance of the police and fire departments to whom she placed a call to seek their assistance in which they participated in having a food can drive to help her out. When all was said and done, she had enough to make up between two to three hundred food baskets, which then were all delivered by the police department. That is when she first met Officer Mario Perez, as he contributed his time with making the deliveries for the shelter. She then had some of the women from the local churches volunteer their time to help organize these functions. LaVonda would throw tea parties on the porch with lemonade and Long Island iced teas to get their guard down and hit them up for donations, along with snacks, sandwiches, and her favorite peach cobbler as dessert. She also threw cocktail parties in the backyard with hors d'oeuvres and drinks as she planned these events. She was not a dummy when it came to raising money for the shelter. She had a way of getting her hands on money when she needed it. That was one of her gifted qualities that no one knew about her, the knack for making money. She especially liked the cocktail parties she had in her backyard; there were plenty of "child pleases" at those gatherings. Some were lawyers and accountants, and some of the contractors who helped with the renovations of Dixie Arms would be invited, along with several of the local firemen and some of the local police officers who helped distribute the food baskets who would attend. Some of the men brought their wives, others girlfriends or lifetime partners, and some came as singles, hoping to meet someone there. There was always a large crowd of people invited to these charity functions, who wanted to help in the community.

Officer Perez told her that he always drove by her house when he was on duty. He would make it a point to go out of his way from the other side of town when leaving the station when on duty to just drive by and check on her house and on the way back into the station just before he got off duty. He loved the charm and style of the house and wanted to know who had purchased the house and wanted to see how the progress was coming on this old Victorian. He also had an interest in her, which she did not know anything about. As for her, she had a fancy for him. She would always toss her hair back and bring out that Southern accent along with the charm whenever she was around him. They became good friends over the past year, but neither one of them had pursued it any further than that. Was it because he was always on duty? On the other hand, was it because she was always too tied up 24/7 in the operation of her shelter? He would, from time to time, bring homeless people in to her shelter, whom he would find wandering the streets late at night, so they would get a nice meal and bath and find a place to crash for a night or two. This was when she would offer him some coffee with a little conversation as they grew to know one another. This was what LaVonda wanted to do. This was her calling, to take in those in need of help. No wonder she had no time to date Office Perez. She had lives that were broken and messed up, and she had to devote her time to getting these people back on the right track.

CHAPTER THREE

Just a few miles away from the Dixie Arms on the other side of town was the Broward County sheriff's office. As the sunrise was just peering through the sixth-floor frosted glass window, which were reinforced with steel bars, there was a dazed and confused Donald Freeman who was just waking up on an army cot from what he thought was a bad nightmare. He then realized it was really happening, along with several other cell mates who were also picked up for drinking and driving the same night.

The ages ranged from anywhere from a twenty-one-year-old male, which is the legal age to drink in Florida, to a man who was around forty-five years old. Most of them woke up with the look of disgust on their faces. As two police officers stood by the cell door, one called out their names from a sheet that he was holding on a clipboard, and they were instructed to step out of the cell one by one as they were handcuffed once more before being led over to the courthouse. The odor of booze just reeked off some of the inmates as they walked out of the jail cell. It was obvious that this was the reason why they were in there in the first place. They were led by the officers, one officer leading the way and the other officer following behind. They were on their way over to the county courthouse, which was just across the street from the main jail connected by a glass-enclosed walkway right into the courthouse, down some narrow hallways, which led them behind the courtrooms. They were to appear before Judge Curtis Lopez, when Donald will hear the charges brought against him.

One by one their names were called to approach the judge's bench, where they were read the charges brought against them. If any of the prisoners before him had prior arrest, they were sure to get the book thrown at them. Judge Lopez would then set bond, and then they would be released. If not, then they were taken back to a cell until they could meet bond. All of them bonded out with a twenty-five-hundred-dollar fine and had to do community service depending on the circumstances of their arrest. Since most of them were for drunk driving, they were going to have to go to driving school and watch the horrible movies on what drunk driving can do to you, then report to different schools throughout the county to stand up in an auditorium and talk to the students about why they should not be drinking and driving and what the severe consequences would be if caught, or worse, if they had killed someone. Donald had to do this, and since it was his first offense and with the charges of animal cruelty added, he had to spend the next two months doing community service for the county shelters. His service included the helping of cleaning out the cages and pens where the dogs were, assisting in the feeding of the animals, and helping out with adoptions throughout various pet stores around town and just maybe have the chance to ride with animal control to pick up those lost animals just roaming the streets. He was hoping that this would be part of his community service. He was going to have to try to make amends for what he had done to Freeway, which was always on the back of his mind, hoping they would cross paths once again. He wondered whatever happened to Freeway as the arresting officer Mario Perez drove him to the county jail in the back of the police cruiser. Where did Freeway go?

He no longer had a job because that was about to end due to Lisa's decision, since her brother's untimely passing. The business was about to be closed for good. Therefore, until he could find a real job, this community service was going to help him focus and move on with his life.

Drinking and driving was not ever going to be a part of him again. He learned his lesson the hard way, and it only took one night behind bars to realize it. He was to come before Judge Lopez, who had ordered Donald to report to the local animal shelter in one week to start his community service, after posting bond and getting his friend Lisa, who was still in town making final arrangements for her brother's funeral and having him flown back to San Francisco, who was willing to pick him up from the courthouse and take him down to get his car out of impound. She was glad to be of assistance, and it kept her mind off the arrangements and her brother, who praised Donald often to her for being such a good manager of his shoe store.

Besides, she felt partially to blame for having let him go and could understand the circumstances why he ended in jail for drinking. She obliged and picked him up in front of the courthouse, where he would wait in front for her. Within an hour Lisa had pulled up in her rental car and took Donald down to the impound lot so he could get his car and pay that hefty fine, where he thanked her so much under the circumstances, when he had no one else to call that he wanted to tell the trouble he got in. She told him not to worry; it's the least she could do for all the bad news she had given him that day.

Donald just wanted to go home and forget this night ever happened and to take a long hot shower and get rid of the awful way he felt from spending the night in jail.

Donald wanted to start going over his finances for the next few months and see if he can save himself from having to file bankruptcy. Did he have enough money in savings and whatever cash he had left coming in from the job before it ended? Did he have enough till he found another job? He would have to flimflam a few bills around and pay only the minimum requirements until he found a job so it would not affect his credit and he would still be able to make the mortgage payment on the townhome and keep a roof over his head.

It was going to be tight for a few months, but he was going to survive the mess that he brought onto himself. Donald also needed a good night's rest so he could start job hunting as soon as possible prior to him serving his time at the shelter. Morning had finally arrived, and Donald was up and ready to hit the streets to find a job.

First thing he needed to do was run to the convenience store, pick up the local newspaper, and see what was available in jobs with his qualifications. He picked up a cup of coffee as well as several packages of beef jerky. After the ordeal he just went through, he was craving a cigarette, and he knew that the jerky would help him through this moment. Donald drove back to the town house, where he could focus, and he sat down on the sofa and placed his coffee on the coffee table before him and started to look through the want ads and found several retail positions available that he could apply for. He wondered if they would do a background check on him. This would not be a good. He found three positions that interested him; one was in the mall as an assistant manager for a shoe store, the other was a store manager for a jewelry store at the outlet mall, and then there was one as a salesclerk for a men's clothing store with the chance of advancement to a store manager. He placed several calls to set up appointments and started applying right away. Donald had set up the job interviews one day apart so he could start the community service immediately. After all, he had figured that it would take at least two weeks before the jobs he applied for would finish looking at other candidates for the position, which gave him enough time to figure out what his next step was going to be while he started working at the shelter.

Donald had to report to the local animal shelter at nine o'clock in the morning and report to Ms. Kitty Fisher to hear the details of what he will be doing for the next several weeks at this shelter. Donald arrived on time the next morning after dealing with the horrific traffic on I-95, getting from Sample Road in Coral Springs to Griffin Road, which was south of town and about a twenty-five-minute commute as long as there were no accidents or a road construction to deal with. It was not going to be a fun commute, but it gave him time to focus on what he was going to do when he completed his sentence. Ms. Kitty greeted him as he approached the entrance to the building. She was talking to one of the volunteers at the front desk when he approached them and said that he had an appointment with Ms. Kitty, and she said that she was she and that he must be Donald and that she was expecting him. Donald's first impression of her was that she reminded him of a security guard at an all-women prison; she was five foot four, with short brown hair, somewhere in her mid thirties, about hundred sixty pounds, and she was very stern and yet pleasant to talk to and with a kind smile.

They managed to get through the initial formalities and knew it was time to deal with the truth. He was about to start serving his community service. Ms. Kitty asked him to walk with her through the shelter to see what area he would be working in and told him to report back to her by end of day, which then she would do a walk through to see if Donald had done his job, which she then wrote in a journal and called in to the parole office at the end of the week unknown to Donald. They then proceeded to walk past the front desk to a double glass door that led them to the kennel area where the cages for the dogs that were up for adoption are. Ms. Kitty told Donald that he was now going to have to report in at seven o'clock in the morning from now on unless told otherwise by her. His first duty of the day was to start out by hosing out the dog cages, followed by giving them fresh food and water each morning before they opened up the shelter at ten o'clock in the morning. There were at least sixty cages that he could see while walking through that was in need of cleaning. Half of them already had dogs in them. The only good thing so far was that Donald was now going to miss the morning traffic or at least the major part of it.

He was shocked on how many dogs there were. Donald had not a clue that there was a separate area for the felines, where they kept the cats and kittens. Those were also up for adoptions. He was more saddened after seeing those that were there and the shape they were in; some of the dogs looked like they only had a few years left in them. Others, only weeks, for no one wanted to adopt him or her. Then there were the ones that were noted with a specific date that they were going to be put down, which was posted on the card, because they had been there for a longer period of time, and no one wanted them. All this information was on an eight-by-ten index card that was on the front of each door of every cage. It told the adoptees the age of the dog, the breed, sex, and any other traits that needed to be told and if they had been fixed or spayed as well as any health issues. Some cards noted if they were strays, others more detailed with a reason like "previous owner moved not able to take with them." Another one said "owner just had a newborn baby and was not able to keep," and the most touching one was "owner passed away," which really tugged at his heart. Every one of the dogs was given a name, whether it was from a previous owner or by the shelter—if they were brought in as a stray with no tags or license. The index cards read like tombstones. This was upsetting for Donald to see as he and Ms. Kitty walked through the kennel area toward the back office to fill out some papers as he starts his community service. Donald, having to hold back the tears, looked at the dogs from cage to cage to see what was there. One dog was a blonde cocker spaniel named Sassy that looked to be about ten years old and had cataracts and looked like she was up there in age and yet still had some life in her for someone to bring her home.

It was a shame that her previous owners had to move and could not take this dog to the retirement home with them because the place would not allow pets. Donald stopped at her cage and got down on his knees and spoke to her and said he'd be back to see her as soon as he was settled in.

The look on her face and by the lick that she gave the back of Donald's hand seemed to let Donald know that she understood him and that it was a deal with her. Donald would come by and see her as much as possible while he was working there and bring her a treat.

She looked to have had a few more good years left in her if only given another chance by being adopted out to a caring and loving home. Sassy reminded Donald of his grandmother's dog, Ashley, back in Sutton Falls when she was alive and how he would take her to the campground for walks and let her run around chasing the squirrels and how she loved to swim in the pond near the covered bridge with him. Ashley had to be put down when his grandmother passed away because she was never the same when she died. She had lost all her zest in life as well as her playfulness and spunk that kept her going, and she spent most of the time sleeping. It was as if she had a broken heart by the passing of her owner. She had been a part of the family for twelve years, and it broke his heart having to go with his dad to put her down. Donald saw this as the opportunity to make sure someone would come in, adopt her, and give the few years she had left to a caring and loving person who needed some companionship in his or her life, before he completed out his community service. In the back of Donald's mind, he could not help but wonder if Freeway was safe and where he was. He prayed that he was not injured or hurt and not still out on the expressway where he left him. Was there a chance that he would be there in the shelter already, or just maybe animal control would bring him as a stray that was just wondering the streets?

Donald wanted a second chance, just like Sassy, if given the opportunity to give his love back to him and make up for the way he treated him and for abusing him the way he did by tossing him out of the car on the expressway before this whole mess led him to the shelter. Unknown to Donald, Freeway was hanging out around a rest area off the expressway just a mile down the road from where he left him. Freeway was eating leftovers by people who stopped to take a break from the long drive into South Florida or by truckers who had stopped to spend the night while hauling goods or merchandise into the South Florida area for distribution to businesses, which were purchased for resale or wholesale. He spent the nights inside of the restrooms, cuddled up in a corner for a good night's rest. When daybreak came around, he would venture out into the wooded area just behind the restrooms, where he would lie and watch as the cars and trucks would pull off and take a break at the rest area. Freeway just kept his eyes on the trash receptacles where people would walk over to and throw stuff in, and when they left, he would make a dash for the receptacle and leap at it so he could knock it over and look for any food that he could get into his stomach. Once someone yelled at him to get away from there, he would dash off into the woods again so he would not be bothered. Well, today was going to be Freeway's lucky day, as one of the truck drivers who pulled off the expressway and stopped to use the restroom had just left the door to his cab wide open. This gave Freeway the opportunity to jump out from under the bushes and make a dash with a jump into the back of the cab where the sleeping quarters were for the truckers when they wanted to sleep on these long-haul trips cross-country. The license plate on the cab was from the State of Texas. Freeway snuggled his way into the blankets and made himself comfortable as the truck driver of this rig just climbed in and closed the door to the cab, unaware he had a passenger with him along for the ride. This trucker only had a few miles to go to his exit in Weston where he was going to drop off his last load of goods to a new wholesale company. The wholesale company that was opening soon specializes in canine pet products like beds and toys as well as food products—all the stuff that people purchase for their dogs at retail stores. Then the trucker was heading back home to Dallas where he needed to be in the morning so he could pick up the next shipment and head to Arizona to a wholesaler out there where he would receive a thousand-dollar bonus if he got the shipment to them in a day and a half. The load pays truckers, or rather, delivery, and this trucker was all about the money. After this delivery, this trucker could take the long-awaited vacation he has scheduled off at home in Dallas where he lived. So he was determined to make no stops and drive straight through. Freeway was sound asleep in the back of the cab with no chance of interruption unless the driver did stop and crawled back there and found him.

Donald was just finishing the paperwork with Ms. Kitty when a volunteer interrupted them to let Ms. Kitty know that animal control had just pulled up and had just brought in two more dogs that needed her assistance. Ms. Kitty asked Donald to join her so he could see how the process went when the dogs where brought into the shelter, and he was obliged to join her.

The first process was to take them directly to the examining room where they first have to examine them for any injuries or sores as well as any kind of identification such as a dog tag or license if they were wearing a dog collar. If no identification was on them when brought in, they then look for tattoos or even microchips. This is where they use the national scanner, which is hooked up throughout the country for all shelters and vets offices for the use of identifying animals that are lost, stolen, or injured—in some cases even runaways that could end up cross-country, which then can be reunited with their rightful owners. They are then scanned over their entire body with a handheld scanner, which looks for any microchips with an identification number, which if detected would send a beeping sound and up pops the identification number in this little window on the scanner, which is then entered into the national database system on a computer. A search is done in a database and if located would bring up the information on the dog from the breed to the sex and who the owners are and where they live as well as phone numbers for contact. If they registered their dogs, they would be in the system; then the rightful owners are then notified by phone or e-mail if they have an e-mail address listed for contact that they have their dog and can come down and claim them. If unsuccessful in locating any identification, they are all then given a manila file for the chart of records on the dog along with a name. They are then brought over to the grooming department located in the shelter where they are then given a flea bath as well as checked over for ticks. From there they are taken over to the quarantine area in the shelter for twenty-four hours of observation for any behavioral problems, and they are then fed and given water. After the twenty-four hours have passed and there are no signs of unusual behavior, they are then released into the main kennel with the other dogs and are put up for adoption. If a dog shows signs of any behavioral problems, they then contact several shelters across the country and tell them that they have a dog with a problem and ask if they could take the dog in and try to help correct the problem with rehab. Most cases they are willing to take them in, and the dogs are then sent to their facilities with the help of volunteers that are driving through the state where they are located; otherwise they would have to be put to sleep. This is the last resort they like to take.

Charitable donations given by the local community, which they depend on for food, and bedding and medical supplies as well as the equipment they need to take care of these animals, keep these facilities running.

Donald was very impressed with how the system worked and wanted to learn more as he was to spend the next few weeks there doing his community service. Donald now had very little hope in finding Freeway because there was no microchip implanted in Freeway that would identify his owner unless he still had his tag and license on him. Someone was bound to have found him by now and taken him into their home, and if not, then just maybe some animal control officer driving around town would pick him up and bring him into the shelter where they would be reunited again as long as he still had his tags on him.

CHAPTER FOUR

Just a week into his community service, Donald was getting to know just about everything he wanted to know on how an animal shelter is operated—from the process of having the canines or felines brought into the shelter, up to the adoption process, and right down to the unfortunate task of having to put some of them down. This was truly an eye-opening experience for him. Ms. Kitty was very pleased with his work and reported this back to the parole office together with how he took interest in the canines up for adoption. She was more pleased to see that he took an interest in helping find a great home for Sassy. She was finally adopted out to a retired couple, who must have been in their mid sixties, that just moved down from the Boston area. This couple had made a decision to move to Fort Lauderdale to get away from the cold, harsh winters to enjoy the sun and warm weather in their villa, which they purchased, overlooking a golf course in Pompano Beach. They had lots of time on their hands to be able to give a dog a loving home; they both had donated to various pet organizations throughout the years but never had the opportunity to become foster parents to one because they were too involved with the jobs at the time. They decided to take a drive down to the shelter and see what was available for adoption. There they met Donald who was a just a few pens away from them as he was cleaning one out that was being hosed out. By eavesdropping on their conversation, one could tell they had a Boston accent and were from the same area as himself He immediately dropped the hose he was holding to clean the pens, walked over to them, and asked if he could be of assistance. Donald happened to mention that he, too, was from Massachusetts and that he, too, had just relocated down to South Florida a while back himself. After they talked awhile about New England and the areas in which they both came from, Donald said, "Let me take you over here to meet someone who I think would be the perfect dog for you."

He took them over to Sassy, who was curled up on a blanket in the back corner of her cage when she bolted up and ran to the front of the cage once she heard Donald's voice. She remembered Donald from day one when he came to serve his community service at the shelter. With a whimper and with the raise of her front right paw that she placed through the chain-link fence of the door, she looked up at Donald and this retired couple as if she was trying to say hello to them. Sassy remembered Donald since he promised he would come by, see her daily, and bring her a treat, which he did faithfully from day one. Donald introduced Sassy to the couple who immediately fell in love with her brown eyes that had a sparkle in them that Donald hadn't seen in her the entire week when he came to see her. This must have been a sign that this was the right couple for her. Donald gave them a few minutes alone and watched from a distance as they patted her on the head and how she shook her body like a bowl of Jell-O and wagged her stubby tail with excitement. The couple then motioned Donald over and said, "Could you please direct us to the adoption center. We would like to take her home."

With a smile on his face and a bit teary eyed, Donald had taken them over to the adoption desk, and they proceeded to fill out all the required paperwork needed to take her home. Twenty minutes later and a brand-new leash from the shelter's gift store, the retired couple from Boston were walking out of the shelter as one big happy family, but not before Sassy had stopped in her tracks and looked back as she walked through the front doors of the shelter to see Donald wiping the tears from his eyes.

Sassy then let out several loud barks that Donald never heard from her before, as if she was saying, "Thank you for being my friend and for finding me a new home," as she walked toward a black Lincoln Town Car and climbed into the backseat. The car door then closed behind her, and the retired couple then got into the driver's seat and passenger seat of the Town car. They started the ignition, put the car in reverse, and pulled out of their parking space and drove off into the direction of the expressway, never to return. Donald's emotions at this time was upside down right side up; he was happy and yet sad at the same time. He realized just then for the first time in his life what it felt like having to say good-bye to a dog once you attached yourself to one, having to let go of that special bond you built with them in such a short time of knowing them. Not for some stupid reason of being angry and wanting to punish them for chewing up some old video collection, which is what he did with Freeway. Whatever the reasons—from being adopted out to a good home to be loved and spoiled or just a companion to someone in need, or because they have to be put down because they were ill or old, and maybe the spark in their life they once had was gone, forever. They would be better off in a better place in the afterlife in which you would see them once again if you truly were an animal lover as they wait for you to come to them. Once Donald had his composure back after that heartbreaking adoption he just saw, he continued to head back to the kennel area to finish his duties, but not before Ms. Kitty who was watching him from a distance had approached him and asked if he was okay. She said, "It's always hard to have to say good-bye to the dogs that come and go from this shelter on a daily basis, that you will eventually build up a wall within you to keep you from having these feelings you're feeling right now. Think of it like this. Once they leave this shelter, they are going to be going to a home where they can be loved and spoiled and you've done your part in finding them the right home." With a smile on his face and a pat on the back from Ms. Kitty, she asked if he would like to continue with the duties if he felt much better. Donald took the information to heart and proceeded to go back to cleaning the pens.

It was a heck of a first week. Donald was enjoying it very much, and not even being paid for his duties, the drive to the shelter was much better this week since his hours were changed. He was also grateful for that. He was looking forward to the weekend and was hoping that he would have at least one voicemail on his home phone from the job applications he applied for so he could see them on Saturday if that was possible. Donald finished his duties, clocked out for the day, and headed home to see what he was going to fix himself for dinner. Money was still tight, but he was able to keep some groceries in the house and cut back on eating out like he used to until he had another job with income coming in. On the way home, he decided to stop and gas up his car and pick up a pack of beef jerky, which he was out of and needed earlier in the day after having said good-bye to Sassy, which was hard for him. Donald pulled into the convenience store around the corner from his townhome, and the first thing he saw when he approached the door to go in and pay for the gas and beef jerky was the flyer of Freeway posted on the inside of the door. He stopped for a moment, then went inside, and asked the clerk if anyone had inquired about the dog on the flyer, and the salesclerk responded by saying not that he knew of because he had just started his shift and would be there until midnight. Donald said, "Thanks anyway, but if you happen to run into anyone asking, please give them my cell phone number," which he jotted down on a business card that was in his wallet, as he took out his credit card to pay for the gas and beef jerky.

Donald had noticed that he had a dollar bill tucked away in his wallet, which was given to him by his grandmother many, many years ago. When he was much younger and had lost a tooth and asked about the tooth fairy, she told him that if he put his tooth under the pillow while he slept that night, he would wake up to find money that had replaced it, left by the tooth fairy, which he found that following morning under his pillow and had been carrying ever since, for years, with him. It was a remembrance of her story that she told him that he cherished, which in his case at that young age, a gift of cash for a tooth. This dollar has seen its days from being moved out from an old wallet and put away into a newer one, not to mention the times his wallet might have gotten a little wet from him jumping into the pond back in Sutton Falls with his clothes on. As Donald glanced over at the cash register, he could not help noticing that the sign flashing near the cash register said the next lottery for Saturday night was up to 125 million dollars. He said, "Oh, what the hell." He walked over to the ticket counter and pulled one of the cards that he had to pick six numbers from one through sixty-nine. Donald reached over for one of the pencils on the counter and covered up the six numbers that he wanted to play. He played the number sixty-seven, the age of his grandmother when she passed away. He also played his birthday, which was on April 1, April Fool's Day, so the numbers four and one was then played—four was the month, and one was the day. He also played the day he first met Freeway, which was on a Saturday, and he was sure it was the eighteenth, along with the day, which happened to be today, March 21, so he played three and twenty-one in honor of Sassy being adopted today. He marked the lottery card 1-3-4-18-21-67. He then placed the pencil back into its holder, walked over to the sales counter, handed the clerk the card, and asked him to play these numbers for the lotto. Donald then reached into his wallet and pulled out that old dollar bill that had seen its final day, but not before he brought it to his lips and gave it a kiss. It was his way of saying good-bye and good luck as he exchanged the dollar bill for the lotto ticket and thanked the salesclerk. As the salesclerk responded back with a "good luck," he put his wallet back into the back pocket, along with the lotto ticket, of his dirty jeans, which smelled like dog since he was cleaning dog cages most of the day. Donald then walked out of the convenience store and filled up his car with gas that he just paid for and jumped in and drove off toward home with a piece of beef jerky he was enjoying on the way. Once Donald hit home, he placed his car keys and wallet on the kitchen counter near the stove, unaware that the lotto ticket was stuck to the back of the wallet as he pulled it out and placed it down on the counter. Donald then walked into the bathroom and stripped down and climbed into a nice warm shower to get rid of the smell of dog, while he figured out what he was going to make for dinner. Donald then stepped out from the nice warm shower and dried himself off with a huge bath towel that he once used to dry off Freeway, which was now cleaned after washing it first and which he put back into the hall closet as it crossed his mind while drying completely off. He then threw on a pair of gray sweatpants, with a pair of white footie socks and a tee shirt that said "Is It Friday Yet," which he had made up when he was out and about at the local flea market looking for things to furnish his townhome with when he first moved into it. This was Donald's favorite saying for he lived for Fridays after a long week of work. He then went over to the kitchen cabinets and decided that a box of mac and cheese and fried hot dogs would be his dinner tonight.

Donald then bent down to one of the cabinets below the counter that was next to the stove to pull out a medium-size saucepan and a ten-inch skillet, which he kept below with the other cookware that he had. When he noticed his wallet as well as his car keys were just a little too close to the stove as he proceeded to turn it on to start dinner, Donald casually slide them away from the burner so they wouldn't catch fire, unaware that the lotto ticket had fallen off the counter and into one of the other pots on the shelf under the cabinet, which he was just closing the door of. Donald proceeded to cook his dinner when the phone rang; it was Ms. Kitty wanting to tell him that tomorrow morning he would be riding along with one of the animal control drivers in their van, which he would be doing for the next several days instead of cleaning the cages. He was thrilled as could be, just knowing he would be able to ride around in the nice weather outdoors, compared to feeling like one of the dogs caged up in the shelter.

He said, "Thank you!" As he told her that, he told her he'd see her early in the morning and wished her a good evening. Donald then finished cooking his dinner, loaded up a plateful of the macaroni and cheese along with three of the pan-fried hot dogs and headed over to the sofa. He then turned on the television to watch a bit of the local news during his dinnertime and before he knew it had fallen asleep from exhaustion headfirst into his plate of macaroni and cheese only to discover what he had done when he happened to wake up about a half hour later. This community service was kicking his butt between the long drive, and the cleaning and feeding of the canines was a full-time job alone. Donald was oh so ready to take on his new duty, which he was so looking forward to.

Riding along with one of the animal control drivers to pick up dogs or cats or whatever animals that were running loose around the streets with no tags or license and terrorizing other residents in the area starting first thing in the morning was a great way to start the weekend, which was just a day away from that. He would have time to rest up and be ready to start all over again for the next several weeks, unless he could get off for good behavior, which it looked like it could possibly happen with the way this past week has been and with Ms. Kitty telling him he is doing a fine job. Donald was hoping that, just maybe, he would be lucky enough to run into or find Freeway while he was out patrolling the streets the next day or at the beginning of next week when he was still going to ride along with the animal control officer. Donald then got up from the sofa with his plate of mac and cheese, which by the way was also on the sofa, washed his face with a wet paper towel, and cleaned up the sofa, hoping to get the cheese out from the cushion if it was not too late, where it would have left a permanent stain. He then turned off the television and headed for the bed, but not before making sure his teeth were brushed and that there was no more mac and cheese in his hair. Morning finally arrived, and Donald who had just gotten a full eight hours' sleep was ready for another day—a good day, he felt in his bones. It was going to be the day he was going to be bringing Freeway home. He still felt like something good was about to happen, and this could be the day. Was he going to get an early release from community service from Ms. Kitty?—which he wouldn't mind since he had to start looking over the want ads again in this weekend's newspapers, since he had not gotten any callback on the jobs that he applied for this week. Maybe that was why he felt so good. He was probably going to be hearing about one of the jobs he applied for, so he could start bringing in money once again. In the meantime, Donald had gotten up, showered again, and threw on a pair of button-down jeans and a pair of comfortable sneakers along with a navy blue polo shirt that no doubt he would have to switch out of once he got to the shelter because the proper uniform that the animal control officers are to wear consist of a pair of navy blue khaki pants and one of those dull white short-sleeved uniform shirts. He was so excited about today that he had a grin from one side of his face to the other. Donald had a feeling that something good was about to happen to him and couldn't figure out yet what it could be. He did know that he needed to hit the road before traffic built up if he was going to get to the shelter on time. Meanwhile Ms. Kitty was at the shelter already talking to several of the animal control officers to see which person would be the right choice for Donald to ride along with today. There was Mr. Jose who spoke very little English and more Spanish, who was in charge of working the Spanish communities of town where he could speak fluently to the residents when he is radio dispatched to an area for what could be an animal problem. He would not be suitable for Donald; there would definitely be a communication problem in that vehicle today. Then there was Ms. Weinstein who worked with radio dispatch for handling the felines that were loose in the neighborhoods or sometimes stuck up on a roof or tree in which she then placed a call to the closest fire department where they would come out with a ladder truck to assist her in rescuing those that were up high and in need of help. The last animal control officer available today was Mr. Otto since the other three officers were not at work today. One had called in this very morning, while the other two officers were working the West Palm Beach area because of the recent pit bulls running amuck up there and terrorizing the residents and their dogs, which Ms. Kitty forgot all about until she looked at her calendar on her desk this morning when she came in and said, "Damn!" She had forgotten about the call she had received from the Palm Beach Animal Control Office earlier in the week; they asked her if she could spare two of her officers to help out there until they could get the situation under control. Ms. Kitty was obliged to be of assistance. She said that it would not be a problem and was glad to assist in any way possible since the Broward County had not had as many calls. She then had penciled them into her calendar "send two officers to Palm Beach Friday" and forgot about it till this morning. She had no problem with lending them to their office to assist them for a day or two; it wouldn't be a problem whatsoever. Therefore, it looks like Mr. Otto was the only choice left to be the animal control officer that Donald would be assisting today. He was a gentle man who had worked for the shelter for several years and was good at his job. He was a little strange though. He was bald and had a slur in his voice and kind of looked like a "mother killer"—even better, he reminded Ms. Kitty of one of the kinfolks from the movie *Deliverance*; he was good with catching the dogs that were loose on the streets. He also enjoyed catching the possums and raccoons that were running around subdivisions twice a week. They seemed to come out only on the trash days, which was twice a week when the local garbage trucks picked up the trash from the front of the homes that was left on the curb for pickup in the early morning hours.

This was not one of the normal shelters functions, but she looked the other way when it came to Mr. Otto because he was doing this on the side by helping out a cousin of his who happened to own a critter control business in which he was being paid by. The extra income was helping Mr. Otto through the economic hard times, having to raise six children and being recently widowed eight months ago, by bringing in these possums and raccoons; these critters have been known to carry rabies and destroy rooftops in homes so they could get into the attics and make a home for themselves. Just as long as Mr. Otto didn't let it affect him from picking up the canines that had been running loose or terrorizing residents and which needed to be off the streets running around loose.

Just then Donald had walked in to the shelter, and she then introduced them to one another. Ms. Kitty then asked Donald to please go to her office and take the white shirt that was hanging up on the back hook of her office door that was clean and change into that so he could then hit the streets. Donald knew he was going to have to change out of his polo once he arrived at work this morning into that tired old uniform shirt, but it was okay with him. Within seconds Donald was back with the clean uniform shirt on his back, and they were ready to patrol the streets. They had already received two dispatched calls—one was for a pack of raccoons that were on the north side of town in a residential area, knocking over trash containers left on the curbside for trash pickup today. In addition, the other call was for a barking dog that was up throughout the night, which kept a neighbor up. Donald was ready for the change, which gave him a break from cleaning dog pens even if it was only for a day or two. When they first arrived at the first call regarding the raccoons in the subdivision, Donald asked, "Why do you like catching these animals?" Mr. Otto said that he was getting twenty dollars for each one that he brought into his cousin who then turned them over to some medical firm, which he did not know why or for what. It was the extra cash that was helping him keep his roof over his six kids' heads; his house was about to go into foreclosure due to several back payments that he was not able to catch up with. Upon arriving at the first dispatch call, there was a raccoon hanging halfway out of a trash bin in front of a home. Mr. Otto put out some scraps of food that he carried around in a cooler that was in the back of the van, which when he opened up smelled liked the local dump. He first put on a pair of rubber gloves and reached in and grabbed a handful of the smelly garbage and placed it inside of a cage that had a trapdoor.

Once the raccoon stepped into the cage through the opening in the front, the door of the cage would close instantly, trapping them inside. So they sat and watched from the van for about thirty minutes when all of a sudden another raccoon that came out from the side of the house crawled into the cage as the other one was sitting on top of the trash bin, eating a piece of corn on the cob that was in the trash. Mr. Otto yelled, "Yahoo!" Then Mr. Otto stepped out of the van and walked over to the trapped raccoon, picked up the cage, and loaded it into the van and drove off to an area of the expressway down by the everglades, where he asked Donald to wait in the van and told him that he'll be right back.

Mr. Otto unloaded the caged raccoon and brought it in to a business that looked to be a bit seedy. Within a few minutes, here comes Mr. Otto with a handful of cash that he so conveniently tucked into his front pocket minus the raccoon he had gone in there with and carrying just an empty cage. After that, Donald and Mr. Otto were off to the next dispatched call to see why there was a barking dog all night in one subdivision. Once they approached the residence, they continued to hear the barking but with a little less bark; it was as if the dog was losing his vocal cords as he dashed from the front chain-link fence to the back of the house just around the corner. The dog did this for several minutes just back and forth to the back of the house, so Donald and Mr. Otto pried open the gate and proceeded to the back of the house to only find an older man who had fallen and hit his head on the patio steps. It looks like he had fallen coming down the steps to feed the dog when he fell back and hit his head on the steps because there were two dog bowls on both sides of him that looked like they had been tossed into the air as he was stepping down and fell.

He was lying there all night long talking to his dog, saying, "Go get help. Go get help." That's why the dog was barking all night long—he was trying to get help for his master. No one would have seen this injured man lying there hurt on the patio because he was around the corner in the back of the house, and anyone who had looked over the fence would have never seen him. It was pitch dark, and with no lights in the backyard, they would have never seen the hurt man who was lying there unless they did what Donald and Mr. Otto had just done—find some way into the yard and investigate. Donald immediately dialed 911 from his phone, and within minutes the paramedics had arrived to help save this man and bring him to the hospital. As for the barking dog, Donald then took him by the collar over to the animal control van and loaded him in there where he was going to be transported down to the shelter until they could contact the owner once he was released from the hospital to see if he was capable of taking care of the dog. This was a day that Donald would never forget since he helped in the rescuing of a man who might have died if they had not gone out to check out the barking dog. He just wanted to get back to the shelter and call it a day since he only had two dispatched calls and nothing else for the day. He did spend the other six hours of the day just riding around the streets, looking for stray or lost dogs, but it just didn't turn out that way; there were none to be found. It was an uneventful day with the exception of saving one man's life.

CHAPTER FIVE

It was just around nine o'clock in the evening when the phone rang over at the Dixie Arms, and LaVonda was in her office at her desk, surfing the Internet for local employers that had posted jobs and were hiring. She was looking for a job for a woman who had been staying at the shelter, named Ms. Honeycutt. She had taken her into the shelter a few weeks back when she found her homeless and living in a cardboard box just a few streets down from the Dixie Arms. LaVonda answered the phone and said, "Good evening, the Dixie Arms, may I help you?"

"Yes, you may. I am inquiring about the job you have for an assistant from ten to three." She then realized who it was on the other end of the phone. It was Mario, who was on duty.

"Hey you," she replied back. "Where you at?" she asked.

Mario replied, "I'm sitting here just off the expressway and thought I'd give you a call from my cell phone while I'm waiting for speeders or drunk drivers or any vehicle that was out of the norm to pull over. I'm just killing time and I just remembered I was supposed to call you back regarding the assistant's position you had opened at the shelter to help you out."

She said in a pleasant voice to Mario, "I was just getting ready to lock up for the night and call it a day and curl up in a warm bubble bath with a glass of wine followed by a good book while tucked into bed. So you didn't forget to call me after all." She asked, "So how's your evening going so far tonight?"

Mario replied, "Slow, nothing to write home about. The streets are safe tonight so I hope it stays that way!" Mario then asked, "Would you consider hiring me part-time as your assistant to help out in the shelter?" LaVonda was silent for a moment on the other end of the phone. "You there?" Mario asked.

"Yes, I am," she replied back. "I was kind of shocked for a moment that you would be interested in the position."

"Why?" he asked.

She replied, "Well, with you working the late shift that you do and then heading home to unwind a bit and then get some sleep before heading back to work that you would be spending time doing other things."

"Well, to tell you the truth I'm looking to be around other people where I can interact with others. Just sitting here night after night in a police cruiser by myself waiting for my next traffic stop, it gets pretty lonely out here at night, so I thought that spending some time during the day helping someone like you and your cause to help others gave me an idea that what a better way to be around others and it would be only be part-time, right? I would still be able to get in my sleep and then work part-time and still have time to do the things that I would need to do like errands, pay bills, or whatever I need to do before having to go back on duty. Besides, it would give us a chance to spend a little bit more time together instead of our normal phone calls from time to time or by me ringing your doorbell all hours of the night when I have someone in need of shelter that I found wondering the streets."

LaVonda replied, "To tell you the honest truth, it would be nice to have a man around here in this big old house. I get a little nervous when I'm here with some of the houseguest that stay here temporary. They look a bit scary and I know it's not their fault that they ended up where they did. Some of them give me the creeps being alone in this house with them. I almost broke down a week ago and decided to head down to the animal shelter and get me a dog to keep me company."

"Well, that might be a good idea a bit down the road when you don't have anyone staying with you," Mario sympathized with her; she really did not know these people or their past. LaVonda had a few questions for Mario about his qualifications to be her assistant, which he had no problem answering over the phone.

First question was, "Do you know how to operate a computer and spreadsheets?"

"Yes," he replied.

"Do you mind assisting me in doing some of the chores to keep the Dixie Arms? Clean from time to time?"

"Do you mean like vacuum, sweep, and dust?"

"Yes," she said. "Finally, do you like your morning coffee freshly ground or prepacked?"

"Well, to tell you the truth I like freshly ground flavors from time to time."

"Well then, I guess you passed my requirements and are officially going to be my first part-time employee for the Dixie Arms."

"So when would you like me to start?" Mario asked.

"How about coming by tomorrow around ten o'clock and go over what your job functions then and I will have a pot of freshly brewed coffee waiting and you will have to figure out what the flavor of the day is then!"

"Great I'll 'see you then. Have a nice evening," Mario said.

"You too enjoy your bath and book and we'll see you in the morning!"

LaVonda was thrilled that she was going to have an assistant and a man around the house. She shut down her computer and decided to finish looking for a job for Ms. Honeycutt in the morning and proceeded to the pantry for a bottle of wine and a chilled wine goblet as she then headed toward the staircase to retire in her bedroom and have a warm bath that she was so looking forward to. Mario on the other hand had no sooner hung up his cell phone and looked up, when there was a speeder that just passed him, and off he was with the sirens running and flashing lights to pull this car over.

He only had a few more hours to go until he was off his shift and ready to head home for he was so looking forward to seeing LaVonda in the morning as he started his first day as her new part-time assistant.

As LaVonda approached the top of the staircase on the way to her bedroom, she could hear Ms. Honeycutt snoring so loud from her room, which was just a few feet away from the landing in the first bedroom that she was staying in since she came to the Dixie Arms. LaVonda stopped outside of the door to her room to listen to make sure she was okay, when she recalled on how they crossed paths and how Ms. Honeycutt came to the Dixie Arms. She was living in a cardboard box just a few streets down. She was about five feet tall, a blue-haired woman in her late fifties or early sixties. She was pushing a shopping cart filled with plastic bottles down this alleyway about four thirty in the afternoon; she was no doubt collecting the bottles for money to get food was her first notion. She had been wearing a gray sweatshirt that was frazzled and rather torn with red cardinals painted or embroidered on the front—from where she was watching her, she couldn't tell for sure. Her wardrobe consisted of an ankle-length skirt that was red and a pair of white ankle socks and holey sneakers that looked to be a bit bigger as she was dragging her feet to try to keep them on. She was wearing a red matching pillbox hat with feathers sticking out of the sides, which made her look like a cardinal bird. She looked tired from pushing her shopping cart. LaVonda followed her down this alley from her car as she drove very slow not to startle the woman and watched her go into this old refrigerator box that was just sticking out from behind a dumpster, which she had parked her shopping cart beside of. She then crawled into this box and pulled out an old sheet that she was holding on to and covered her shopping cart and then crawled back into the refrigerator box. LaVonda was horrified to see her in these conditions as she was watching her from a distance from her car. LaVonda put her car in park and shut off the ignition and climbed out of the front seat and walked cautiously over to the refrigerator and yelled, "Hello! Hello!" toward the box.

"Who's there?" the lady from the box shouted back.

"My name is LaVonda Georgia and I own a shelter named the Dixie Arms just a few streets down from here and was wondering would you like to come with me for a nice bowl of chicken soup and a sandwich over at the shelter? I can give you some food and warm shelter and a nice bed to sleep in instead of this box. I also have a roomful of nice clothes where you can pick out something else to wear and sleep in. Let me help you out. LaVonda asked, "Would you come out please so I can speak to you?"

Within a few seconds, LaVonda thought what she heard was this woman crying, who crawled out of the box all teary eyed and looked up at LaVonda and said, "God bless you!"

"What is your name?" LaVonda asked.

"My name is Ms. Honeycutt."

"How long have you been living here in this box?" LaVonda asked.

"I don't recall because I don't know what day it is or what month it is. I do remember a day when I heard fireworks in the sky and horns blowing for a long time."

"That must have been New Year's eve then," LaVonda said.

"Could be. I had been here since that night after I found this box to keep me warm and safe that I had dragged down here behind this old dumpster that never seems to move. I hide behind here in the box."

"Oh my God! It has been at least four months then."

"I guess so. I collect bottles for money so I can get something to drink and cans of food that I open with this can opener that I have on a chain around my neck. See!" She pulled it out from under her gray sweatshirt that reeked body odor.

"Okay, what have you been eating besides can food?"

"Anything that I can beg for from the strangers on the street when I see them eating as they are walking by me. Some people have been nice and gave me French fries, chicken tenders, half of a hamburger, ice cream sometimes. I go up to the Three Juanitas down the road and look for anything that they toss out the back door into the garbage can from their day-old leftovers."

LaVonda held back the tears for it was just a matter of minutes before she let go with a flood of tears for this woman. LaVonda reached her hand out and asked her to take her hand and to please come with her. It would be a lot safer for her than being out here on the streets. She didn't hesitate for a minute and reached out for LaVonda's arm to hold on to as she was escorted back to LaVonda's car as LaVonda helped her get into the passenger seat and helped her with the seat belt. She knew she was going to have to have her car detailed in the morning after taking Ms. Honeycutt for the ride in her car.

The smell was unbelievable, which was coming from Ms. Honeycutt, her body odor.

La Vonda said, "Hang on to your hat, honey," as she rolled the electric windows down in the front and backseat to air it out. There was no way in hell that she was going to be closed in with Ms. Honeycutt smelling as bad as she did without tossing her cookies all over the dashboard. So the windows went down, and Ms. Honeycutt grabbed her red pillbox hat and said, "Weeeeeeeee!" as LaVonda drove like a bat out of hell to get her home to the shelter to clean up Ms. Honeycutt and get her some decent food and clothes and a well-needed bath the thought of using gallons of tomato juice to bath her in had crossed LaVonda's mind. Ms. Honeycutt smelled as if she had been sleeping with skunks! Just minutes away from the Dixie Arms, LaVonda knew that they would bond; she felt it in her heart. LaVonda had put the Dixie Arms downtown for reasons like this—to help people like Ms. Honeycutt who had hit rock bottom and have no place to go or food to eat. Ms. Honeycutt said, "Oh my," as they pulled up in front of the Dixie Arms where LaVonda could see from the smile on Ms. Honeycutt's face as she looked up to see how grand the shelter was from the moonlight that had bounced off her face from the front windshield it reminded her of a deer caught in headlights look.

LaVonda helped Ms. Honeycutt out of the car and up the walkway to the front porch where the Dixie Arms seemed to have a glow as they approached the front doors where all the lights on the first floor were on and just two lights could be seen coming from the second floor, sort of like a smile on a jack-o'-lantern at Halloween time. LaVonda escorted Ms. Honeycutt up the staircase to the guest bathroom and assisted in helping her get out of those rags she was wearing and into a warm bubble bath that Ms. Honeycutt said she couldn't recall when was the last time she had one. LaVonda asked her if she would be okay for a few minutes so she could run down the hall to the women's boutique she had set up in one of the vacant bedrooms. LaVonda recalled seeing a long nightshirt and a baby blue bathrobe and a pair of white slippers that was on one of the racks that was perfect for Ms. Honeycutt to wear after she had taken her well-needed bath. Then they were heading down to the kitchen for some soup and sandwiches, while LaVonda tried to learn more about Ms. Honeycutt and why she ended up the way she did on the streets in a refrigerator box. LaVonda found what she remembered in the boutique as she was getting that room ready with all the donations she had received and grabbed them and headed back to the bathroom where she found Ms. Honeycutt soaking in the bathtub with her eyes closed and humming a catchy tune when she opened up her eyes to see LaVonda standing there with clean clothes in her arms and a nice pair of white slippers in her hand. Anything would feel good on her feet compared to those holy sneakers that were several sizes too big for her feet, which LaVonda had picked up with two fingers and tossed over into the wastebasket in the corner of the bathroom. Ms. Honeycutt broke down in tears and thanked LaVonda for giving her this nice bath and for the nice clothes; she said she felt like a brand-new woman thanks to her.

LaVonda reached for the big bath towel off the towel rack and held it up in front of Ms. Honeycutt so she could stand up from the dirty water that was left behind and wrap herself up and step out of the tub. LaVonda suggested that she would really feel clean if she stepped into the shower to rinse off with clean water to remove any residue left behind on her body from the dirty tub before she helped her put on the nightshirt and bathrobe. Ms. Honeycutt laughed and said, "Sure, darlin', anything to please you! You're right. I would feel much more refreshed." With a little more spunk in her step, Ms. Honeycutt walked over to the shower by herself and proceeded to rinse off. While she was in the shower, LaVonda pulled out a trash bag that she had a box of in the bathroom cabinet to toss out those rags Ms. Honeycutt was wearing to get them out of the house and into the trash in the morning for trash pickup. The red pillbox hat she saved. She thought that Ms. Honeycutt would like to keep this; after all, it did look cute on her blue hair.

She would have to find a way to get it cleaned for her, but that was the least of her worries; she wanted to get Ms. Honeycutt downstairs to the kitchen for some soup and sandwich and pump her for information as soon as possible because it was rather getting late, and she wanted to get a few hours of sleep for herself, after getting Ms. Honeycutt out of la-la land on a full stomach.

LaVonda helped Ms. Honeycutt out of the shower and into her nightshirt that Ms. Honeycutt said was a bit more appropriate for a younger woman than for her. LaVonda said that she would help her look for a housecoat in the morning that would be more her style; it would be just for tonight. Ms. Honeycutt said that would be fine.

LaVonda helped finishing getting Ms. Honeycutt dressed and couldn't help but notice the smile as she put on the white slippers on to her feet. She must have felt some relief on her tired feet from having worn those holey old sneakers she had been wearing.

They were off to the kitchen, and Ms. Honeycutt asked if it would be okay to hold on to her arm as she was taken downstairs. LaVonda said that she'd be honored to help her downstairs as she looked into her light blue eyes that glistened with hope that she was going to be safe and had nothing to worry about because she felt safe and secure being in the care of LaVonda. As they entered the kitchen, LaVonda asked, "What kind of soup would you like with your chicken salad sandwich?"

"Do you have chicken noodle?" Ms. Honeycutt asked.

"I have tomato, clam chowder, white only not the red, and vegetable soup. I may have one can of chicken noodle. I'll look and see if I do."

"That would be nice. Thank you!" Ms. Honeycutt replied as she was seated at the kitchen table and nibbled on some green grapes from the bowl of fruit lying on the table as her dinner was being made for her.

"Would you like a glass of milk with your dinner or some sweet tea?"

"Oh, I'd love a glass of sweet tea," Ms. Honeycutt replied.

"Coming right up. Would you like a slice of lemon with that?"

"No, that would be just fine."

"So tell me, Ms. Honeycutt, what is your first name?"

"My name is Gloria. You can call me by my first name if you like. Ms. Honeycutt sounds so formal and reminds me of the students I used to teach way back when I was a teacher."

"You were a teacher?" LaVonda asked.

"Yes, I taught a class in business marketing and office essentials, to students who were going to be graduating from high school and going out into the business world with the knowledge of using certain office equipment such as the typewriter, mimeograph machines, with copy paper that you had to hand crank before they came into the age of copiers and fax machines. I taught shorthand, the proper way of filing folders into file cabinets by the name or by business, the proper way to answer a phone in a business, take messages. It was many years ago that I did that. The times have changed since then with the new and updated office equipment that they have today. We didn't have computers. We had to go to the library to do research or book reports back then. Today is so much more sophisticated, I wouldn't even know how to turn on a computer."

"Well, while you're here and staying with me, I'll find some time to show you because these days you will need to use a computer whenever you look or apply for a job."

"At my age who will hire me?"

"You would be surprised. Someone with your knowledge would love to snatch you up to run a small office to answer phones. We'll deal with that when the time comes but don't let that worry you right now, okay? Just enjoy your chicken soup that I did have just one can of and this nice chicken salad that I had picked up the other day at the market. Would you like it on white or a croissant, the chicken salad?"

"Oh my, I'll have the croissant. It sounds so much more fancier."

"So where are you from?" LaVonda asked.

"I grew up in New Orleans and I lived there most of my life until I met Andre, who was my husband, and we got married when I was in my twenties. I met him at a jazz bar on Bourbon Street. I had gone down to the French Quarters with some other teachers one evening for dinner and drinks and he was sitting at the bar drinking a hurricane, which they are known for in the French Quarters.

"He was a dashing young man with wavy jet-black hair and blue eyes that caught me from across the room. He had the waitress bring over a drink to me with something he scribbled on a cocktail napkin that said, 'You are a breath of fresh air, please call me for a dinner date' and gave me his phone number. Since I was with friends and coworkers I looked up at him and nodded my head to say thank-you and made sure he saw me put the napkin in my purse. And a few days later I came across this napkin in my purse when I decided to call him. It wasn't something I would normally do, but what the hell, I took a chance. And to my surprise he had answered his phone after I dialed the number and while it was ringing I didn't know what I was going to say when he answered the phone. Before I knew it he was on the other end, saying, 'Hello, Andre speaking.'

"'I don't know if you remember me but I was the breath of fresh air that you scribbled down on a cocktail napkin while I was out with several of my friends a few nights ago down on Bourbon Street at the jazz bar.'

"'I do remember you. I just wanted to say that you were stunning and had me in awe. I didn't want to interrupt your party so I sent the drink over with the message. I hope you didn't mind. I said to myself I have to meet this woman.'

"'So I had you in awe.' I asked, 'May I ask what you do for a living?'

"'I own a beauty salon down on Canal Street and I was on my way home from closing shop and decided to stop for a drink and relax after such a busy day, so I went over to the jazz bar and after sitting alone at the bar for about twenty minutes you came in with your party and had me at awe when you walked in and passed me on the way over to your table.'

"'That's so sweet.'

"'Would you like to meet for coffee and beignets down at Café DuMonde, Saturday morning, before I have to open up shop?' Andre asked.

"'I'd like that,' I replied.

"'So it's a coffee date. How about eight o'clock?' Andre asked. 'Is that too early for you?'

"'No, that's my normal day to run errands since I teach at the high school. I don't have time during the week to do them.'

"'Great, I'll look forward to seeing you then.'

"Well, before you knew it, we had met for coffee and talked about each other's careers and things we like to do when we are not working and several months later after we started dating he asked me to marry him and I did. We spent a wonderful thirty years together until he passed away from a heart attack in the salon when one of his workers came into work and found him lying on the floor by the rinse bowl in the back of the shop. He loved making women feel beautiful when he cut their hair. I think that the smoking and the chemicals that he inhaled all those years from owning the salon did him in. So after that I had to close up the salon because I didn't know the first thing about doing hair and then with my teaching position, which I was let go of because the school was downsizing and my class was no longer needed and I couldn't find another teaching position. I had to work wherever I could to make ends meet since Andre had no life insurance so I just had a breakdown and ended up in a mental hospital for several months and then let go from there and ended up homeless and here I am today."

"You poor thing! You have had a rough life since than, haven't you?" LaVonda asked.

"I've only broken the ice with you, dear. There's so much more you haven't heard. I know you have to get to bed and get some rest so we'll talk more later, if you like to hear my story."

"I'd love to hear more and you're right I need to get to bed. Have you had plenty to eat? Would you like something else?" LaVonda asked.

"No, dear, this was just perfect. Thank you so much for the dinner and for caring. If the world had more people like you in it, it would be a better place."

"Well, thank you for the compliment," LaVonda replied. "Now let me get you up to your room and into a nice cozy bed."

"That would be just wonderful, much more comfortable than a refrigerator box."

"You won't have to worry about ever going back to that. I'll make sure of it. So you ready?"

"Yes, ma'am, I'm exhausted and ready for a long night's sleep."

"I'll just clean up these dishes in the morning. Let's head up to bed!" LaVonda said. So Gloria held on to LaVonda's arm as she escorted her up to the bedroom and shut off the light along the way. Gloria was a remarkable woman in LaVonda's eyes who was determined to help her out in any way possible so she could enjoy the rest of her golden years with some pride.

As they approached the top landing of the staircase to the second floor, Ms. Gloria Honeycutt turned to LaVonda and gave her a peck on the cheek and said, "Thank you for such a wonderful evening. I can't remember the last time that I felt this good."

"You're welcome!" LaVonda replied back. "So here we are. This will be your room and if you need anything I'm just down the hall last door on the right. The bathroom you already know where that is. You have a brand-new bed that no one has slept in and fresh, clean sheets and a quilted comforter on the end of the bed if you get cold in the middle of the night."

"Thank you again for everything!" Gloria said.

"Sweet dreams," LaVonda said back as Gloria closed the door behind her as LaVonda dragged her tired butt to her bedroom, where she decided to take a quick shower and skip the bubble bath and wine. She then crawled into her bed, but not before picking up her paperback book that was lying on the nightstand to read a bit before she could get through the first few pages before nodding out like a light.

This was how she first met Ms. Honeycutt who has been with her for a few weeks, and from the sound of her snoring on the other side of her bedroom door, she was off in la-la land once again. LaVonda had to get to bed herself for tomorrow was going to be another busy day, and she wanted to look her best for when Mario comes by to see her in the morning. She had to finish looking into a job for Ms. Honeycutt to get her grounded on her own two feet with a stable income and eventually a permanent roof over her head.

The Dixie Arms was just a stepping stone to get her back there. She wanted to make sure she would be able to take care of herself before releasing her into the world on her own with dignity and pride. She needed to build up her self-esteem a bit more, so getting her employment and into a working environment with the help of interacting with others would hopefully do that for her. She had been a loner for some time and separated herself from others that it was time to get her on the path to start caring for herself; it was up to her to see where she wanted to go from there, and hopefully she won't take the path back to being the homeless woman she had found in an alleyway once again.

CHAPTER SIX

The highway sign read Food and Gas next to two exits just before crossing the state line from Louisiana into Texas. Truck driver Bubba Higgins was craving a cold bottle of soda and a couple of bacon cheeseburgers with a side order of French fries, so he pulled off of the interstate because he knew it would be a great distance before he had the chance to stop again. He pulled over at the designated area for truckers only and parked his rig alongside of two other truckers who where there and heading into the direction he was just leaving away from Texas. He climbed out of his cab and stretched a bit before heading into the fast-food restaurant area to take care of his taste buds after he made a pit stop for the restroom first. A few minutes later, trucker Bubba was ready to hit the road again with a paper bag full of hot French fries, two bacon cheeseburgers, and a large diet soda in hand—as if that was going to balance out the two burgers and French fries, NOT!

As Bubba climbed back into his cab, the other two truckers were pulling out as they tooted their loud horns; it was as if they were saying so long to him as they were exiting out of the rest area onto the interstate heading out across the country to wherever they were heading. Bubba tooted his horn and sat a few minutes, sipping his diet soda with one hand and chowing down on his bacon and cheeseburger with the other, unaware that just behind him a woken Freeway was peeking out from under a blanket, sniffing the French fries and burgers that had awaken him, or was it the sound of the loud horn that had awaken him from his long, long nap back there in the sleeping quarters of this cab?

Bubba placed his cold drink in the cup holder and took the burger from one hand and placed it in the other and reached over to the bags of French fries, only to notice that Freeway was already headfirst into the bag of fries and scared the living hell out of him. He jumped up from his seat and hit the top of his head with the roof of the cab over him and yelled, "What the hell!" as Freeway came up for a breath of fresh air from being headfirst into the bag of French fries. Bubba rubbed his head from hitting it on the roof and said, "Where did you come from?" as Freeway was eyeing the bacon cheeseburger in Bubba's other hand. Freeway whined a bit and begged for a bite of the bacon cheeseburger, which Bubba broke down and gave in, with a smile on his face from ear to ear, just puzzled on how this beautiful black-and-white border collie ended up here in his cab. He looked for a collar and hopefully a dog tag, but none was to be found on Freeway. Bubba then said, "So I guess I'm going to have to take you with me to Dallas and once we get home, we're going to have to try to find you your rightful owner if that's possible." Freeway then climbed into the passenger seat and sat up as Bubba shared his meal with him. Freeway then laid his head down between his two front paws and closed his eyes to take another nap on a full belly, but not before filling the cab with a bad smell coming from his hindquarters that Bubba said, "Damn," as they pulled out of the truck stop onto the interstate heading home to Dallas.

Donald on the other hand was thinking of Freeway as he was sitting on the edge of his bed, looking down at one of the chew toys that were lying on the floor near the bed. It was one of Freeway's favorite chew toys; it was the one that he used to greet Donald at the door with that was always clinched between his mouth, wanting Donald to take it and throw it so that he could play fetch the minute he stepped through the door.

Donald leaned over and picked it up and held it in his hand close to his heart and said, "One day, Freeway, we'll be able to play fetch again. Just be safe wherever you are," as he took the toy and placed it on his nightstand by the side of the bed. Donald was pretty down in the dumps because his answering machine had no messages for him. He was hoping that maybe one of the jobs that he applied for had panned out, and he would be able to start something that would bring in cash for him after he finished doing his community service for the animal shelter. He like being down there a lot and like being around the dogs that were in the kennel area that kept hope in him that maybe one day while he was there that Freeway would show up. All he had was hope, and right now he had to hope in finding himself a job, or he was going to lose his townhome.

So he picked himself up from the side of the bed where he was sitting, walked into the kitchen, grabbed his car keys, and headed down to his car to make a run over to the convenience store and pick up today's newspaper. It was the weekend edition that had plenty of want ads from local companies that were hiring, so he could start searching all over again since the other three jobs fell through. Once he got to the convenience store, he happened to recognize the salesclerk who was on duty again that he asked if anyone had inquired about Freeway; the salesclerk also recognized Donald and asked how he was doing and if anyone had called him also regarding being the owners of Freeway. Donald said that he hadn't heard anything either, just that Freeway has been on his mind, and that he just found Freeway's favorite toy.

"That's what brought me down to the store to see if you have heard anything and to purchase today's newspaper if you have any left. The newspaper stand out front was empty." Donald asked the salesclerk if he just might have an extra copy behind the sales counter.

The salesclerk said that he had only one left, and it was his copy, but he was willing to give it to Donald since he looked so down in the dumps. "This one's on me," the salesclerk said.

Donald couldn't thank him enough for giving up his own newspaper for him. Donald noticed from the corner of his eye that tonight was the night for the 125-million-dollar drawing and realized that he had purchased one ticket with his old dollar bill from his grandmother but couldn't recall seeing it after he got home. Donald thanked the salesclerk again and said he would be back soon as he ran out of the store and jumped into his car and headed home. Donald was on a mission to find his lottery ticket with the numbers that he played a few days back.

He started in the bedroom, went through all the dresser draws, and then the nightstands. Nothing! Next his closet, he looked in the pockets of his jeans, his pants pockets, went through the dirty-laundry basket, nothing! Next to the living room, looked all over out there, checked in between the sofa cushions under the sofa, around the television stand, nothing! He went to the kitchen area last, looked in the drawers, along the countertop, behind the appliances on the counter, nothing. He turned around and noticed that he had just turned the town house upside down, and no sign of the lottery ticket. He was now going to have to put everything back the way it was before he called it a night, but not before making himself a grilled cheese sandwich, which he was craving for. Donald put everything back to normal and went to the kitchen cabinet, the one near the stove that has all his pots and pans, and reached in for the griddle pan and to his surprise saw the lottery ticket just lying on the inside of a saucepan that was on top of the griddle pan. He busted out into laughter and said, "I'll be damn!"

Donald then put the lottery ticket on top of the television stand where he would hopefully be able to stay awake until eleven o'clock in the evening when the drawing was on. Donald then went back to the kitchen and continued to make his grilled cheese sandwich and then sat down on the sofa and started flipping through the want ads in the newspaper

He had only a few more weeks left to serve on his community service, just weeks away from finding a full-time job after. If he couldn't find something by the end of his service, he was heading in the direction of a financial crisis because his money was dwindling down. Donald spent the rest of his Saturday evening looking through the want ads as well as surfing the web for online job sites from his computer in his bedroom.

Before Donald knew it, as he glanced over to the alarm clock on his nightstand, it was just a few minutes after the ten o'clock hour and decided to call it quits and head off to bed.

He felt pretty good after sending out five resumes online and had four that peaked his interest from the newspaper that he was going to call on Monday after leaving the shelter. While Donald was nodding off in Florida, Freeway was just an hour away from his final destination in Dallas. He had woken up from his nap after sleeping on a full stomach from trucker Bubba's bacon cheeseburgers and French fries and was sitting up with his nose to the wind as the passenger window of the cab was lowered just enough to keep him from trying to jump out of the cab to breathe in some fresh air.

Bubba turned and looked at Freeway and said, "Hey, fella, not too much farther to go before we get there and then I'll get you a big bowl of water when we get home. In the meantime here's some ice that I can give you from this minicooler," which he pulled up from the passenger's side floorboard and opened with one hand and reached in and grabbed a few pieces with his hand as he drove his rig with the other. Freeway turned around from having his nose out the window and lapped up the ice bits until there was no more. "This should quench your thirst until we get there, which won't be much longer, okay? What am I going to call you? You don't have a tag with a name, so I'm going to have to give you a name instead of just calling you Fella. How about French fry since that's how we met with your head in my bag of fries!" Freeway cocked his head to the right and just looked at Bubba, like he was going to give him more fries. "Oh no, I don't have any. I'm thinking of calling you that. What about Stowaway?" Freeway cocked his head to the right and turned around and looked back out the window of the cab. "No, huh? Didn't think so. What about these names: Highway, Roadway, or Freeway?" That got his attention as he turned around from having his nose out the window and let out a loud bark and looked at Bubba and continued to bark as he kept saying "Freeway."

"So you like that name, huh? So Freeway it will be." He put his front paw on Bubba's leg and gave him a lick on the face. Bubba and Freeway were becoming good friends in the cab, but Bubba was going to have to explain to his girlfriend Darla how he left Dallas a week ago with no dog and comes back home with one. Darla wasn't a dog person; she was a cat person. "I'm going to find a way and talk her into letting me keep you. It looks like in the short time that we have spent together, I've enjoyed your company. Let's hope that Darla feels the same way and lets me keep you. You could be my traveling companion on the long-haul trips so I won't have to be alone on the road. Well, we are almost home. Just a few more miles to go and you get to meet Darla. If you want to stay with me, then you best be on your best behavior like you have been with me on this ride home.

"I still have no friggin' idea how you ended up in the back of my cab. But it has been a pleasure having your company and we'll just have to see what Darla has to say about you!" Bubba and Freeway finally reached their final destination as they drove down the long dirt road toward the house that was sitting in the middle of ten acres on a dry and desolate land. Darla could be seen walking out the front door onto the front porch and was standing there waving her arms as if she was guiding a plane into a gate at the Dallas Airport. Bubba honked his horn to say hello as they approached the house. There were no neighbors for miles from them, so the sound of the horn from the cab of the truck wouldn't bother anyone. It would spook the armadillos or any other critters that may be on the property in the evening. Bubba parked his rig next to the house, and as he opened the door to his cab, Freeway had already jumped over his lap and down to the ground and sniffed his way over to a fence post and peed like a racehorse. He needed to go really bad.

Bubba then climbed down from the cab to be greeted by Darla who was standing there waiting to give Bubba a hug and to welcome him home from being gone for a week. She couldn't help but notice and comment on the dog that jumped out of the cab and nearly scared her to death as she approached the cab. She first hugged Bubba, welcomed him home, and then said, "What on earth was that?" Bubba said that Freeway, his new riding companion, had stowed away in his cab, and he had no friggin' idea how he got there in the first place. He continued to fill her in on how they met and how he enjoyed having his company on the way home and then asked, "Darla"—like a little boy would ask his mother—"can we keep him? Can we keep him, please!"

Darla said, "For the night it wouldn't be a problem, but the discussion on keeping him after tonight would require further discussion. But for now let's get you settled in and cleaned up and have something to eat, then we can talk about Freeway." Who was, by the way, just sitting on the ground beside the both of them on his hind legs, looking up at the two of them after taking care of his long overdue business, waiting for Bubba to look down at him to introduce him to Darla and then invite him inside of their home.

Bubba agreed with Darla and said they would discuss it later and that he was just glad to be home and happy to see her. Darla said, "You go take a shower and I'll be getting you something to eat if you're hungry and a nice cold beer for afterward."

Bubba said he wasn't really hungry, but the ice-cold beer sounded great, as they both headed back into the house as Freeway followed once he heard Bubba's voice say, "Come on, Freeway, you have a place to stay for tonight," as they entered the house. Bubba headed toward the bedroom and bathroom and Darla toward the kitchen for a cold beer. Freeway didn't know who to follow as he just sat in the middle of the living room floor, watching as the two of them just disappeared out of his sight, when he heard Bubba's voice from down the hall and around the corner yell, "Freeway, come on!" Freeway dashed in the direction to Bubba's voice, which was coming from the bedroom as he was just going into the bathroom to shower. Freeway jumped up onto the bed and made himself comfortable by digging into the bed pillows and tossing them around and making himself a place to rest his head as he waited for Bubba to come out from his shower.

Darla, who just happened to walk into the bedroom, saw Freeway up on the bed and said, "Oh hell no! Sorry, Freeway, you are not sleeping in our bed. You got two choices—one is sleeping on the floor or the other is outside on the front porch."

Freeway lifted his head up from the bed and directly looked at her as if he was saying to her, "You kidding me?" She yelled at him to get down, but not before Freeway stood up and peed again, but this time in the center of the bed right in front of Darla, who was horrified and started screaming louder at him as he dashed out of the bedroom and down the hall to the front door. It was Freeway's way of saying, "Bitch, I'll take my chances outside than being stuck inside with you."

Bubba came rushing out of the shower with a towel wrapped around his waist, yelling, "What is all the screaming going on in here?" as Darla is stripping the bed linens and blankets off the bed to be washed.

She yelled back at Bubba, "It's that damn dog you brought home. He just stood up and looked at me as I told him to get down of the bed, that he was not sleeping up there, and told him he was going to either sleep on the floor or on the front porch, when he looked at me, stood up, and just peed and ran out of the room." Bubba had a grin on his face from ear to ear as he wanted to burst into laughter for he wished he could have been in the room just a few minutes earlier to see that scene. Darla was not amused and told Bubba to wipe that smirk off his face or she was going to do it and to go find out where in the hell Freeway ran off to.

Bubba, still wrapped in his bath towel, headed out of the bedroom and down the hall toward the living room area where he saw Freeway sitting on the floor in the entryway, looking up at the door as if to say, "Let me out."

He bent down, looked at Freeway, and said, "Well, I guess you told her, didn't you. Thanks for making my homecoming a bit more than I expected this trip around. I gather from where you're sitting right now you chose the front porch! Let me get you a blanket from the hall closet and a bowl of water and you can then go outside on the porch. I'm sorry this happened but I told you earlier that Darla was a cat person and not a dog person. You know that by you pulling your little stunt has made it harder for me to persuade her into letting me keep you." Bubba then opened up the front door, laid the blanket on the lawn chair that was up on the porch, and placed the bowl of water by the door as Freeway climbed up into the chair and with his head between his paws looked at Bubba to say, "I'm sorry," as he was patted on the head and told by Bubba that he was going to try to fix this and to get a good night's sleep outside on this lawn chair and that he would see him first thing in the morning and hopefully have some good news after he calmed Darla down. Bubba then turned around, still wrapped in his bath towel, and headed back into the house where Darla was waiting patiently for Bubba to return to help flip the bed mattress that just happened to get a little soiled from Freeway. It was going to be a long night for Bubba and just as long for Freeway who could not get settled in the lawn chair and decided to head over to the tractor trailer parked on the side of the house and crawled underneath to try to get some sleep. He dozed off with flashbacks of Donald who let him sleep on his grandmother's old quilt at the foot of the bed and his chew toy that was nearby as he dozed off into doggy dreams.

As the sunrise was peering through the blinds of the bedroom, Bubba was waking up next to Darla after they spent last night getting the bed back to normal after Freeway's stunt and a few beers and conversation with Darla that he had lost his fight to keep Freeway. He was going to have to get up and tell Freeway that he had to have to go to a shelter in Dallas as soon as he got up and dressed and had his morning caffeine. Freeway was still sound asleep under the truck and was just waking up at the same time and crawled out and stretched and walked back up onto the porch for a drink of water when he heard voices from the other side of the door. It was Bubba telling Darla that he would take care of Freeway and bring him into Dallas today and try to find him a good home with the assistance of the Dallas Animal Shelter. Within minutes the front door opened up. Bubba was standing there with a cup of coffee, dressed in blue jeans and cowboy boots and a buttoned-down shirt, and said good morning to Freeway and asked how he slept and said that he didn't sleep very well, that he had tossed and turned, and that he was going to take him for a drive this morning and that he was going to help him locate a new place to stay. "Darla made it clear that it was her or you. And since I have been with her longer and only knew you for a couple days that I have to say I chose her. I'm sorry, Freeway, I would have loved to have kept you around to be my companion on my road trips but it just wouldn't work out with Darla. So we are going for a ride this morning in my pickup truck and not the cab this morning into Dallas where I promise I will find you a good home. So let's hit the road, okay?"

Freeway looked up at Bubba as if to say, "I understand. I don't like it, but I understand," and turned around and waited for Bubba's command to follow him.

Darla in the meantime was peering through the blinds and watched as they both climbed into Bubba's pickup truck and drove down the driveway and said, "Sorry I had to do this, Bubba, but we just can't take on something that needs love and attention constantly and with you on the road a lot and me working in town in Dallas with late night getting home wouldn't be fair for Freeway. It had to be this way.

"One day when we are both home full time or you are, I will promise to get you a dog then. However, not right now." She closed the blind, turned around, and wiped her cheek for she felt bad for Bubba, having just watched him say good-bye to Freeway and to see them both drive off, knowing they already bonded was going to be hard for Bubba. Darla might have been a bitch the night before, but she was trying to avoid the heartache that comes with losing a pet.

She was not only a cat lover but was also a dog lover. She lead Bubba to believe otherwise and didn't want him to know that she once had a springer spaniel who was her best friend for many years, which was a gift from a friend, who helped her though some difficult times in her life and unfortunately had been hit by a car as it was chasing an armadillo in a park as they dashed across the street.

This woman who was running late to a cookout in the park and in a rush hit her spaniel as it dashed into the street. The woman apologized, stopped, and assisted in getting her and her dog to the vets and paid all the medical bills, only to have to put the dog down several weeks later when she lost all movement and was not able to walk again or have control of her bowel movements.

It was the hardest thing she had to do, to say good-bye, and swore that she would not ever get another dog again. She felt the pain that Bubba was going to experience, but it's not as bad as if he had Freeway longer than the few days together that they shared; it would have been worse.

CHAPTER SEVEN

Donald had such a restless night sleeping, with him tossing and turning, with all that he has going on these days, with worrying about finding a job after he completes his community service at the shelter, finances, and then on the whereabouts of Freeway, that when he opened his eyes and glanced over at the alarm clock on the nightstand, it was flashing five thirty in the morning on this rainy Sunday morning in South Florida. He took his sweet time from getting up from his bed when he realized that he had nothing going on today and was just going to hang out at home and watch television and a few movies today to rest up for another week at the shelter and calling about the job interviews he saw in last night's paper and circled to call Monday afternoon when he came home from the shelter. Donald took his time and moved into the kitchen and poured himself a glass of orange juice and made a pot of coffee and then walked over to the living room and turned on the television and sat there most of the morning, channel surfing till he found something that caught his eye and decided to watch when he came upon the local news that had stated that the last night's lottery in South Florida for the whopping 125 million dollars was won by one person from the Coral Springs area from the Saturday night's drawing and that the next drawing was going to be for 25 million dollars on Wednesday night's drawing at ten o'clock that evening and to watch your local news channel for the winning numbers.

Donald then remembered that he laid his lotto ticket up on the entertainment center and got up and walked over and picked it up and then walked into his bedroom and over to his computer on his desk and proceeded to search the Internet for last night's drawing to see what the numbers were drawn and to see if he had the winning ticket.

With the rain that was going on outside, he was not able to get any reception or connections to the World Wide Web to find out any information. So he just laid his ticket in the top draw of his desk and turned off his computer and went back to the living room to watch television. It was about three o'clock in the afternoon, and after watching two movies and a few television shows that he found interesting, he noticed that the sun was starting to come out and it had stopped raining. Donald decided to stop being a couch potato, took a shower, and got dressed. He needed to run to the supermarket and pick up a few things to get him through the week for meals. He would also pick up today's newspaper to see if any other positions might have been posted that wasn't in the newspaper from yesterday that he could add to his phone call list for the week.

As he walked into the supermarket, he glanced over to the customer service counter and noticed that it wasn't busy and headed over in that direction and picked up today's newspaper that was stacked up on the counter and paid for it with the few loose coins he had in his jeans pockets. He had noticed that the lottery drawing was on the front page in small print and looked down at the numbers when he noticed that the numbers looked too close to his numbers but not in the sequence that had been printed out on his ticket. Donald, with newspaper in hand, walked back over to the entrance of the store and took one of the shopping carts and headed back into the store to get a few things that would get him through the week for lunches and some frozen dinners for dinners at night when he got home from the shelter.

The frozen food aisle has some great deals where you buy one and then get one free. Donald had enjoyed having one or two of the dinners a while back and with money running short would take advantage of the sale.

He picked up several dinners from the frozen food cooler and one frozen pizza and then headed over to the bread aisle and picked up another loaf of white bread and dashed over to the lunch meat aisle and picked up a package of bologna and sliced ham and a package of all-American cheese, but not before picking up a jar of peanut butter on the end cap before heading to the cashier to check out. He now had enough food to get him through the week for both dinners and lunches. Donald paid his grocery tab, which came to the amount of thirty-five dollars and change, which now left him ten dollars for the remainder of the week for drinks and jerky. Donald then headed home and unpacked the few groceries he had, which took a mere five minutes to put away, and then walked into his bedroom over to his desk and pulled out his lotto ticket from the top draw and went back to the kitchen area where he had laid the newspaper down and checked his ticket against the newspaper, one number at a time. The first number was one, followed by the number three and then four. He got three numbers so far; then there was the number eighteen, followed by the numbers twenty-one and the last number sixty-seven.

Donald's hands were trembling so hard he had to verify the numbers again. He then dashed into his bedroom and turned on his computer, which now was working fine since the rain had stopped a bit earlier.

Donald searched the Internet again and came across the lottery site that indeed matched all six numbers on his ticket. Donald felt his chest; he thought he was going to have a coronary.

He then let out one hell of a scream and jumped up and down in his bedroom, up on the bed, and said, "Holy shit! I'm rich! I'm rich!" He then took some time to compose himself and realized that he had to now collect this money as soon as possible. With 125 million dollars at stake, he had to be careful and discreet; otherwise, the "crazy train" was about to hit town with long-lost friends and cousins and acquaintances and then the media—it was going to be a circus. He wanted to tell someone, but whom? He tried to call his parents back in Sutton Falls, but they were not home. The house sitter said that they were on a well-deserved vacation from running the campground and were on a cruise ship in Greece. It would be another few weeks before they would be home and that if they happened to call, the house sitter would make sure they got the message he had called.

Donald's parents never knew or will not ever find out about his arrest and what he had done while living down here in South Florida. If they knew, it would upset them; both of his parents have heart diseases, and the stress of keeping up with the campgrounds has finely taken a toll on their health. That's probably why they got far away from the campground and took the well-deserved vacation they so desperately needed. He would find out more on how they were feeling when he spoke to them in a couple of weeks when they got back. Donald had great news and wanted to scream it from the rooftop of his town house but couldn't. What was Donald going to do with this large amount of money once he collected it?

When would be the right time to go to Jacksonville and get it? Should he go with a lawyer? Should he wait till his parents got back from their trip and tell them to fly down so they can drive up together to collect it? He did know that he had to finish his community service, or it was going to be jail time, and he didn't want to go back down that road. Besides, his parents would find out then.

That wasn't an option he was going to take. Hell no, jail was not going to be the option for Donald to take! Besides, it was only a few weeks away till he finishes his community service. Donald enjoyed being around the shelter and liked Ms. Kitty; being around all the dogs opened his eyes on how to be more compassionate and kind to the canines. Donald had learned a lot in the short time being at the shelter, and he wanted to do his part to make more people aware that there are too many canines taking up space in the shelter and all across the United States that needed a good home before it's too late for them when they would eventually have to be put down.

Freeway in a way helped Donald see clearly that he did have compassion for all living things and that canines were there for companionship in someone's life, which brought smiles and joy to those who were handicapped, used as guide dogs for the blind, helped in the therapy for people who just gave up on life and never talked until the first time, and made others smile. They have helped people who were in shells to come out and be alive once again. They'll give their loyalty and love back with just a lick or snuggle under your chin. They'll greet you at the front door after a long day away from them, all happy and excited to see you arrive home.

When you have a bad day, they put a smile on your face and make you forget about the bad day you had. They'll help keep your blood pressure low and make you relax just after a few minutes from being with them. They don't talk back. They don't ask for money; all they have is unconditional love for someone in need.

He continued to find ways to find homes for all of them before he left the shelter. He now had enough money that he could build a huge house on a large lot of land and adopt them all. He could afford to feed them; money wouldn't be a problem anymore.

He could also offer a huge reward to find Freeway, but then the "crazy train" would bring out all types of people with all types of dogs, saying that they had Freeway. Donald wanted to make up for the awful way he treated him and for Freeway to give him another chance as well as his love.

In return they just want your unconditional love, for you to take care of them. Unfortunately for Donald, he was a little late to learn this compassion, by having to spend time in county jail, and doing community service at the shelter was not the way he wanted to find out.

Donald now had to find a place to hide this lotto ticket until it was time to collect his winnings. Where would you hide a 125-million-dollar winning ticket until you were ready to collect? Donald looked all over the town house for a save spot to hide the ticket.

He realized that it was his grandmother's dollar, and he remembered Freeway, and he went to the linen closet and pulled out his grandmother's quilt, the one that Freeway slept on; it was the best place to hide it. He unfolded the quilt and found several places on the quilt where the stitching had fallen out and where he could slide the ticket in between the top layer and bottom layer on the batting and then folded it back up and put it back in the closet. "Thanks, Grandma, may you rest in peace."

Once this was hidden away and secure, Donald couldn't stand still anymore. He had to get out of the house and went for a drive to clear his head. He had all kinds of plans running through his head on what he was going to do with the winnings. He wanted to help out his parents and get help with the upkeep of the campground, maybe hire people to take care of the grounds for them. He wanted to pay off their house but remembered that Grandma's will and insurance took care of that. He was debating on whether to pay off his town house and keep it or yet build a bigger house and give the town house to his parents as a second home for them to get away from the cold winters in Sutton Falls and which they now would be known as what is called in South Florida as snowbirds, who are people from the East Coast who come only in the winter months to get away from the cold and snow and return back to the East Coast when the first sign of warm weather is here to stay, only to return several months later once the chill was back in the air for the winter months.

Would he purchase a new car? How much money would he donate to charities and organizations, if any? Donald had so much on his mind that he needed to go for a drive before heading back to the shelter in the morning without causing any suspicion that he was now a millionaire.

Donald drove down University Drive, one of the major streets near his townhome, and headed south until he came upon Commercial Blvd. and headed west toward the expressway, which he was familiar with since it was where he got into trouble in the first place. He could not help but notice as he drove toward the expressway that all the vacant land that was once there was getting sparse, for the land was being filled up with new shopping centers and retail stores as well as restaurants and a school and even a church as he got closer to the expressway. Donald then realized he could own one of them if he wanted to; he had the money to build and then rent out the retail spaces and make money as a return on his investment for being an owner or landlord. His mind was still on spending the money, and he needed to focus away from it for the time being and needed to concentrate on getting through the next few weeks at the shelter.

Donald was just approaching the ramp to the expressway but not before noticing a huge billboard that said "for sale ten acres zoned for building commercial, call this phone number posted." Donald jotted down the number on a piece of paper that was on the console of his car. It was the last piece of property this size that was left on Commercial Blvd. that had not been taken up with development already. It was backed up to the access road before leaving the interstate. On the other side of the access road were the everglades.

That was the only concern that there'd be a lot of traffic at this intersection, but the land was the first thing you saw once you got off the interstate or the last place seen before getting onto the interstate. Donald was going to hang on to this phone number; he was also pondering buying the land to build a state-of-the-art animal shelter for canines so that the dogs in the northern part of the city would have a place to go if they were abandoned or strays. The residents in this part of the county wouldn't have to commute south for forty-five minutes if they wanted to adopt a dog, and it would be larger than the one south of town, with more room for outside kennels and more that Donald would have to sit down and plan.

This was just another idea rambling through his mind with all the others, and it was just overwhelming at the time. Donald entered the access road and was about to do a U-turn when he noticed a police cruiser just parked over to the side of the road to the right of him, staking out the cars getting on and off the interstate at high rates of speed, and he was not going to do the U-turn that he thought would send the police cruiser in his direction. He had enough of dealing with the police and was not going to take the chance of being pulled over for an illegal turn at the stop sign. So he just decided to take the access road up to the interstate and then get off at the next exit, which would be Oakland Blvd., and head east for about five miles, which would be University Drive, then head north back toward Coral Springs to head home to get some rest before he had to go back to the shelter in the morning, but not before he stopped and took care of his craving for a bucket of fried chicken and a side order of mashed potatoes and gravy with a few biscuits before heading home.

CHAPTER EIGHT

As the full moon lit up the sky over the Dixie Arms, LaVonda was just in a sound sleep around midnight when she heard a loud scream coming from down the hall from Ms. Honeycutt's bedroom. LaVonda jumped up from her sound sleep and tossed her bed linens aside and dashed down the hall to Ms. Honeycutt's bedroom and opened the door to her room to find Ms. Honeycutt lying on the floor next to her bed. She had fallen out of her bed. LaVonda turned on the light to the room and ran over to assist Ms. Honeycutt and to make sure she had no injuries or bruises from falling off the bed. "Are you okay, Ms. Honeycutt?"

"Oh, darlin', I'm fine, just a little stunned from the fall. I had a bad dream that someone or something was trying to get into my refrigerator box while I was sleeping and I heard a scratching sound coming from the top of the box when I crawled out to look what it was and there was this huge raccoon sitting on the box, looking right down at me from the edge of the box and was wearing a mask, which was their eyes looking down at me. It was holding some kind of sharp object and I couldn't make out what it was. I started to scream thinking it was a burglar that was going to attack me. Then I started screaming and fell out of the bed onto the floor."

"You poor thing," LaVonda told her. "It was just a bad dream and you're safe and will be from here on in. You never have to worry about going back to that refrigerator box again behind that dumpster. Give me your hand and I'll help you back into bed," LaVonda told her.

Ms. Honeycutt reached her hand out to LaVonda for her assistance on getting up from the floor. "Thank you so much for coming to help me. I'm sorry I interrupted your sleep with my scream."

"Oh, it's okay," LaVonda told her. "I was just in and out of a light sleep watching the clock roll by. I have so much on my mind these days, running the Dixie Arms and then looking for part-time help. It has just become a bit overwhelming but I'm used to being overwhelmed. I'll be fine in a day or so and be back to normal Are you sure you're fine?" LaVonda asked Ms. Honeycutt. "No cuts or bruises from the fall?"

"No, I'm fine. It's my pride that is a little hurt from falling off the bed. I have never ever had a dream that caused me to fall out of bed in my lifetime. This is the first."

"Don't worry, I won't tell a soul about this," LaVonda assured her.

"Thank you!" Ms. Honeycutt replied back.

"Well, it's just a little after one o'clock in the morning. Would you like me to get you a glass of warm milk or a glass of water maybe? Before we try to get back to sleep and at least get a few more hours of sleep in before sunrise."

"Oh, I'd love a glass of warm milk if it wouldn't be a problem."

"No problem at all," LaVonda replied. "I'll just run down to the kitchen and heat you up a glass of milk and I'll be right back, okay? You'll be all right?"

"Yes, dear, I'll be just fine now that I'm back in the bed."

"I'll be right back in a few minutes with your milk," LaVonda said as she walked out of the bedroom, heading toward the kitchen, mumbling under her breath, "Stupid bitch, now I won't be able to get back to sleep. Why did I even offer warm milk? I should have just kept my mouth shut and tucked her back into bed and left it at that. A raccoon my ass! She was drunk. I could smell the Jack on her breath and the hidden bottle under the pillowcase. Who does she think she is fooling? I'm going to have to make sure that this doesn't get out of hand. A nightcap is fine once in a while, but a whole bottle? That's a bit much. She'd be tossing her cookies after she mixes the warm milk with the Jack and about a half an hour and then I'll have to deal with that real nightmare. Oh, what the hell, it's her first night here and she has gone through a lot in her life and being in a strange place compared to a refrigerator box, and not knowing me is a lot to take in a night.

"God forgive me for I shouldn't be bitchin'. That's what I'm here for, to help those misfortunate, not make fun of them. I'm just cranky, that's all it is, just tired and cranky. Well, here I am in the kitchen warming a glass of milk and the time now is one forty-five by the clock over the stove. I need to be on my best and look my best in the morning when Mario comes over in the morning to start work. I'll need a beauty mask or tons of Olay to get rid of the bags I'll have in the morning if I don't get my ass back to bed soon. I think this milk is ready," she said as she poured it from the pan to a glass and then shut off the burner and placed the pan in the sink and headed back up to Ms. Honeycutt who was graciously waiting until her next nightmare happens in about thirty minutes when she mixes it with the Jack in her system. As LaVonda approached the bedroom where Ms. Honeycutt was sleeping, she could hear her snoring like a truck driver. As she entered the room, she noticed that Ms. Honeycutt was sound asleep, so she tucked her in and placed the glass of warm milk on the nightstand and said sweet dreams and headed back to her own room to get some well-needed sleep, or the morning was not going to be pleasant for her or anyone else that she comes in contact with in the morning.

It was now seven o'clock in the morning when LaVonda glanced at her alarm clock on the nightstand and jumped up from her bed and said, "Shit! I overslept. I wanted to be up by at least six o'clock. Oh well, I needed the sleep. I hope Ms. Honeycutt is doing better than she was last night." She threw on her bathrobe and headed out of her bedroom, heading down the hall toward the staircase to get her first cup of coffee in the morning, when she noticed that Ms. Honeycutt's bedroom door was open and the bed was made up. She smelled hazelnut coffee as she headed down the staircase toward the kitchen as she could hear voices coming from the kitchen. She said, "Shit! I look like a hot mess and now I have to meet whoever's in the kitchen looking like this." It was just Ms. Honeycutt, who was listening to the local radio station as she was sipping a cup of coffee at the table.

"Oh, thank God, it's just you in here. How're you feeling this morning after your fall from the bed?" LaVonda asked her. "You sore at all?"

"No! Just fine and dandy and ready for another day in paradise. I never slept so good," Ms. Honeycutt told LaVonda. "It must have been that comfortable mattress I slept on."

"Yeah, that's it," LaVonda said as she had a smirk on her face and thought to herself, *No, it was because you were drunk on your ass and passed out.* But she was nice and left it at that.

"Well, what would you like me to do today for you since it's going to be my first real day here at the Dixie Arms with you. Would you like me to help you with some housekeeping? Maybe a little dusting, vacuum the floors, clean up a bit here in the kitchen? Do some office work like filing or make phone calls?

Oh, aren't we just full of piss and vinegar this morning?

Oh, it's just that I'm a morning person and the sooner you get the things you hate to do out of the way early in the day, you can then relax and enjoy the rest of the day doing what you like to do."

"What is it that you like to do?" LaVonda asked as she poured herself a cup of hazelnut coffee that Ms. Honeycutt made a pot of for her and LaVonda to enjoy when she woke up this morning.

"Well, I used to like to run errands in my earlier days then putter around the yard and weed and garden. I'd do the housework that needed to be done and then spend the rest of the day reading or visiting friends. Most recently was collecting bottles for recycling to make some money to feed myself and get me something to drink from time to time."

"Oh really," LaVonda replied, knowing she already drank and had a bottle under her pillow from last night's escapade. LaVonda wanted to know if she would come forward and admit she might or might not have a slight drinking problem. "So what do you like to drink?"

Ms. Honeycutt replied back, "Soda pop, iced tea, coffee, and from time to time a pint of Jack Daniel's to take the edge off from walking all day collecting. There were days that I would get so numb that I hoped that I wouldn't wake up in the morning. I had no life anymore, nothing to show for it but a few raggedy clothes that were hand-me-downs and a shopping cart filled with bottles and a box that I called home. I had no friends anymore. I had no job. I had no one in my life to keep living for. It was the bottle from time to time to get the edge off that kept me going until you came along and saved me. I don't know how I can ever repay you for all you have done for me. So if there is anything that I can do to help out around this big old house, I'm willing to help to show you that I appreciate all that you have done for me." LaVonda, already teary eyed from hearing that, told her that she was not to worry about paying her back and that since it was her first day at the Dixie that she was going to go shopping for new clothes in the spare bedroom that was set up with donations, to go and pick out a new wardrobe that she could keep; and then she was going to take her down to her hairstylist and get her hair done up after she met with Mario and got him started on his first day of work for her, and then they were off.

Ms. Honeycutt was so thrilled that she was getting new clothes that she got up from the kitchen table and walked over to LaVonda and gave her a big hug and a kiss on the cheek and thanked her for being her guardian angel. LaVonda reminded Ms. Honeycutt that she had nothing to worry about and that she was there to help her and get her back on her feet and eventually find her a job with the skills that she had, and eventually she would have a new life of her own, and that would be the payback that she wanted to see from her if she put her mind to it and tried to pick up where she left off before she became the local bag lady. Ms. Honeycutt said that she was going to do exactly that and that LaVonda would be proud. LaVonda replied back and said, "That's all I want to see," as she placed her coffee cup down on the counter and took Ms. Honeycutt's hand and walked her out of the kitchen and up the staircase to go shopping for something to wear from the donated-goods room as she went and took a shower and got dressed before Mario came.

Once they reached the bedroom where all the donated clothes for women were, LaVonda said, "Go on in and find yourself something pretty to wear and I'll be back in a few," as she headed to her bedroom to get showered and dressed. Ms. Honeycutt was in awe; there were so many clothes, and some of them still had price tags on them. Some of the clothes were too big for her to wear, and others were too small, but she managed to find several skirts and blouses and a couple of long-sleeved, buttoned sweaters and several pairs of designer shoes that she loved and fitted just right. They, of course, were low heeled, very low heeled, and she had also picked a nice pair of slippers and a pair of running shoes to replace the ones that were tossed out last night in the trash. She found several pieces of costume jewelry that she liked to wear as broaches and a pearl necklace, and then she almost peed on herself when she saw the hat racks that were set up from one corner of the room with hats that only reminded her of Minnie Pearl from *Hee Haw*, some still with price tags on them. She took one hat to wear with her new outfit and several others for later dressing. She loved her hats. She missed her red one that she was wearing when she came into Dixie Arms last evening. She made a mental note in her mind, what was left of it, to ask LaVonda what had happened to it. She was going to wear the just-below-the-knee-length navy blue skirt with the pale yellow-colored ruffled blouse and a broach to top it off and this navy blue pillbox hat with yellow Bedazzled stones that edged the top of the hat and with yellow and blue feathers that came out from the side. She was now heading back to her own bedroom with her arms filled with new clothes and hats. LaVonda peeked out from her room with a towel wrapped around her, for she had just gotten out of the shower and was looking for Ms. Honeycutt as she came down the hall humming a happy tune. LaVonda asked her if she found something to wear and that she'd be ready in about twenty minutes to come help her get dressed if needed. Ms. Honeycutt replied back, "Yes, dear, all is well. I found everything and then some. I will be ready myself in about twenty to thirty minutes. I'll meet you downstairs when I get dressed for another cup of hazelnut coffee in the kitchen with you if that's okay."

"I'd like that," LaVonda told her.

"I'll meet you downstairs then." Ms. Honeycutt shuffled into her bedroom and placed all the clothes on the bed and started to get dressed. She had taken a bath last night so was going to skip that this morning but was going to wash her face though and then get dressed. Within a matter of minutes, she was dressed and heading down the staircase to the kitchen to meet LaVonda who was already dressed and sitting at the kitchen table sipping her coffee when she looked up and saw Ms. Honeycutt enter the kitchen all dressed like she was going to church on Sunday. She was pretty as a picture, as pretty as anyone can be who just left a refrigerator box in an alley and was on her way back to self-esteem.

"Damn !" LaVonda spoke out. "You look incredible. The clothes fit just perfectly. The hat's a bit much though."

"Do you not like it?" Ms. Honeycutt asked.

"No, I like it. It's just that I haven't seen a hat like that since *Hee Haw*."

"That's how I felt when I found it," Ms. Honeycutt told her. "I just like big festive hats. It gives me a lift. I feel like the queen mom when I wear them." With a smile on her face, she modeled it for LaVonda who was about to bust a gut with laughter but controlled herself so she wouldn't make Ms. Honeycutt feel bad. She had a lot going on, and laughing at her was not going to help any.

So she said, "Oh, it's just fine and does match the rest of your outfit though, so go ahead and wear it if it makes you feel good." LaVonda had to change the subject from the hat conversation to something else before she did lose it with laughter. "Oh, I called my stylist Andre who is just a few blocks from here in his salon and was able to squeeze you in about eleven thirty this morning for a makeup and redo."

"Oh, I can't wait. I can't remember the last time I was pampered," she said as she took her cup of hazelnut coffee and sat down at the table with LaVonda.

"Oh, he is really good. He does wonders with my hair!" *I can't wait to see what he does to you rats nest*, she was thinking to herself, which was just tragic. She envisioned mice running all through her hair and on top of the hat. "Oh, you'll feel like a new woman by the time you leave his salon. I thought we could go for a drive along the beach so you can see the area and then I need to stop at the store and pick up a few things that we need here and you can come along for the ride. Would you like that?" LaVonda asked.

"I'd love it as long as you don't drive too fast like you did last night. I hate to lose my hat along the beachfront."

"Oh, I'll drive slow," she said. *Darn!* LaVonda said to herself, *I thought for sure I could get rid if that hat. It would have just flown off her head and out the window down to the beach area.* "I have a gentleman named Mario who is coming here at ten o'clock who will be working for me part-time and is also a traffic cop for the county sheriff's office."

"Oh my," Ms. Honeycutt replied, "a man in uniform here with me!" with a big old smile on her face.

"Oh, not to worry, he won't be in his uniform and he's volunteering to help me out here at the shelter so I can run my errands and keep the shelter open without having to lock up every time I leave here. He will answer the phones, do some clerical work and stuff for me on the computer and odd things around here. Speaking of computer, I'd like to show you how to use one sometime soon. It will be something that most companies have and use these days and you'll need to learn how to operate one when you get back out into the working world."

"Oh, nice, you're going to try to teach this old dog new tricks you could say!"

"That should be a real treat for you." LaVonda chuckled back. "In time we'll get to that. I'll either teach you how or maybe I'll have Mario teach you."

"Oh, will he be wearing his uniform?"

"Oh, I don't think so."

"Darn it. I just love a man in uniform," Ms. Honeycutt replied.

"I can tell!" LaVonda told her. "So he will be here shortly and I will introduce you to him and then I will take him around the shelter and show him where he will be working and then we can be off to get you all gussied up."

"I'll be ready. Do you mind if I take a stroll outside in the backyard and just sip my coffee and look around?"

"No, I don't mind. Let me show you the way to get out there, so then you can go out whenever you like. It is just around the corner over here on the other side of the walk in the pantry just a few steps away to the door that leads into the backyard. Just make sure you hold on to the stair railing when you go out. I wouldn't want you to slip and fall."

"Oh, I will, dear. These old legs have been around the block, literally. I will make sure I hold on to the railing. They ain't like they used to be. They are finally wearing out on me. Anything to lean on from time to time helps a great deal. Even a man in uniform helps me a lot better." LaVonda chuckled once again at Ms. Honeycutt. The doorbell rang, and as LaVonda was finishing showing Ms. Honeycutt the way out to the backyard, she glanced down at her watch and realized it was exactly ten o'clock on the dot.

"This just might be Mario and on time too." She walked with Ms. Honeycutt to the front door and through the frosted glass doors saw Mario standing there all dashing and very good looking.

Ms. Honeycutt couldn't help herself but to say, "My heart be still."

LaVonda said, "I know the feeling, but what you might want to say from now on in is 'CHILD, PLEASE!' It's another way of saying 'what a hunk.'"

"Oh, I like that saying," Ms. Honeycutt told LaVonda. "CHILD, PLEASE!" LaVonda opened the door to welcome Mario who couldn't help but overhear Ms. Honeycutt say it!

LaVonda burst into laughter as Mario came into the Dixie Arms. LaVonda introduced Ms. Honeycutt to Mario and told him that she was the most recent guest at the Arms and that he'd be seeing her around the shelter. To herself she said, *Yeah, and maybe more.* She has a uniform stalker on her hands as she grinned from cheek to cheek.

"How nice to meet you," Mario replied back.

"Likewise," Ms. Honeycutt replied back as she excused herself from the two of them so they could get on with their business and she could find her way out to the backyard alone.

"Oh, I can smell hazelnut. Is that the choice that you chose to brew for me?"

"You've got the flavor right, but it wasn't me who made it this morning. It was Ms. Honeycutt who made it this morning. She was up before me and found her way around the kitchen and to my surprise."

"Surprise?" Mario asked.

"Yeah, I'll fill you in later on that," she replied as they headed toward the kitchen to get Mario a cup of hazelnut coffee and a refill for herself so she could get started on getting Mario settled in on his first day at the shelter by showing him the office and the kitchen and the living or sleeping quarters for the homeless as well as the donated goods in the two bedrooms that she set up as a store for those in need of clothing.

LaVonda asked Mario if he wouldn't mind assisting the gentlemen when they come in, with getting them fitted for clothes. He said there would be no problem with helping them. She mentioned that she had made an eleven-thirty appointment with her stylist to have him do something with Ms. Honeycutt's hair and that while she was gone, would he get familiar with the files and the vendors she calls on for donations and to answer the phone while she was out and that this was her password to get into the computer system to update the spreadsheets and the vendor list and donations. He said he had no problem keeping himself busy while she was out and that it was already a little bit after eleven and that she needed to go get Ms. Honeycutt and get on the road before she missed her appointment.

LaVonda said, "There was a reason why I hired you. Because you are so efficient." Mario made himself comfortable in the office as LaVonda headed back to the kitchen to see if Ms. Honeycutt was done with her walk in the backyard and if she was ready to go. As she approached the kitchen, Ms. Honeycutt was sitting at the table and waiting. She mentioned to LaVonda that the backyard was so big and that if it was okay she'd like to plant some colorful plants along the border when she had time if she likes it. "I don't have a problem with that but you will probably be busy with training on the computer and then there will be the job interviews down the road. The weekends I will be glad to take you to the garden center for plants. That will be the best time to do that."

"That would be fine," Ms. Honeycutt replied back. "I will enjoy the gardening then and it will help me relax and give me time to ponder on what I want to do with my life. I look forward to getting myself on the right track and back to work with your assistance and guidance getting me there. I don't know how I'll ever repay you for all you're doing."

"Don't worry about that. We just want to concentrate on getting yourself together and speaking of that we need to get going to make your hair appointment on time."

"Oh yes, dear, I'm so looking forward to the hairdo. Maybe I will go with a dark color. This blue makes me look old and I want to look younger especially when I go out on interviews for a job."

"I think a darker color would definitely make you look younger." LaVonda envisioned Ms. Honeycutt's rat's nest being redone and couldn't help but put a big smile on her face to keep herself from laughing. "So are we ready to go," LaVonda asked Ms. Honeycutt.

"Yes, ma'am, I'm ready. Let's go." As they both passed through the parlor area on the way out the front door, Ms. Honeycutt noticed Mario sitting in the office and said, "See you soon, Mario!"

"CHILD, PLEASE!" followed after that good-bye greeting, and LaVonda shook her head and said, "Honey, you're a mess but you're a cute mess."

CHAPTER NINE

As Donald fumbled with his keys to get into the town house, he could hear the phone ringing on the other side of the door. He dashed for the phone, and by the time he answered it, they hung up. Donald said, "Who would be calling me at this time on a Sunday night? Well, if it was important, they'll call back." Since they left no message on his answering machine, it couldn't have been that important. Donald poured himself a glass of milk and took out a plate from the cupboard and started making himself a plate of fried chicken and the rest of the fixings when his mind wondered off again, wondering where Freeway would be and that he would be at his heels right now, looking up at him, waiting for some chicken or at least the crumbs if any had fallen to the floor.

Donald was ready to call it a day and get some rest for he had to head back to the shelter in the morning. He pondered, *Should I or should I not tell Ms. Kitty that I'm wealthy? Should I tell her that I'm thinking of buying the lot to build a new shelter north of this one for people who live north and don't have to drive to adopt or drop off the dogs who no longer would be wanted by their owners or even those lost on the north side of town that were running lose.* He thought that she might like the idea of having two shelters in the county area than just one. Would she be interested in working for him since she did help make him more aware of the problem with so many unwanted or homeless animals in shelters that are around the country and that more needs to be done to find them homes. They could work together since they both got along well, and she knew the operation of running a shelter.

He pondered these issues for a while, but he realized that no matter what amount of money he had, he had to finish his service so he wouldn't have to go back to jail unless Ms. Kitty and his parole officer released him sooner. It really depended on that, which meant he could go collect his 125-million-dollar winnings minus the government's take. Donald just finished taking his last bite and looked over at the clock and said, "The hell with it. I'll call it an early night for tomorrow may be the beginning of another hectic week at the shelter or may not be."

Donald had to hang in there a few more days; that's all he had to do, and then it would be the beginning of new and better things to come. Donald jumped in the shower and got ready for bed and within minutes, on a full stomach, dozed off with the vision of Freeway in mind just running through a field, barking out loud.

This must have been déjà vu because at that moment somewhere in Dallas, Freeway was running through a field under the stars, barking at an armadillo that he came upon as he was with his new owner. He was an acquaintance of Bubba's who also was a truck driver named Derek Waters that was from New Orleans who was visiting his sister in Dallas. They ran into each other in town while Bubba was driving around trying to locate the local shelter to bring Freeway, when they both were at a red light, and they glanced over at each other at the light and realized they knew each other as they chatted, waiting for the light to change. Derek asked who the good-looking dog was in the pickup, and Bubba told him his name was Freeway and that he was driving around all day, avoiding having to drop him off at the local shelter because his girlfriend said he couldn't keep him.

Derek said, "Oh hell no. Just follow me over her to the gas station and we'll chat. I want him. I'll take him off your hands, instead of dropping him off at the shelter, which is now closed by the way since it is after 6:00 PM."

"I know," Bubba said. "I couldn't bring myself to do it."

"Just follow me. It's just a block up on the right."

"Will do," Bubba said as the light turned green, and he pulled behind Derek's SUV and followed him up to the gas station. As Bubba pulled into the gas station, he looked over to Freeway who was just staring ahead and said, "You're one lucky dog. I believe that where you're going is going to be a hell of a lot better than the shelter. Who knows, maybe we will see each other again at one of the truck stops along the interstate. I hope you will remember me."

Freeway turned toward Bubba and approached him and gave him a couple of licks on the face as if he was trying to say, "I will remember you," just as Derek approached the passenger side of Bubba's pickup and climbed into the front seat. Derek told Bubba that he had lost his border collie named Sheba to his ex-wife in a divorce six months ago and that he wanted to take Freeway off his hands and that he could provide him with a good home—if you want to call the apartment he was temporarily living in a home until he got his house back from the divorce and that he had plenty of room and land for Freeway to run around in and that he would be a great companion on his long-haul trips.

"I know how you feel. That's how we met on the interstate at a rest area," Bubba told Derek his story on how they met.

After a twenty-minute conversation, Derek gave Bubba his phone number and said, "You can call anytime to see how Freeway's doing if you want."

"I will from time to time if you don't mind."

"Mind? What kind of person would you be if you didn't check in from time to time? I can see he was getting attached to you and you to him. It just shows you that you do have a heart for such a beautiful creature like this canine."

Bubba said, "Well then, I better get this over with Freeway".

"You see you are going to have to go with Derek right know. He will take good care of you since I can't. You will be in a good place and remember what I said. I hope we meet again on the interstate at one of those rest areas like we did the first day but with Derek by your side this time."

Freeway let out a loud bark as he looked at Bubba who was teary eyed as Derek climbed out and said, "Don't worry. He'll be in good hands."

Bubba said, "I know," as Freeway climbed out and followed Derek and climbed into his pickup as they departed ways. Derek talked to Freeway on the way back to his sister's house, which was just a few miles away. She owned several acres of land where he was at the time, barking at an armadillo on her property in the field. So Donald wasn't dreaming; he was really connecting in mind with Freeway.

Bubba drove back to his house where Darla was waiting, worried, since he was gone all day and not a single phone call or word from him. *Was he really upset with me? Did he have an accident? Will he be coming home with Freeway?* Finally he walked into the house and said, "He's gone and that's all I'm going to say on the subject. And yes, I'm still pissed about not being able to keep him but I will get over it and in time it will pass. I do love you, I really do, and you know I can't stay mad at you for long. So that's why I was away all day just spending time with Freeway. I couldn't bring myself to saying good-bye to him."

Darla said, "I know how you feel. I really do." And she went into her story about her springer spaniel as they both hugged each other and walked the hallway toward the bedroom. It was a long day for Bubba and a long day for Darla worrying, so they decided to call it a night and watch television from the bed just in case they both dozed off early. Freeway was now being introduced to Derek's sister where he was staying who also noticed that Freeway did indeed look similar to his dog Sheba before the divorce. She was happy for him that he had found a new friend and that Derek wouldn't be alone again and that he would have company on the road trips while he worked. Derek took Freeway to his room where he was staying, but not before telling his sister he was going to head back to New Orleans early in the morning to his apartment and that he had to meet with his attorney in a day or so. He wanted to get his house back from his ex as soon as possible, who was, by the way, not able to meet the mortgage and bills with her income and decided to sign the house over to him.

It wouldn't be long, and Freeway would have a place to run around in and call home.

Over at the Dixie, Arms LaVonda was on the phone with Mario, who was calling from his cell phone while he was sitting in his patrol car off I-75 interstate, waiting for traffic violators. "Just thought I'd call. I wanted to touch base with you, and see how Ms. Honeycutt was doing"—who was already tucked into her bed upstairs after a long day of running around with her to the stylist and the market and then accompanying her as she had other errands to run and didn't want her to be around Mario with her drooling at him, making him feel uncomfortable. LaVonda said she was a handful but had a lead on several positions for her to look into for work, which tomorrow she was going to check out. Their conversation ran over an hour, and Mario, who was now on duty at the sheriff's office, had to get back to work and said he'll see her in the morning. He mentioned he would bring some donuts in when he came in to work to have with their coffee in the morning and to make sure she had a pot of coffee on. She said she'd make sure and told him again thanks for watching the Arms while she was out and that she would see him in the morning and to have a good evening. "Sweet dreams," he told her as they hung up the phone, and she locked up the shelter and called it a day. She had a long day with Ms. Honeycutt who by the way was no longer blue haired and was now a raging redhead, and the rat's nest was no more, and any hat she chose to wear would really look good on her. Now to concentrate on finding her a job was another situation that she was going to start dealing with in the morning with the help of Mario assisting her.

LaVonda peeked in on Ms. Honeycutt before she went to her room to make sure she was okay, and as she opened her bedroom door, she saw her sitting up in bed, snoring away. It was as if she slept this way so she wouldn't mess up her new hairstyle.

With a smile on LaVonda's face, she sneaked into her room and gently tucked Ms. Honeycutt down and under the covers; otherwise she was going to have a stiff neck in the morning, and LaVonda wouldn't want to see her that way. In the meantime, Mario was checking the tags on automobiles of drivers from his laptop in the front seat, passenger's side. He could possibly come across one or two, and maybe more if it was his lucky night, who would have warrants or outstanding tickets or suspended driver's license. It could turn out to be just another fun night in the Sunshine State.

CHAPTER TEN

The alarm clock was beeping six o'clock; it was time for Donald to rise and shine as he rolled over and pushed the snooze button on. Donald always dreaded Monday mornings, just having to get up and face reality and that he had to work for someone else to make a buck to stay alive and had no choice but to deal with it and go on. But in this case he wasn't getting paid for his service at the shelter; that made it more unbearable. He didn't want to get up from his comfy bed. But with a smile on his face as he rubbed his eyes, he knew he wouldn't have to do it much longer, and he had finally decided to purchase that piece of land that is west on Commercial Blvd. near the I-75 expressway.

Donald was going to call the number that he jotted down, which was in his car, later today to make inquiries on the land and what the asking price was. He didn't want to put it off any longer since the property in the area was being developed quickly, and that piece of land could go quickly, so he needed to act fast and get the ball rolling ASAP. He would have the money to purchase the land; he was getting it once he cashed in the winning lottery ticket, which was going to be this week.

He couldn't wait to hear back from his parents while they were on holiday, so he was going to do this on his own with or without their assistance. With being such a large amount of money, he would need some legal advice, so he was going to ask Ms. Kitty this morning at the shelter who they used for legal advice for the shelter for when they needed one to hire to represent them. Maybe she could refer someone when it comes to collecting a large sum of money and how he should go about collecting it without having it broadcasted all over the news that he was now a millionaire.

Donald jumped out of bed and dashed into the kitchen to make a pot of coffee, and while it was brewing, he was going to head to the shower and get dressed and then sit and enjoy the first cup of the day while watching a little bit of the early morning news before heading out to the shelter. It wasn't five minutes after he sat down to sip his coffee when his phone rang. He jumped up to answer it, and on the other side of the line was Ms. Kitty who called Donald if he could stop and pick up some donuts or bagels on the way to work and that she would reimburse him when he got in. She told him that she forgot, but today was going to be an open house for adoptions at the shelter, and she thought that this morning they should have refreshments for those who would come in. He said he wouldn't mind and that he'd see her in a about an hour. She thanked him and said, "I'll see you soon then." Ms. Kitty then hung up the phone and turned around to the other volunteers who were hanging up a banner in the break room that said Congratulations Donald she then said, he fell for it and he'll be there in about forty-five minutes to an hour with his drive. The volunteers then mentioned that they will miss him and that he had done a lot in his short stay at the shelter and how he persuaded the adopters to take all those dogs that only had a few more years left in them.

He was surely going to be missed. Ms. Kitty agreed and said that her surprise was when she tells him that it was really a going-away party for him for it was his last day at the shelter and that the parole office had called her last night and told her that he was going to be relieved from his community service with the information that she had reported back to them on Fridays when she called in on his work progress weekly.

He was given an early parole, and he was free to go by day's end. Ms. Kitty couldn't wait to break the big news just as Donald had some news of his own, which was going to be an even bigger surprise to her. Donald then finished his cup of coffee as he was channel surfing for the traffic watch on the weather channel, which at the time was just broadcasting on how the hurricane season was only a month away.

June 1 was the start date until the end of November when hurricane season ends; it was going to be a very interesting year with eighteen named storms, and four would be major hurricanes, which was not good for anyone living on the East Coast. Donald said, "Yikes, I hope we don't have any at all here in South Florida."

The state cannot take any more devastation like they've seen a few years ago. Donald then turned off the news after getting the traffic report and headed out while the interstate was clear and free of any incidents in which it would then be a smooth drive south.

Donald then grabbed his car keys and headed out the door and was hoping that the donut shop just before the exit to the interstate was open early so he could get the refreshments for the shelter, or else he would have to go out of his way to find one that was open before heading down to the shelter.

The phone number that Donald was going to look for in his car just happened to fly off the sun visor that was over the driver's seat as he opened his car door to climb in to head out to the shelter.

"That's odd," Donald said. "I was going to look for this number later on when I got my morning break so I can call them after I approach Ms. Kitty about a lawyer." It was as if someone or something just happened to throw this number in his face. It might have been an omen to make the call. Donald placed the phone number into his pants pocket with the vision of a new shelter built on the lot he was about to purchase. Donald was no more than a mile from his townhome when he happened to come across a shopping center that had a supermarket, which when he pulled into the parking lot, he saw several people entering the store. "Great, this is just what I was looking for." Donald parked his car and walked into the supermarket and immediately upon entering the store, to his right he could smell fresh bread, and he knew he had found one with a bakery. Donald approached the counter and asked the salesclerk for three dozen assorted donuts and two dozen assorted bagels and asked where he could find the cream cheese. The salesclerk said that it would be in the dairy case along the back wall of the store; he could find it there. Donald said thank-you and said he would be right back to get his order, and he went searching for a shopping cart and the cream cheese. The salesclerk said she would have his order ready by the time he got back. Donald thanked the salesclerk once again.

Upon reaching the dairy case, as he started searching for the cream cheese, he happened to glance up and over to his left side, and he had recognized a familiar face dressed in a sheriff's uniform. It was Officer Mario, the arresting officer who had taken him to jail for abusing Freeway on the interstate.

He stood there for a moment in awe and said nothing; what was he going to say? Should he say hello or just continue on with his business looking for cream cheese and avoid him totally or be civil and acknowledge him if Officer Mario recognizes him just standing a few feet away from him. Well, it was too late; they both happened to make eye contact, with a nod from both of them as if to say hello.

Donald said to himself, *I'll be the bigger man and approach him and say hello, and I also wanted to thank him.* "I don't know if you remember me but you were the arresting officer who had taken me to the county jail a while back for abusing my dog on the interstate and the DUI."

"Oh yes, I do remember you. I was just doing my job. I hope you understand," Officer Mario said to Donald.

"I do and that's why I want to thank you! For taking me in." Officer Mario looked shocked and puzzled.

"It's the first time that someone I arrested thanked me for doing that."

Donald explained, "You arresting me had sent me to do community service at the shelter and I have a better understanding on why you arrested me for animal abuse." It had opened his eyes to see what animal abuse can do to living and innocent creatures that can't defend themselves. He has seen a lot at the shelter and has also helped several dogs find a good home with whatever time they have left to make someone happy or put a smile on someone's face who hadn't smiled in months or see a toddler talk for the first time when the parents thought there was something medically wrong with their child. "I have learned a lot so I just wanted to say thank you!" Mario didn't know what to say. He was in awe himself for a few moments. Mario asked Donald if he ever found the dog he was with that night before being arrested.

"No," Donald said, "and believe me, there is not a day that goes by that I don't wonder if he's alive or living with a good family or just wondering around the interstate where I first found him."

"Oh, I'm sorry you don't have him. He looked to be a pretty smart dog from what I saw. Is there a phone number that you can give me just in case I come across him in my travels as I'm on duty on the interstate and I could call you?" Donald gave Officer Mario his phone number and said that he would be grateful if he comes across him while on duty. They shook hands and parted ways.

Donald found his cream cheese and a shopping cart and headed back to the bakery department to pick up his order of donuts and bagels before heading to the checkout counter, when he ran into Officer Mario at the checkout line who had several items on the checkout line that he was purchasing when his cell phone rang, and on the other side was LaVonda who was just getting up and wanted to know if he could come in a little earlier today since she had set up several employers who might be able to help Ms. Honeycutt with employment. He said he had just gotten off of duty and was just on his way home after making a pit stop at the store for a few things and that he could go home, take a shower, and be there about nine o'clock instead of the normal ten o'clock. She said that would be great and that she would have a fresh pot of coffee on for him when he arrived.

She thanked him, and he said, "No problem, it's fine. I'll see you at nine o'clock." Donald couldn't help but overhear the conversation while standing in line next to him.

"So you just got off duty?"

"Yeah! And now I'm going to head into my second job at a shelter downtown."

"Really? So you're helping out the homeless community and me helping the animal community, which will be over in a couple weeks."

"That's great," Officer Mario replied back.

"I thought the sheriff's department paid well."

"It does but I have some free time and I'm working at this homeless shelter called the Dixie Arms and that was the proprietor who asked me to come in early. She had errands to run."

"It really is a gift helping others, isn't it?" Donald said as Mario grabbed his grocery bag and headed away from the checkout line. Donald said, "It was nice running into you again but under better circumstances this time."

Officer Mario laughed. "You're right. Much better than the interstate, huh? Take care," Officer Mario said as he walked away.

"You too!" Donald replied back for he was next in line to pay for his donuts, bagels, and cream cheese to head off to the shelter.

Ms. Kitty was getting ready to open the doors to the shelter after she made her final walk through the facility to make sure all was ready for another day of walk-ins looking to adopt so that the animals in her care would go home to a loving and caring home. And she was hoping that there would not be any more brought into the shelter due to financial or hardship times where their owners couldn't take care of them anymore and brought them down to the shelter to be adopted out. The shelter was 80 percent full due to this problem. She needed to do something to make the public aware of the situation, and if she did a story on the shelter through the local news station, it would possibly bring more people in to take care of the problem. She needed someone who had experience in marketing who could assist her in trying to find homes for these dogs.

She was going to post an ad under the shelter's Web site for someone to fill that position as well as the local newspaper in the employment section for someone with marketing experience and the love of animals. This would also be a cry out to the public on how serious this issue was and how many animals are in the shelter and that they need loving and caring homes. This was going to be one of her top priorities when she found a free moment in the day. Just as she was getting ready to unlock the front doors, she noticed that Donald was pulling into the parking lot and was about to enter the shelter. She then ran back to the office area, telling the volunteers that Donald was now entering the parking lot and asked everyone to go to the break room and yell, "Surprise!" when he comes in. She told them that she was going to run out to the parking lot to assist him in carrying in the refreshments so he wouldn't suspect anything.

Donald was just a few feet away from the front entrance when he saw Ms. Kitty coming out of the front door to assist him and asked her to take the two dozen bagels from his one hand as he carried the three dozen donuts in his other hand, trying to avoid from dropping them onto the ground. She said, "Oh my, I didn't realize that you would have bought so much."

"Well, you said enough food for the visitors who'd come in today."

"Yeah, you're right," she said, which was to cover up her little white lie and to surprise him by telling him he was being released from community service by day's end. "I'll reimburse you from the petty cash draw if you give me the receipt after we put these in the break room."

"Okay, that will be great." This would be the time he would ask her about the legal advice once they freed up their arms.

Ms. Kitty leading the way went first into the break room, followed by Donald, when all of a sudden he heard screams of "SURPRISE!" He looked around and saw the rest of the volunteers in there and the large banner on the back wall that said Congratulations. He was stunned and speechless. He turned to Ms. Kitty and said, "What's this all about?"

"I have good news for you that's what this is for. It's going to be your last day here at the shelter. I tried calling you last night but got no answer. It was late."

"So you're the call I missed getting."

"You were there?"

"Yes, I was busy doing something and by the time I got to the phone they hung up."

"I wanted to tell you that you have completed your community service on good behavior and that you no longer have to come back unless you want to visit us or volunteer." Donald was surprised all right and speechless and said nothing for a few moments. Then one by one the volunteers started to approach him and shake his hand and give him a hug to wish him luck and to say that they enjoyed working with him and not to be a stranger as they then broke into the donuts and bagels to have along with their morning coffee or tea before starting their workday at the shelter.

He turned to Ms. Kitty and said, "May I speak to you alone for a moment."

She said, "Sure, let's go to my office. I'll get you your money back from the refreshments as well while back there." Donald was going to break the news about the lottery winning to her and ask her about the legal assistant question and ask her if she would like to help him with the plans of opening the state-of-the-art shelter north of town, which he thought about on the way down to the shelter this morning; who would be better to oversee this project but her?

It was now her turn to be surprised, but not before he grabbed himself a chocolate-covered donut and a cup of coffee before heading over to her office so he could sit back and enjoy both of these things at the same time. Once in Ms. Kitty office, Donald asked her the first question regarding the legal advice on whether the shelter had a legal team or lawyer representing them if ever needed. The look on her face with that question had raised her eyebrows. "Why?" she asked. "Did you do something that I need to be aware of?"

"Oh no! It's just that I have some exciting news to tell you, but before I do, you promise right here and now that you will not tell a soul."

"Cross my heart and hope to die, stick a needle in my eye."

Donald let out a chuckle. "I haven't heard that in years. You remember last week that the lottery was up to 125 million dollars?"

"Yes, I recall I didn't play that week. I forgot to stop and get tickets," she said.

"I won!"

"You won what? Did you match three or more numbers?"

"Yes."

"So you won. How much did you win if I may ask?"

"Well, it's more than four numbers."

"Great," she said. "So you got a couple of hundred dollars. That's the usual pay with four numbers."

"No!"

"You got five numbers? That pays a couple of thousand dollars! Oh my God ! That's great."

"No!"

She stood there and looked shocked and mumbled, "Tell me you didn't hit all six numbers, tell me you didn't hit all six numbers."

"Well, I didn't hit the five numbers."

"So what did you hit?"

"I'm just busting your leg. I did, I picked all six numbers and I'm going to be filthy rich and I need some legal advice and assistance on how I should go about collecting this without the local news knowing about this. I don't want to be hounded by press, and worse, the nuts coming out of the woodwork looking for donations." Ms. Kitty stood there in shock with her mouth wide open. Then she reached out and gave him a big hug and congratulated him on his winnings.

"Please do not tell anyone about this."

"I promise, I told you, I wouldn't tell a single soul. So now you have to get yourself a lawyer who can advise you on what your next step is to collect the winnings. We have a legal department that is part of the Broward County government to assist us. You don't want to go there then. The whole county will know. I have a friend who is a lawyer downtown that I used for legal issues like making a will, closing on my home. I'll give her a call and ask her if she can assist you on this."

"Great! I appreciate that. Then maybe she can assist me with the next question that I have for you. Since she does closing on real estate."

"Already in the market to purchase a big old house?"

"No! I want to buy a piece of land that I saw off of Commercial Blvd. near the expressway and want to build a new shelter for homeless dogs sort of like this but with the state-of-the-art equipment and on-staff veterinarians on staff and groomers, with room for boarding so people can go on vacations and take trips and not have to worry about their dogs while gone.

"I thought that since this is the only one in the county, that having another one north of here for those people who want to adopt wouldn't have to drive so far and just maybe we can take some from here to lessen up the capacity. But before I do this I want you to come work for me and help with the building plans and the layout and the whole operation of running it. With me funding it."

"Of course," she said.

"I would pay you a seventy-five-thousand-dollar salary, and medical insurance." Ms. Kitty then fell back into her chair. She didn't know what to say. Donald told her that it was because of her that gave him the inspiration to do something with his life and being around these amazing canines and seeing the joy in the people who left here with an adoption and the excitement in the canines that they thought their days were numbered.

"I can do so much good with this money and want you to be part of it. So what do you say?"

In a daze, Ms. Kitty said, "Yes! Yes, yes. I would not be more pleased and honored to be part of this or even think twice about passing up this experience." They extended out their hands and shook to close the deal. Donald knew that this was his last day here at this shelter. So Ms. Kitty being so excited herself told Donald that he could spend his last day by just visiting and talking to the other volunteers and say good-bye to them as well as the dogs in the back and say nothing of their conversation and that he could sneak out early like at noon. "Which would give me time to get a hold of my friend the lawyer and make arrangements to go see her right away. So you can head up to Tallahassee to collect your winnings."

"Great! Then I can call on the property and set something up with the realtor so I will call you later so we can go over plans and have dinner, if that would be okay with you?"

"I'd love that. I can't wait to get started on this new adventure for the both of us." Donald thanked her for everything she had done for him and will call her later with the dinner plans. He wanted to get out of her office. He was craving another chocolate donut before they disappeared from the break room; besides, he wanted to say good-bye to the dogs out back in the pens before he said good-bye to the volunteers that he enjoyed working with.

Donald saw a couple of volunteers that peaked his interest to come on board with him and Ms. Kitty when they were up and running at the new shelter and wanted to make sure he got their phone numbers before he left the building. In the meantime, Ms. Kitty had to place her phone calls as well as look for a marketing person for this shelter to bring on board so they could bring more people into the shelter to adopt these precious creatures, now that it would be about six months or more before she would have to turn in her notice and say her very own good-bye to those she worked with for so long and cherished their dedication and time volunteering at the shelter.

CHAPTER ELEVEN

Six months have flown by, and once again South Florida was spared from a bad season of hurricanes that was predicted with only a couple of weeks left till the end when it is officially ends. Freeway was living in New Orleans, running free along with Derek in the home that his ex-wife signed over to him, and she then downsized to an apartment, which was more in her budget. He would walk the canals with Derek as he fished off the sides and bark loud at every boater that came by on their fishing boats on the way in from deep-sea fishing. He lived like a king and more now that he had found his perfect mate, Sheba—yes, Derek's first dog that his wife took from him in the divorce; she realized that her apartment building did not allow dogs and was forced to give her up and had no choice but to let Derek have her back, which she knew would be better off than living in an apartment. Freeway and Sheba spent all the time together; they were inseparable. Neither one was far from the other. They played and ran and chased each other and slept next to each other all the time. They were a handful when Derek would take his long-haul trips; he now had two dogs along for the ride. Thank god for his large cab in the back of his rig that they all fit just comfortably for sleeping.

LaVonda back in Fort Lauderdale was busy as a bee. She had found Ms. Honeycutt the perfect job. As long as she remembered to make several bus changes on the bus route to get her to work on time and was up at the crack of dawn to meet the first bus that picked her up in front of the shelter with several changes along the way that would get her to work on time. The company had just opened up several weeks ago and was in need of staff, and with LaVonda's charm, she was able to place her with them as a temp and after thirty days' probation could become a full-time employee.

She was now working as a receptionist answering phones and helping with filing and sometimes taking orders for customers for the distributor of Everything Canine Inc., which sold everything from food and toys and dog beds to kennels and even clothing and accessories to the public and some elite and well-known actors and actresses whose pride pooches wore some of these goods that they specialized in, which sometimes were spotted and photographed by the paparazzi and later found on covers or gossip rags and magazines across newsstands everywhere. Who knew that the pet industry would bring in so much money?

LaVonda still had Mario working for her part-time and then some. They have become best of friends, and Mario also spent extra hours on his own time on his days off with helping with the amount of guests that had come and gone through the Dixie Arms that were coming and going that were helped out by her charity and seeking shelter, as well as those misfortunate who needed a place to come every time they issued a hurricane warning for the county to be prepared and seek shelter. The homeless would then come out of the woodwork, seeking shelter and a roof over their head so they wouldn't be stranded on the park benches or under the overpasses, hiding from the storm.

She fed and clothed them with the help of a couple of volunteers from the downtown business who boarded up and closed up shop and headed to her place to help out. They all bunkered down in sleeping bags all over the Dixie Arms; the shelter was huge, so there would sometimes be wall-to-wall sleeping bags up and down the halls till the storms passed or went in a different direction and away from Fort Lauderdale.

It was then that Mario helped out with his extra hours to make sure LaVonda was safe and not alone with these houseguest at any time because some of them were looking a bit scary, and she was not about to turn them away, so he hung around longer hours to make sure she was safe on her own. After dealing with these homeless people, she would not turn anyone away in time of need and safety, which was another quality that Mario loved about her.

Donald had received the legal advice that he needed and purchased the land from his winnings from the lotto. With the assistance of Ms. Kitty over the past six months had a groundbreaking ceremony for the new shelter with food and balloons and music on the lot., They named the shelter, the Freeway Shelter for Lost and Abandoned Canines.

With r the right amount of money, he was able to contact all the appropriate sources in purchasing the right equipment needed as well as hire a contractor to build his state-of-the-art canine shelter, which was going to be having its grand opening in just a few days.

Ms. Kitty had turned in her notice at the shelter and had found a marketing director who had turned the shelter into a place where more animals were now being adopted out and made the public aware of how many animals are being abused and need rescuing from the shelter in which local supermarkets were holding adoption days in front of the stores. They held walks for the animals to raise money to help with keeping the shelter open and those in need of surgeries with help from local donations.

Even Donald secretly donated one million dollars to keep the shelter running as an anonymous donor, which made the local news stations and newspapers. Donald's parents put the campground up for sale back in Sutton Falls and were going to retire and do some travel abroad and enjoy life a little more after all the years of running the campground. Donald was just waiting for the occupancy certificate to come in from the county before he could open the doors. They had hired a local band to play music on the grounds, and there was going to be hot dogs and burgers with cold drinks and ice cream for all who attended, with local newspapers and television coverage from a couple of local stations to promote their opening. There were clowns and artists to entertain the kids with face painting and games. The shelter itself was unbelievable with a state-of-the-art veterinary clinic with three DVMs on duty, a grooming salon of four groomers, and two dog bathers. There was a outdoor in the ground pool in the shape of a bone where the dogs could swim if they wanted, if boarding is requested, they'll have separate kennels with their very own doghouse in different shapes and styles in the room for them to sleep in with room for playing with toys. Each kennel is temperature controlled to keep it between sixty-eight and seventy degrees in each one. A dog park was available for those residents wishing to take their dogs out to play and run, with obstacles for them to run around on. There were fire hydrants throughout the park area for those needing relief. Trash receptacles and waste stations with pooper-scoopers and wipes were near each one for the owners to pick up and dispose of after using them. There was a refreshment stand open for the dog owners who could sit and chat at tables like in Paris and drink soft drinks or coffee if early in the morning was your choice to go to the dog park. It was something different and unique, just what the county needed for those canine lovers. The adoption and kennel center had over one hundred cages for those canines that would end up needing a new home if brought in and abandoned, and it was just a few feet away from Donald's office, which he wanted to be close by so he could say good morning to them as the first thing he does when he comes into the shelter each day. They had a special kitchen area built where meals were prepared for those who needed special attention when it came to diet plans to keep them healthy or had to eat special foods, with two food preps, or rather "Doggy Chefs," on duty.

All they needed was a good sunny day with no chance of any rain or showers in the forecast, or worse, any hurricanes on the horizon to be heading their way to ruin it.

It was hell waiting for the certificate of occupancy to come down from the county. The employees were on standby just waiting for the one call: "We are open and you can come in and start work." Ms. Kitty's office was equipped with a camera overlooking the entire facility, so while she was on duty, she could see how the operations were running and if needed could use the overhead intercom to page someone to the office or to report anything unusual on the grounds if needed. Donald's office was near the boarding area where the dogs would stay and down the hall from the kitchen area. He, too, had cameras in his office where he could watch the shelter's operation from every department and all over the grounds. He even had a flat-screen television in his office where he could do e-mails and watch the cameras as well as watch television when he wanted to. The facility was just yards away from the expressway, which was accessible to the center from the north or south of the county, depending on which way you were coming in. There was an old power plant just on the other side of the expressway before it became the everglades, which was old and dilapidated and was under county scrutiny because the environmentalists wanted it taken out because it would affect the wildlife that was diminishing from its natural resources from the rusted and falling down structures. From time to time there were always news cameras with their high towers pointing into the direction of the power plant that could be seen from the dog-bone pool area, which was in the center court of the boarding areas for the dogs. He was hoping that with the news crew out there from time to time, it would bring in more interest to the area and possibly traffic to his shelter since they were just yards away from the exit to the shelter.

It was around four o'clock in the afternoon on this hot and muggy Wednesday when a county clerk had come buy the facility and just happened to catch Ms. Kitty and Donald walking the grounds when they spotted someone carrying a yellow clasp envelope in his hands and approached them and asked if they were the owners of the property, and Donald said yes. The clerk introduced himself and said, "I think you have been waiting for this," and gave him the clasp envelope, which he opened up.

And Donald jumped ten feet off the ground and screamed, "YES, YES!" and grabbed Ms. Kitty and picked her up and spun her around, stating that he had just received the certificate of occupancy and to start placing phone calls from her cell phone to the future employees to report to work in two days.

Donald started making calls with his own cell phone to the power company to have the power turned on to the building, then the call to the phone company to turn on the phone lines ASAP. He was now going to open the Freeway Shelter for Lost and Abandoned Canines in just a matter of two days. Next they called the vendors for Friday's grand opening and the local news channel to make sure they have someone there to cover it. It was finally falling into place, and he was excited as hell. Donald and Ms. Kitty spent the next several hours trying to get a hold of everyone they had phone numbers of, to call to make the grand opening day, hoping to catch those businesses before the close of day, which was just now approaching the six o'clock hour. After all were said and done, they decided to go out for a celebration of steak and lobster at one of the new restaurants that just happened to be down the road on Commercial Blvd. They had finally pulled it off, and all was a go. As they entered the restaurant, they were standing in line for dinner, so they headed over to the bar area for a glass of wine while waiting for their table to be ready. When they looked up at the television that was over the bar area, the locals news was on, and the weather report was just wrapping up, but not before the local forecaster reported that there was a disturbance in the Atlantic and that they were going to send a plane into it tomorrow to investigate it just to make sure that it was not going to become somewhat a threat to the Florida coastline, just before the sports segment came on. Donald looked at Ms. Kitty and said, "Oh hell no, this can't happen. It's only two days away from grand opening and they suspect a damn storm. Please don't turn into anything. Please, let it be just a thunderstorm and nothing else."

Ms. Kitty grabbed his wrist and said, "It will be fine. I have this gut feeling it will not bother your grand opening day whatsoever."

"I hope you're right," Donald told her. Just then they were called to their table for it was ready for them to be seated so they could eat. They both left the bar area and followed the waitress to their table where they were given a menu and were asked if they'd like to have their drink replenished. They both said they were fine for now and that they already knew what they wanted to order for dinner, and they placed the order with the waitress.

She said, "Would there be anything else you'd like to order, maybe an appetizer before your meal?" t Donald, said he was fine., Ms. Kitty then asked the waitress for her phone number and said that would do just fine. With a mouthful of wine, Donald spit it out all over the table for he was shocked that she said that to the waitress as she smiled and gave Ms. Kitty her phone number. Donald then asked the waitress for a bottle of wine to be brought to the table for he was going to hear all the details on Ms. Kitty before they finished their dinner; besides, they were celebrating, and this night was going to get even better after he got the 411 on Ms. Kitty. Donald who was wiping off the table with his napkin just laughed.

"So what's so damn funny?" Ms. Kitty asked Donald.

"Nothing," he replied.

"Oh, you just want me to spill my guts to you, don't you?"

"No, your business and lifestyle is yours and no one else's business."

"I couldn't help it. It was the wine and the excitement and besides she looked good and my gay dar went off so I just blurted it out. I didn't think she'd give me her number but look I got it!" And she placed it into her bra for safekeeping. As the dinner was winding down, Donald had gotten all the news he wanted to hear about Ms. Kitty and had no problem with her lifestyle and was glad that she had come into his life and was thankful for having her as a great friend and coworker; as long as she didn't flaunt her business around the shelter, she had nothing to worry about, because there would be people who come and go who would disapprove of her lifestyle and could be assholes if they wanted to be. She said he had nothing to worry about as they ordered a cup of coffee each and decided to split a piece of cheesecake for dessert with two forks. It was now approaching ten thirty, and they both needed to head home and get some rest, for the next few days were going to be hectic for them with the grand opening on Friday and all.

Donald drove Ms. Kitty back to her car, which was parked at the shelter since they went to dinner in his car. As he pulled out onto Commercial Blvd., he saw Officer Mario giving a ticket to someone whom he had pulled over for a broken taillight as he left the parking lot of the shelter. In the back of his mind, he was reminded of the night he was pulled over for a DUI, and it brought back unpleasant memories of that evening, and he wanted to get the hell out of there since he had just put away a bottle of

wine; and though he felt okay to drive, he wasn't going to take the chance
of going back to jail again.

The next morning, Donald and Ms. Kitty met at the shelter and did
a walk through around the shelter and grounds area to make sure that
everything was on schedule for the grand opening tomorrow. He had
remembered he needed to have giveaways to the visitors that came through
the shelter and had nothing to give away yet and needed to make a quick
call for these items from his office and placed a phone call to the Weston
distributor of Everything Canine Inc., which was just down I-75, about
twenty minutes away from the shelter.

He spoke to Ms. Honeycutt who answered the phone and who was
more than happy to give him directions to get to the warehouse where
he could come in and place an order after going through their catalog of
products, and then he would have to wait about an hour till his order was
pulled from inventory and placed at the pickup area where he could then
pay for the goods. He said he'd be there within the hour and thanked her
for her assistance; he was looking forward to meeting her when he got
there. She sounded like a character over the phone and wanted to see what
she was all about.

He spotted Ms. Kitty who was just walking by his office and was
heading over to the adoption and kennel area to make sure that the area
was ready for the arrival of fifteen canines from the south shelter where
she left and met Donald. They were being brought down to fill some of
the cages in the kennel area with the hope that they would be adopted
out tomorrow during the grand opening. She kept in touch on a daily
basis even after she left there several weeks ago when it was her turn to say
good-bye to take on her new position with Donald. They were more than
happy to help out by sending some of their canines and more if she wanted
them. They were just about up to maximum capacity and were probably
going to have to send them north to their shelter. Donald couldn't wait to
get back to see them. Ms. Kitty said that she had everything under control
and to take his time that she had plenty to do while he was gone and not to
worry. If she had any questions, she would call him on his cell phone and
vice versa if he needed anything. Donald then headed out to his car, but
not before noticing an ominous dark cloud over the shelter, which meant
rain was on the way, so he decided to turn on his car radio to see if he could
get the local forecast.

He prayed that the good weather would hold out for at least a few more
days so that the grand opening would be successful and not a washout.

Donald focused on the weather alert that was being broadcasted. There was a tropical depression forming in the Gulf, which meant that the dark clouds could be feeder bands that he saw as he left the shelter. He called Ms. Kitty back at the shelter and told her what he just heard on the radio and to please turn on the television in his office and to check from time to time on the storm in the Gulf. She said she would do it right after she got the dogs into their cages and that he just missed them by minutes when he left and that she would do it then.

"Great!" Donald already was at the warehouse in Weston and just about to meet Ms. Honeycutt who was sitting outside on a picnic bench, eating her lunch, as he pulled into the parking lot of the Everything Canine Inc. He exited his car and approached this older woman and asked for assistance on where he could go to place his order.

She recognized his voice from the phone and said, "I think I just spoke to you not too long ago on the phone."

"Are you Ms. Honeycutt? The woman I spoke to on the phone?"

"Yes, I am the one and only." She stood up from the picnic table and introduced herself to him. She was an older woman, not what he had envisioned by her voice over the phone. She had short red hair and was wearing a bright yellow dress and a hat with matching netting and a miniature stuffed bird like a blue jay perched on the top. Donald couldn't help but stare at her hat. It was something you don't see in South Florida, which was more like something you would see at the Kentucky Derby. He was amused as Ms. Honeycutt stood up and asked him to follow her in from her break to assist him in placing his order. Donald extended his hand out to introduce himself to her as she did the same, and they proceeded into the building to take his order, but not before she had to place her hands on a security pad that read fingerprints that then would make a buzzing sound that let her in to the building.

He followed to the waiting area where she excused herself as she went looking for a catalog that he could use to place his order if he would just write down the item number and quantity on the order form she had given him with a pen. She then could enter the order in the system for him, which would be ready in about an hour if he cared to wait for it, or he could run an errand and come back if he liked. He said he would wait. She asked him if he'd like something to drink while he was waiting, and he said a cold soda would be nice. She then went to her desk and pulled out a couple of quarters and proceeded to a back door at the end of this huge office and in seconds returned with a diet soda, which she made an excuse for not having a regular soda due to the beverage company not coming in till tomorrow to refill the drink machine. He said, "No problem, this would be fine." He found her to be very pleasant and personable, although a bit overdressed for such a small office, which had about ten cubicles set up with phones and computer screens, which from where he was sitting and waiting could see. They were all emptied though, and he asked Ms. Honeycutt where everyone was. She said there were a couple of other people working in there but were at lunch now and that they had recently opened up and that she was taking applications for the staff that they needed to bring in and asked if he would like to apply. He said, "No, thank you. I have my own business that is opening up tomorrow and that's why I'm here to get some goods as giveaways to the visitors that come in."

"Oh, how lovely. What a nice gesture from you."

"Yeah, I thought it would be nice."

"Well, take your time. When you are finished, just come over to my cubicle that is right up front and give me your order and I will take it from there." Donald thanked her for her assistance as she went back to her desk. Donald looked through the catalog and wrote down a bunch of items and quantities and asked Ms. Honeycutt if he could take the catalog with him when he was finished. She said, "Sure, darling, anything you like. You can take me too if you like." Donald just smiled back at her and said nothing for he was shocked that she was hitting on him. She must have been a cougar looking for a younger man was his first thought, as she mumbled, "CHILD, PLEASE."

Donald then said that he was finished, placing his order that she could then place the order for him She graciously took his order from him and said that she would see what she could do to push the order through quickly since there was not much else going on this very moment. She entered the order from her computer at her cubicle and than got up and walked away from her desk and went around the corner. He heard a door close and assumed she went to the warehouse, but a few minutes later, here she comes with a long piece of toilet paper trailing behind her on the floor. She had gotten it stuck in her panty hose and was trailing it behind her as she approached her desk and did not know it. He busted into laughter and said, "Excuse me. But you have toilet paper dragging behind you."

"Oh my lord. I did it again. I just can't get used to wearing these damn panty hose. I usually go commando." Donald was beet red for she just gave him too much information.

He asked her, "Where do I go to pick up my order?"

Ms. Honeycutt said, "Just drive around the back and up the stairs and through the door and ring the bell and someone will be more than happy to bring you your order from the back." As he asked how much his order came to, she pulled it up and said, "It would be $269 even." She asked if he was going to place it on a credit card or pay cash. He said he was going to place it on his business credit card and proceeded to give it to her as she rang it through. Ms. Honeycutt then gave him his receipt and said, "Thank you for shopping at Everything Canine Inc." Donald thanked her for being so helpful and gave her back the pen and the empty soda can, which he guzzled down fast so he could get out of there. Donald then left and headed to his car and to the back to get his merchandise to head back to the shelter before the dark clouds that was now hanging over this building.

Donald called Ms. Kitty and asked if everything was okay at the shelter and that he was going to be back within twenty minutes if he didn't get caught in the rain that was now approaching him. She told Donald that she saw on the television from his office that there was indeed going to be a hurricane developing in the Gulf and that Texas and New Orleans would be in its path and that South Florida would be experiencing feeder bands in several days but tomorrow was still going to be sunny for the grand opening. It was news that Donald wanted to hear and yet somewhat not. He signed for six boxes of merchandise and loaded them into the backseat of his BMW and headed back to the shelter.

CHAPTER TWELVE

LaVonda and Mario were just sitting outside on the front porch, drinking and enjoying a glass of iced tea and iced coffee, taking a well-deserved break from the phones and seeing off their last houseguest that just left the shelter. The gentleman was heading back into society with a full-time job and a place he can call his own from overcoming a gambling addiction at the casinos in Hollywood. They were talking on how well the shelter was doing and about some of the characters that had come and gone through the Dixie Arms over the past several months and those that they helped find jobs and homes and how nice it was to get a break now that the hurricane season was coming to an end.

Mario was so thrilled that this time of year was over; it had been a busy season for him as well ticketing careless drivers as well as several road rage incidents he had to deal with. The sheriff's department was busy keeping crime off the streets was more crazier than usual for them. He just wanted to get back to a normal schedule once again.

Mario's cell phone rang, it was his captain at the sheriff's office asking if he could report to his shift a bit earlier than normal. It was sudden but was needed to relieve the first-shift deputy, a little earlier today. The deputy was heading to the airport to pick up his daughter who lived in New Orleans and was evacuating to his home due to a hurricane on the horizon that was taking aim on the Texas and Louisiana border

He said he wouldn't mind and that he'd be in as soon as he went home and changed into his uniform. The captain thanked him. Mario then turned to LaVonda and told her he needed to leave and that he was called in early. And he said, "It was nice while l as it lasted," t He had to cut their relaxation time short out on the veranda and told her to brace herself for a possible unexpected wave of housequest due to that call he just received regarding the weather on the Gulf Coast. He said that it could get a bit crazy just one more time before the hurricane season ended.

LaVonda replied, "That's what I'm here for to help those in need." He said he'd call her later once he had more news on the storm and that she might want to turn the weather channel on the television to keep an eye on this. She said she would and then would check her supplies and food to make sure she didn't need to run out and get more supplies just in case the Dixie gets another full house.

In the meantime, Donald was just finishing up unpacking the free goods that he was going to give away for the grand opening. Ms. Kitty was going through her list of things to do while listening to the television, hoping that the grand opening tomorrow would go off without a hitch and that the weather would not stop them. Donald then asked Ms. Kitty if she would walk with him to see the dogs that were just brought in over in the kennel area. She said she'd be more than happy to. She had so much going on, but to see those cute dogs took away any stress she was feeling to get through tomorrow. She jumped at the invitation just to be around them.

Donald was in awe the minute he walked through the kennel area and saw the fifteen adorable faces just barking away as they approached their kennel. There was a mix of canines up for adoption that had come over from the shelter south of town, which ranged from a year old up to three years old, which were now going to be in his care. There was a Benji type-looking dog, a beagle, a Lab mix, two terrier mixes, a shepherd mix, and several other medium-size dogs and three full-size dogs. He was overwhelmed that he got teary eyed to the point that he was now realizing that he was giving them a second chance, which he wanted so badly to do with Freeway. All was set for the grand opening tomorrow. Donald said that he was going to call it a day and asked Ms. Kitty to make sure that she asked the other employees whom they hired to report to the shelter about an hour earlier before they were supposed to start, for a brief meeting to go over a few things before they unlock the doors of the new Freeway Shelter. She said she would take care of it and practically pushed him out the door. Ms. Kitty could see he was tired and stressed; after all, it was going to be an expensive adventure, and she wanted to make sure she was around for the ride. After all, she was getting a nice salary and enjoyed what she did and didn't want to see it fail.

Donald said good night to Ms. Kitty and left it in her hands, and he headed home to his town house, which was now paid off clear and free

from his lotto winnings. Donald decided to keep it since it was about a
fifteen-minute drive to the shelter so that he could be close just in case
of an emergency, and he could be there in a matter of minutes. Ms.
Kitty paged all the employees to the front of the building so she could
double-check on their duties and see how they were doing and to tell
them that tomorrow was going to be a big day and that they were going
to a big part of this shelter from here on in and that she and Donald were
pleased with their work and to let them know about reporting in a bit
earlier and that they would be paid the overtime for coming in earlier.
She told them that if tomorrow goes off without a hitch, they would
all be getting a bonus in their first paycheck, and they needed to be on
their best behavior and act professional around the adopting families that
would be strolling through the shelter tomorrow. They all looked at each
other with a smile on their faces because they knew that a bonus was
just around the corner. After a brief meeting, she told the employees to
finish up and that they could go home a bit earlier today to be rested for
tomorrow. She was going to head out after she made sure the dogs were
feed their dinner and the lights were out.

In the meantime, Mario was arriving on duty as he was asked to help
out a fellow officer who, by just minutes he would have missed, was leaving
the parking garage and was getting in his own car and heading to the airport
to pick up his daughter. He waved to Mario and yelled out the window,
"Thanks, Mario! I'll call you later," as he drove out of the parking garage.

"Later!" Mario yelled back. Mario placed a call to LaVonda at the
shelter to check in with her before he started his shift and asked if she was
okay and told her that he would be out on the streets in about an hour and
if she needed anything to call him on his cell phone. She said she was good
with food and supplies and that she'd be okay as she was finishing up some
last-minute things in her office and was on the computer.

"No, Mario, I'll be fine," she told him. He said he'd check with her
later, and she said that it would be fine. As he hung up the phone and
walked into the sheriff office's to report to work, LaVonda was on her
computer looking for potential employers and checking on the storm in
the Gulf to see what was going on with that and where it was heading. Her
phone rang again, and LaVonda answered the phone, "Good afternoon,
the Dixie Arms, LaVonda speaking."

"Hi, Mom, it's me Savannah, just checking in on you to see how you
are doing and to catch up on the boys if you have heard from them."

"Hi, honey, I'm fine," LaVonda said. "Just working a lot and keeping an eye on the storm in the Gulf at the moment."

"Yeah, I saw that too on the news up here so I thought I'd check in and make sure you were okay."

"Oh, darling, just doing great. The shelter's keeping me going 24/7 just about. I have Mario working with me now part-time and he is a big help, not to mention my daily dose of eye candy."

"Oh, Momma, you haven't change a bit. That's why I still love you all the way from up here in Tennessee."

"So how is your wheel-bound husband doing?"

"Oh, Momma, you know his name!"

"Okay, okay, Rusty, how could I forget since he has a rusted pipe that you have to go to the cookie jar to replace?"

"What are you talking about!"

"I heard the story from one of the church ladies who told one of the other church ladies who called me who I keep in touch with. I about fell out of my rocker on the front porch that day Laughing my ass off. I would have died of embarrassment if it were me."

"Oh my God, you heard the story. I can't believe that those busybody women from the church have nothing better to do than gossip across the country."

"Well, honey, I told you never trust a Southern woman with a secret or gossip. It'll surely eventually make it to the front page."

"So have you heard from Matthew or Scott lately?" Savannah asked, trying to change the subject with her mom.

"No, darling. Not t in about a month or so. They are doing fine and love what they are doing. I'm sure they'll be calling me any day too if they see or hear about another storm in the Gulf brewing and will be checking in too."

"Give them my love," Savannah asked.

"I will, honey. Hope to see you soon. Take care. My regards to Rusty pipe."

"Mama! Good-bye!"

"Bye, darlin'." As LaVonda tries to get back to her business on the computer, the phone rings again. "Dang phone! I need to put the answering service on," LaVonda tells herself.

"Good afternoon, the Dixie Arms, LaVonda speaking."

"Hey, LaVonda, it's me Ms. Honeycutt. Just wanted to let you know that I will be coming in a bit later tonight. I will be getting a ride home from one of the girls I work with. She wanted to grab a bite out somewhere and didn't want to eat alone. She said her treat. So I said, 'Hell yeah!' Couldn't pass up a dinner. Besides, it'll give you a break from having to feed me tonight."

"No problem. Just be careful and if you end up needing a ride home later for any unknown reason, call me and I'll come get you." LaVonda made a face like, "Oh shit, what did I just say. I could have had a free night alone and not have that crazy bitch following me around all night telling me about her day at the office word for word."

"Will do, honey!"

"You have a nice time," LaVonda said back as she heard the sound of *CLICK!* The phone was hung up. "That was wrong, just wrong, calling her a crazy bitch. I need to find her a place of her own. I'm losing it. I know it. I'm going to lose it if I hear one more story about her day at the Canine—whatever the name of the place is. I'm putting the answering service on right now and if it's an emergency they will call my cell. I'll screen all the others from here."

LaVonda was now free from any interruptions and was going to head to the kitchen for a glass of wine from the wine cooler and relax the rest of the day in front of the computer, catching up on e-mails and surfing the web, something she likes to do a lot when no one is around. She spent a lot of time on the computer whenever it was not being occupied by Mario. She had a special interest in keeping up with the news from the IRS Web site and its newspaper that was posted online. Before she knew it, the clock on her computer read 8:45 PM. Where did the night go? And all of a sudden she heard Ms. Honeycutt being dropped off in front of the Dixie Arms. She peeked out the window and saw a by a broken-down but running AMC Pacer. "Holy Shit! It's yellow, bright yellow, and look at all the windows." She watched Ms. Honeycutt climb out of it. LaVonda had just taken a swig of her glass of wine when she spit it out all over the window sill, holding back from laughing hysterically. "What a hot mess! She looks like a beta fish in her outfit climbing out of a giant fishbowl with her feathered hat just blowing in the breeze. Shit, I made a mess of this window and sill." She looked around for something to wipe up the wine she just spit up from trying not to laugh; she noticed a box of tissues on the desk and grabbed them and wiped it up as soon as possible. She knew it would be at least ten minutes before Ms. Honeycutt got up the walkway and up the veranda and through the front door. This gave her plenty of time to get out of the office and out of sight before she would have to listen to another day and life of Ms. Honeycutt. She finished wiping the wine up and threw the tissue in the trash can under the desk and shut the desk lamp off and dashed to the kitchen where she was going to run to her room up the back staircase from the kitchen to avoid a long and painful evening of conversation, not realizing she had left her computer screen up on the IRS Web site.

Ms. Honeycutt entered the Dixie Arms, humming a happy little tune. No doubt she had a nice evening out with a coworker and was in a very good mood. She called out to LaVonda who was nowhere in sight and was on her way into her own bedroom for a long night's sleep. Ms. Honeycutt went to the kitchen for a nightcap and then off to her room for it wouldn't be several hours till she had to get up and catch the first bus back into Weston for another workday for her.

CHAPTER THIRTEEN

Winds were starting to pick up in the French Quarter, and the signs were all there, from the stillness that was lurking throughout the Quarters. Only a handful of people could be seen walking down Bourbon Street. All the restaurants and bars and stores that are normally hustling and bustling with tourists were far from few. Word on the street was a major hurricane was heading their way, and everyone was home, watching and waiting to see if an evacuation notice would be issued in the next three days. Derek who was home with Freeway and Sheba were cuddled up on his sofa at home with the weather channel on, wondering the same thing. *Do I evacuate or stay?* He had to board up his house in a day and was concerned for both Freeway and Sheba; they could sense that there was something in the air as they kept sniffing and whining. Derek wasn't going to take any chances and made the decision to take the dogs to a local shelter in the morning where they would be safe until everything blew over, and he only had a day to get them to safety because the animal shelters fill up quickly. He needed to take his rig and hit the road and with a few of his possessions that he could put in his rig, which was the main thing that he needed to protect for it was his way and means for providing his livelihood not just for himself but for Freeway and Sheba; and with no room for them, he had to protect them someplace safe. The three of them finally dozed off until the crack of dawn, when they heard the trumpet sounds on the television playing reveille, which meant it was dawn and time to get up. This was not heard of much anymore, but some broadcasting systems to this day still play it. Derek woke up stiff from sleeping on the sofa and not in his bed and had Freeway on one side and Sheba on the other side of him with their heads in his lap looking at each other as if they were saying, "Oh, is it time to get up?"

Derek spoke to them and said, "Okay, time for a cup of coffee and a shower for it's going to be a long day." Freeway and Sheba jumped down off the sofa and followed Derek to the kitchen where he was rubbing his eyes, trying to wake up and make his coffee but not before feeding them two.

While they ate their breakfast, the first meal of the day, Derek jumped into the shower and finally woke up. As Derek stepped out of the shower with a towel wrapped around his waist, he saw Freeway and Sheba lying on the bathroom rug, just waiting to be let outside to take care of their morning business. Derek said, "Come on. I'll let you out in the backyard while I finish getting dressed." They then bolted to the patio doors off the bedroom to take care of business.

After getting dressed in a pair of jeans and tee shirt, he threw on his sneakers and headed back to the kitchen for his first cup of coffee of the day. "Where do I begin? Let's see what's going on with the storm first," and he changed the channel and watched a banner come across the screen that there would be an evacuation in forty-eight hours and that now would be the time to make preparations of things around your home and pets. There was a hurricane on the horizon, and its name was Alden—in the English language means "old friend." So with Alden twisting and turning out in the Gulf, it was time to get Freeway and Sheba to safety first.

Derek pulled out the yellow pages from the top shelf in his pantry and looked up animal shelters in the area and placed several calls. Two of the shelters were filled up, and the only one left did have room for eight more kennels that were open, so he placed a deposit down with his credit card and told them that he'd be down with his two dogs within the hour. Freeway and Sheba were at least going to be together for only a few days, and he was going to shutter up as soon as he dropped them off and hit the road after making a pit stop at the bank for cash on the way out of town.

Derek called out to the dogs who were running around the backyard, frolicking and jumping on each other. They both stopped once they saw Derek and made a beeline right for him. "Okay, guys, you're going on a little trip, going bye-bye in the car, going for a ride!" They both sat on their hind legs, looking up at Derek with their tails wagging and ears perked up as they tilted their heads from side to side for they understood the words "bye-bye," "car," and "ride." They were then jumping up in down with excitement for they knew they were going somewhere.

Before they knew it, they were at the shelter about to enter this brick structure, which looked pretty much secure from the outside. Derek explained to Freeway and Sheba that this was where they were going to stay for a couple of days and that he would be back for them and that there were other dogs inside that they would meet and probably play with if they could accommodate that. But no matter what, they were going to be together in the same kennel and that they have food and water and that it was only temporarily. Derek got all choked up, not knowing whether he was making the right decision, or if they would survive Alden, would he see them again? He had no choice; he was already there at the shelter. And time was running out, and he had more things to get done before hitting the road out of town, knowing that Freeway and Sheba were all taken care of as they were walked to the back where the kennels were by one of the shelter's staff. They both stopped in their tracks and looked back to say bye and not before Derek said to them, "Go on, go on. I'll see you soon." Once they heard and recognized Derek's voice, they then proceeded on their way to the kennel area with the attendant. Knowing that they were settled, Derek was heading to his bank to withdraw enough money for gas and food and anything else he might need cash for. His last stop was home to pack up a few things like some clothes, his personnel papers, and some photos and to close the shutters, which he had installed a few years back after the last major storm hit the Gulf Coast so it would be a quick process and so he could spend more time preparing for the next storm, which in this case was Alden.

Within a few hours, Derek was done preparing and was hitting the road with his rig, his means of his livelihood, and his other car was parked in the garage all tucked in for safety. Traffic on the I-10 was starting to back up because the other arteries into New Orleans were closed off. So he was going to head as far north as he could to get away from the brunt of the storm, knowing he still had to deal with running into rain and possible winds.

The grand opening of the Freeway Shelter was way under way, and the turnout was unbelievable. They had face painters for the children, cotton candy, ice cream, hot dogs, balloons—it looked like a carnival event from the street out front.

There must have been at least 150 people that had already came thru the shelter by noon, and they had only three dogs left from the fifteen that was there, and those who did not leave with a dog from the shelter were directed to the shelter south of town where they had more canines available to adopt out. Ms. Kitty called her old office where she was employed before she left to come work for Donald, and they told her that they had adopted out eighteen dogs today so far.

It was a good day for both shelters. While Donald was walking the grounds of the shelter with a family, his cell phone rang. It was transferred over to him from the front desk at the shelter. It was the shelter were Freeway and Sheba were staying in New Orleans; they wanted to know if they could send some of the overflow of dogs they had at their shelter with relatives that were heading out and down to Florida as they were being told to evacuate from their homes. He said he had plenty of room and would be more than willing to assist, and if needed, he would pay the way to fly more in if needed.

Donald had the means and the money to make sure they would be safe. The shelter had gotten his number from the Web site that was up and running, introducing the Freeway Shelter now open in Fort Lauderdale, Florida. The notices were sent to all shelters across the country, where they could all be part of a network working together to help those misfortunate and in need of a home. The New Orleans shelter was grateful and said they would be sending about twenty dogs and that the need to fly them would not be necessary, and he said that he was more than willing to assist them. So now that the arrangements were taken care of by phone, Donald called Ms. Kitty on her cell phone, who was giving a tour of the facility of her own, and told her to be prepared and that they were going to have more dogs coming in by the end of day tomorrow because they were on the road from New Orleans as he explained the situation to her. She was glad to hear that he was willing to go as far as paying for the expenses and plane flight, which showed her that he was a changed man and a very caring one in fact.

Donald was not aware that Freeway was going to be one of the dogs in the pack that would be coming back to Florida. Sheba was also coming because they came in as a pair and were not going to be separated per the owner's request. Was Donald going to finally see Freeway again?

The phones were ringing off the hook over at the Dixie Arms because the word was out that hurricane Alden was in the Gulf and that Florida would be getting lots of rain and that the homeless would need a place to stay. Mario was taking calls, and LaVonda was taking in those who were already at the front door, seeking shelter. LaVonda was willing to line the halls of the shelter with blankets and sleeping bags once again from the second and third floors to accommodate those in need. LaVonda was not going to turn anyone away. Mario had called in sick to the sheriff's office just so that he could be at the shelter to help LaVonda out. It was going to be a long night and, if not, an even longer day tomorrow as the roads were going to be filling up with out-of-towners who are evacuating to South Florida.

Mario knew he was going to have to find some time to crash because he knew he was going to be pulling a double shift over the next few days with all that was going on with the shelter, not to mention his full-time job on the highway patrol. So he asked LaVonda if it would be okay to crash in her room a bit when things settled down a bit. She said it wouldn't be a problem and told him that whenever he was ready to crash, to go ahead up, that she had it under control. He thanked her for her hospitality and for being a great friend and for getting to know how much this shelter was part of the community for those in need and that she was a real trooper doing this day after day for it was a privilege and pleasure helping out. She was touched by Mario's praise and felt the same working side by side with him and for him taking time from his limited schedule to help out; after all, he was just a part-time employee for her at the Dixie Arms.

LaVonda appreciated it very much, and she would find some way to make it up. Mario said that it wasn't necessary, that he just loved helping those in need, which they both agreed on. "So now that this day has just about ended, why don't you head up to my bedroom and get a few hours of sleep. I have it under control from here."

Mario said, "You sure?"

And she said, "Yes, it's not as bad as I thought it would be. We have at least a dozen or so homeless settling in and I have Ms. Honeycutt who was released from work early because of Alden and was able to catch a ride home today in that yellow AMC Pacer, which I'll tell you about later if I don't forget. I put her to work in the kitchen, making sandwiches and getting drinks for the guests. I'm hoping she will meet Mr. Right as she's helping out and eventually he will sweep her off her feet and out of here on her own."

"Oh! You're bad," Mario replied.

"No! Not really, she's been here at the shelter a bit longer than those who have come and gone and haven't returned. Don't get me wrong. She's a lovely lady and at times a crazy bitch but it's time she found her own nest and moved on. She can't stay here forever!"

"Yeah, you're right," Mario replied, and he commented to LaVonda that he hopes he never ended up in that situation like she did, living behind a dumpster in a box and panhandling change for food or drinks or eating leftovers from people off the streets. "That's just sad."

"I agree. I was at the right place for a reason when I found her and she has come a long way since then and I know it made a difference in her life and she's doing well. She has a job and a roof over her head even though it's mine and has a closetful of clothes that she keeps me in stitches in with those hats that she wears practically with every outfit. I think she's been going into the ladies' room upstairs where I have all the women's things and stuff. You know the room that was a bedroom and converted into a ladies' shop for those who have nothing when they come in."

"Yah! I've seen it."

"I think she goes in there late at night while I'm sleeping and helps herself to more clothes from the donations."

"Really!"

"Yep, I haven't seen one same outfit on her since she's been here. So I think she's hoarding or putting them back after wearing them and that's why I haven't seen them again."

"Oh my God! No wonder you call her a crazy bitch. She is a very colorful person. She just warms my heart every day with laughter when I see her here. I think it started the day I first met her and she said, 'Child, please,' and you told me what that meant. I was flattered and think it was cute coming from a woman her age. Oh hell, I thought she was a cougar hitting on me!"

"Yeah, I would have thought the same thing. Well, why don't you head up to my bedroom and I'll lock up the shelter and we'll chat later."

"Okay."

"Thanks for a nice day!"

"What? I had a nice day spending it with you and getting to have our talks when we can," Mario replied.

"Likewise," replied LaVonda.

"Good night!"

"Good night, Mario!" Just as Ms. Honeycutt walked in and said that she has fed all those that are staying there tonight in the shelter. They all had a sandwich along with a drink, along with either a cookie or a piece of fruit for dessert. "Great!" LaVonda replied. "You've really been a big help to me tonight."

"You're welcome! But you can thank my employer because they sent me home early today. I will no doubt be off tomorrow so I can help out some more tomorrow."

"That will be nice. So are you heading up to your room right now?"

"Yes! My feet are killing me right now. I just want to lie down and kick them up. You know something you might be doing later tonight if you play your cards right."

"Excuse me!" replied LaVonda.

"I may be old, but I have ears like a hawk and I couldn't help but overhear that Mario would be taking a nap in your bedroom. Child, please! I'd be all over that like beans on rice!"

"You're a mess! We are just friends and besides that, he works for me part-time here at the shelter."

"Wouldn't be the first time an employer slept with an employee," replied Ms. Honeycutt.

"Enough! Okay, it's getting late and I, too, would like to get some rest so this conversation is now over, do you hear me?"

"Yes! Loud and clear," Ms. Honeycutt replied as she walked away and headed up to her room, mumbling something like, "If you got some, you wouldn't be so bitchy!"

"Excuse me!"

"Nothing! Just said got some food on my dress."

"Good night!"

"Good night," replied Ms. Honeycutt as she turned and headed out of the room.

CHAPTER FOURTEEN

The road sign said "Now Entering the Sunshine State Florida" as the van carrying Freeway and Sheba along with seven other dogs from the New Orleans shelter crossed the state line from Alabama into Florida. The driver named Steve was a brother of one of the workers at the shelter who volunteered to help with the overflow of canines by taking them out of New Orleans to safety before Alden came ashore. Several other volunteers weren't too far behind them with a few more canines in tow with them that also were evacuating.

Steve told his friend Jeff who was along for the ride with him that they had about eight hours or so if they picked up speed and would be coming into South Florida and it was now nine o'clock in the morning. They were going to the Freeway Shelter first stop, and if it was after closing hours, they were instructed to call Donald on his cell phone since he was only fifteen minutes away, and he would meet them at the shelter.

Donald was up at the crack of dawn because he couldn't sleep from being overwhelmed from the grand opening yesterday of his shelter. He had so much on his mind from now actually owning his own business and not having to worry about money anymore since he was now very wealthy. He had employees and their families—the ones that were married—to take care of, not to mention the canines coming and going that he had to find homes for. But he was young and had a lot to look forward to. He was wondering where Ms. Kitty was after the grand opening because she had received a phone call from the waitress at the restaurant that she had flirted with several days ago, and they were going on their first date. Was it a good day for her in more ways than one?

Donald was restless, so he decided to head to the shelter early since the doors weren't schedule to open until ten o'clock in the morning. He was going to check on everything before the staff arrived and see if Ms.

Kitty would happen to arrive at work on time from her date. He was going to notify her that he was going to take the day off and take care of some personal business that he was putting off, like shopping for a van for the shelter and getting an oil change done on his BMW. Donald arrived at the shelter, and there was Ms. Kitty just sitting in the entryway, crying. Donald asked her what was wrong, and she said her date last night with the waitress had gone bad. He said he was sorry to hear that and asked if there was anything he could do.

She replied, "Yah! Could you please unlock the door of the shelter because I left the keys on my dresser at home and I forgot them."

He said, "No problem!" She mentioned she had a lot to do today. This way she could forget about last night and move on. "Good for you!" he told her.

"I don't know what I was thinking going on this date," Ms. Kitty told Donald. "It was a mistake and believe me I won't let it happen again." Donald who was dying on the inside wanted to know the details on what happened, but he knew when she was ready to talk, he'd be there to listen. With that he helped her up and unlocked the door and turned on the lights as they both went toward their offices, and that was that.

Donald called Ms. Kitty's extension in her office about an hour later to check on her to see if she was all right, hoping she would say something to him. He was also informing her that he would be leaving the premises and taking the day off and that she was in charge and that if she needed anything to please call him on his cell phone. She said she had it under control and not to worry. He said that he'd try to be back in time to meet the van that was bringing the dogs from New Orleans later in the day once he received the call on where they were and that he would meet them here. However, for any reason he was not back in time, he'd call her and tell her what to do with them. Donald wanted to keep the dogs separate from the other dogs because they were not up for adoption, because they belonged to someone and didn't want to mix them up. He was going to kennel them in a special section of the kennel to keep them apart. She said she would be there all day and not to worry.

Over at the Dixie Arms across town was a half-woken up Ms. Honeycutt who was stumbling over the bodies of homeless people that she helped feed last night, who were lined up outside her bedroom door on the floor all the way down the hallway. She was getting up late, but her feet and legs were much better. She was working her way down to the kitchen for some tea when she stumbled across a familiar face that she thought she knew. He looked familiar but couldn't place it. Someone from her past, she thought. As she got through the obstacle course and down to the kitchen, she was greeted by Mario who was in a pair of jeans and shirtless as well as barefoot, pouring himself a cup of coffee.

She was startled, and she blurted out from her lips, "CHILD, PLEASE."

And he smiled and said, "Good morning to you too."

She was in awe; there in front of her stood this handsome sheriff with bulging biceps, six-pack abs, and tanned. She said good morning and asked how his night was.

He said he felt better getting some sleep and that he was just getting a cup of coffee for LaVonda who was already at work and on the computer in her office, tracking hurricane Alden; she wanted to see if there would be any more influx of houseguest that would be coming in to the shelter if the hurricane was going to be bad.

"Oh!" she said. "I just came down through the back staircase because of the bodies of blankets and sleeping bags in the hallway and I didn't want to wake anyone."

"I just woke up myself a few minutes ago and she was not in the room so I looked around down here and I found her in her office and said good morning to her and she said that the coffee was on and here I am getting me a cup as well as a refill for her."

"So in other words there was no SLAP AND TICKLE between the two of you last night?"

"Excuse me!" Mario said.

Ms. Honeycutt wanted to know the story on why a fine-looking man like him was not taking the opportunity to enjoy the companionship of that lovely, kindhearted woman in the other room.

"I respect her and she was kind enough to let me crash in her bedroom since it was busy here last night and that I will have to go on duty tonight because I called in sick last night so I could be here to help her out last night with a full house."

"Well, that was very nice of you," Ms. Honeycutt replied back. "So you're either gay or crazy. Which is it?"

"Neither!" Mario told her. "I just haven't found the right woman that could accept me and my work schedule because of the night shift on the sheriff department working till wee hours in the morning. So I just date from time to time, but I haven't given up on women. I don't really have the time at the moment. As for being gay, I'm very much straight," he said as he leaned over toward her and gave her a kiss on the cheek and excused himself from the coffee pot so he could go put a shirt on and head back to the office with LaVonda's refill and to see if she had found any more updates on the hurricane.

"Oh! By the way, your hair looks fabulous." Ms. Honeycutt was questioning if he was messing with her just then.

"Oh my God! Hair, that's it!" The gentleman upstairs that looked familiar to her was Philip; he was her husband's assistant at the salon in New Orleans when she lived there. "I can't believe it is him." She turned and headed back upstairs, trying to find him and was going to find out if it was truly him.

Mario had put on a tee shirt from the men's store upstairs that was converted at the time the shelter was being put together and went downstairs again to see LaVonda and how she was doing on the computer, tracking the storm. Just as he walked up behind her, she was once again on the IRS Web site. He looked puzzled because this was not the first time that he came across this Web site on her computer, and she casually closed down the site. "So did you find any updates on the hurricane?" Mario asked.

"Yes, it looks like it's going to be a big one. The size of it alone takes up the Gulf but it's going to hit land as a category two with lots of rain. At least there shouldn't be much structure damage to buildings, unless some of those building over there are not able to take it on. I guess we'll just have to wait and see, won't we?"

"Yes, we will," Mario replied back.

"So what's your schedule for today?" LaVonda asked.

"Oh, thought I'd help out and get breakfast for your houseguest from last night and help out with anything else you might need help with before I have to go into work tonight."

"Oh, you're going in tonight for highway duty?" LaVonda asked.

"Yes, going to try to keep the streets safe as possible with the rain from the feeder bands and the winds if we get any. It wouldn't be a good night for anyone to be on the streets. I'll no doubt be stationed at my usual place over at I-75 and Commercial because there's an overpass that I can park under and watch from there. I could call in sick again if you like? . . ."

"No! That wouldn't be necessary. I'll have it under control, no need to worry. I'll call you if I have any problems here," LaVonda told Mario.

"Then I'll feel a lot better knowing that you will call me if you need me," replied Mario. LaVonda mentioned to him that she thought that they might only see one or two more houseguests by day's end.

"I'm running out of room and will only be able to accommodate a couple more. I'll to have to place calls around town and see if any of the other shelters can take any more people in if I get more than two showing up for shelter. I will have to bring them from here to those shelters unless you could find a way to help me in that area of needing your assistance without you getting in trouble while on duty tonight."

"I'll see what my night is like and it's possible I could help you out."

"If not then I can handle it. I've done it before and besides I'm from the South and believe me I can take care of myself very well if I see any signs of trouble. No one wants to piss me off or even try anything with me, or else they'll regret the day they ever messed with LaVonda. I'm one of those women that no one wants to underestimate. I could go crazy on their ass so I think I pretty much have it under control if you cannot help tonight. So don't worry I'll be fine," she told him.

Now, Mario was suspicious on what she meant by that comment. There was another side of LaVonda that he had never seen. There was something in her past that she was hiding, and he was not going to let it go. He was eventually going to find out more about her and her secret.

"Okay then, I'll just head into the kitchen and see what I can rustle up for the houseguest before they wake up," Mario said.

"I think we have plenty of eggs and toast, and I think we have some bacon and hash browns too. I'll be in there with you in just a minute to help you out!" LaVonda replied.

"Take your time, I have it covered," Mario replied back.

In the meantime, Ms. Honeycutt was upstairs, looking for Philip, who had her baffled on why he was here. What happened to him? She finally had run into someone from her past and was thrilled that she wanted to know more. As she approached Phillip, he was rubbing his eyes and waking up. She said, "Excuse me, sir."

"Yes!"

"Sorry to bother you but your name wouldn't happen to be Philip, would it?"

"Oh yes, it is. Did you ever live in New Orleans?"

"Yes! Did you have work at a salon on Canal Street?"

"Yes!"

"Oh my God! It is you!"

He asked, "Do I know you?"

"Yes! My name is Gloria Honeycutt. I was Andre's wife."

"Yes, I remember you! What are you doing here?"

"I'm staying here at the shelter. I have been here for several months. Come with me to my room. I'll fill you in." Her eyes were teary eyed, and she helped him up as she took him by his hand and led him down the hall to her room to catch up.

The aroma from the kitchen where Mario was preparing breakfast was carried all the way up the staircases to the second floor. It smelled like a Southern diner. Only thing missing was grits because they had run out and forgot to order them with their food supply of staples this week. The bacon, hash browns, and coffee woke up the remaining homeless guests as they were getting up. One by one they were folding their blankets or sleeping bags and lined them up along the hallway. This might be the same place tonight that they will be sleeping in again if the rain keeps them off the street. They all came down the staircase where they saw LaVonda standing at the bottom as she was leaving her office and heading toward the kitchen to help Mario out. She greeted them with a "Good morning" as she directed them to the kitchen area for breakfast. She then headed up the staircase to make sure they had all come down for breakfast and that no one would be left behind.

It was going to be the only time that she was serving breakfast. If they missed the breakfast, they would have to wait till lunchtime. Mario had set up a buffet line so they could help themselves. LaVonda assisted them to the dining room as they carried their plates of eggs and bacon, a slice or two of toast, and a helping of hash browns where she was going to bring them their drinks, which consisted of either a glass of juice, a cup of coffee, or a cup of tea, as they all sat down to eat together.

Mario was at the buffet table, helping serve up the food that he had cooked and was just amazed on how many people had come in last night that needed shelter. Mario asked LaVonda if she had seen Ms. Honeycutt this morning. She replied she hadn't since last night when she said good night to her.

"I'll run up to her room and see if she is up and will be coming down for breakfast."

"Okay," Mario replied back. "I still have plenty left." As LaVonda knocked on Ms. Honeycutt's bedroom door and slightly opened it, she saw her sitting on the edge of her bed, holding hands with one of the houseguests that came in last night for shelter.

She said, "Gloria! What are you doing? Who is this gentleman with you?"

"I'd like you to meet Philip. He used to work for my husband Andre in New Orleans at the salon. The one I told you about and had to sell when you first took me in."

! What a pleasure it is to meet you!" she said to Philip.

Ms. Honeycutt introduced Philip to LaVonda and said, "This is my guardian angel, the woman who saved me from the alley."

"How nice it is to meet you," Phillip replied as he extended his hand out to shake her hand.

"Likewise I'm sure. I will let you two get reacquainted. I know you have a lot to catch up on. I just wanted to let you know, Gloria, that Mario has breakfast ready and that if you like to eat to come on down and bring Philip."

"Thank you!" Philip replied. "I'm famished."

As they rose from the bedside, still holding hands, "We'll be right down," Ms. Honeycutt told LaVonda.

"I'll tell Mario to set a place for the two of you someplace special so you can spend some time catching up." They both thanked her and said they would be right down.

"I know you must have a lot of questions for each other!" And she was just dying to find out his story. What are the chances of two people who knew each other years ago both ending up homeless and in the same shelter in a different state?

It was going to get a lot more interesting around the Dixie Arms. LaVonda couldn't wait to tell Mario as she quickly flew out of the room and down the hall to the staircase where she thought about sliding down the banister; she wanted to share the news about the reunion of Ms. Honeycutt and Philip but knew that was not very ladylike and proper for a girl from the South to do. Sliding down banisters was so not ladylike at her age! But she said, "What the hell," and did it anyways. Besides, the banisters needed a bit dusting anyways. Once she hit the bottom of the staircase, who else but Mario was standing there. She was embarrassed that he saw her do that.

"So that's where you disappeared to?"

"Oh! I'm just doing a little dusting," she told him, as he chuckled. "No, seriously, I thought it'd be fun and had to try it."

"I checked the hallway and everyone is gone. So they must be all down here then?" Mario asked.

"All but two."

"Oh?"

"You'll never guess."

"What?"

"Ms. Honeycutt and a friend from her past were in her room just sitting on the bed holding hands and talking. It was so cute."

"What!"

"From what I can gather he came into the shelter last night and he was homeless. His name is Philip and he used to work for her dead husband, Andre, at a salon she, or rather he, owned and had to close down after his death back in New Orleans."

"Are you serious?" Mario asked.

"As serious enough I would be willing to slide down this banister again."

"Oh, that won't be necessary. I believe you." LaVonda asked Mario if he could get two plates for them because they'd be right down. He said, "No problem, be happy to."

He asked her if she would like something to eat, and she said, "No, I'll pass. I could use a refill on the coffee though." He said he'll get it as she sat on the bottom of the staircase, just thinking of the history Ms. Honeycutt and Philip have to catch up on as they were coming down the staircase at that very moment. Mario came back with her refill of coffee and was introduced to Philip as they were ready to go in to breakfast. Mario in the meantime mentioned to LaVonda that the houseguest that stayed at the Dixie last night had "chewed and screwed" and left the shelter. She said, "What?"

"Yep. They all ate breakfast and one by one they walked out the front door. She took her cup of coffee and went out the front door onto the veranda and looked up and down the street, and she saw several of them just disappear out of her sight.

"At least it isn't pouring anymore!" she said to herself. She turned around and walked back into the foyer and told Mario to go ahead and set their breakfast plates in the dining room, which they now had all to themselves. He said it'd be his pleasure as he took one arm of Ms. Honeycutt, and Philip held on to the other as he escorted them to the dining room.

"Oh, by the way," Mario said as he took several steps out of the room.

"Yes?" she asked.

"We will have plenty of room tonight for anyone that needs shelter."

"Glad to hear that!"

"You'll be fine then with less for you to worry about." And they headed to the dining room.

CHAPTER FIFTEEN

Local broadcast was preempting television shows across the Southern states, keeping residents informed on hurricane Alden and its whereabouts as it churned in the Gulf, to all residents from South Florida all the way up to the Texas coast. Alden was to make landfall just after midnight in the New Orleans area as a category two. There would be lots of rain associated with the storm and winds up to ninety-six miles an hour or more. There will be more updates as the evening approached.

Many residents had spent the day bringing out their hurricane supplies, which consisted of flashlights, generators, first aid kits, as well as batteries and food supplies, as well as bringing in their pets that would also need to be protected from the storm. Some residents boarded up their homes while others ignored the warnings but did take some precautions by removing any flying objects from around their home from patios and yards.

Those items could become flying projectiles and were stored away safely into garages or brought inside of homes so they would not cause any further destruction that would follow by Alden's impact as it continued to churn in the Gulf.

Freeway and Sheba were only a half hour away from exiting the turnpike at Commercial Blvd. with their riding companions in the van which Steve and Jeff took turns driving down the turnpike. They would have been tired by now if they hadn't stopped at several rest areas along the way. They, too, needed to stretch their legs as well as the dogs and to take care of business as well as some fresh air and exercise. That was a chore in itself, having to harness the dogs one by one and then leash them up before they walked them.

After the second pit stop along the turnpike, Steve decided to keep the harnesses on them so they would only have to attach their leashes before they took them out of the van. The van was getting to be a bit overwhelmed with the smell of wet dogs from walking them in the rain, which they tried to avoid from the feeder bands that they just happened to run into at several pit stops. The turnpike was not as busy as Steve and Jeff had anticipated. It looked like the residents of Florida were listening to the word of their county officials to stay off the highway and main roads to avoid any accidents.

Steve decided to call Donald on his cell phone to let him know that they were exiting the turnpike and getting onto Commercial Blvd. He needed to know whether to hang a right or go left at the light.

Donald told him to take a right and that he would have to drive for about another ten minutes from that point and to be on the lookout for the following crossroads, Rock Island Road and then University Drive, and once they crossed University, they would be coming up to Pine Island Road. From that point they would see the I-75 at the very end, to continue driving till they got closer to that, and on the right-hand side they would see the sign Freeway Shelter on the top of the building in black letters with a head of a dog next to it. "You won't miss it."

"Great!" Steve said. "We're almost there then."

"Oh, by the way, I'm not going to be able to meet you there because I'm tied up at this dealership purchasing a van for the shelter so I don't know how long I'm going to be. I will call my assistant Ms. Kitty who is there, and she will help you bring the dogs in to the shelter.

"I have instructed her to kennel them up away from the other canines that are up for adoptions since they belong to someone so they would not accidently be adopted out.

"I'm going to call her now and give her a heads-up that you are close and that I won't be able to meet you and remind her of kenneling them separately from the others."

"Great!" Steve said. "Sorry we're not going to be able to meet you and tell you in person how much this means to us over there in New Orleans that you opened up your place for us."

"Me too, but maybe on the way back we'll meet," Donald said. "So, was the trip down bad with the weather?"

"Nothing we couldn't handle."

"Glad to hear that. Well, I'll let you go because I know you're almost there and that you, too, want to get out of the storm and make it to shelter."

"Yes, we have to call our friends and let them know we made it to town and that we'll be seeing them soon."

"Be careful and stay safe," Donald told him.

"You too" Steve replied back. "Thanks I will be in touch after the storm blows through to make the return arrangements on when I'll be picking them up to bring them back to New Orleans in a few days."

"I'll look forward to your call then. Don't worry, I have a state-of-the-art building built with the required codes by the county that is hurricane proof and with plenty of room since we recently open the doors. They will be in good hands, nothing for you to worry about," Donald told Steve.

"Thanks, we'll be touch. Bye!" Steve said as Donald said bye back and immediately dialed Ms. Kitty to fill her in that the dogs were near and to see how she was doing at the shelter and if any more boarders were coming in.

"Hey you!" Ms. Kitty answered her cell phone with, "I was just thinking of you since I haven't heard from you to see how you were doing and to see if you were enjoying your day off."

"Yes," Donald replied, "I got my oil change done and took care of some personal errands and I'm in the middle of purchasing a van for the shelter. That's why I'm calling you. I won't be able to meet the van coming from New Orleans with the dogs we are going to help board until the hurricane blows out of there. The driver Steve just called me and told me he is on Commercial Blvd. and heading your way from University Drive. He'll be there shortly."

"Great! I'll head out front and look for them."

"I think they have six dogs with them from our conversation. I may be wrong. I already have the kennels that are on the far west of the building blocked off just for them. You know the kennel area that we had the outside wall done in a mural of all types of canines so that the traffic exiting off the interstate would see the back of the building and know that this was the shelter as they approached Commercial Blvd. exit."

"Good, that's what I had in mind."

"I knew we thought alike," Donald told her. "This way they would be far enough away from the others that are up for adoption."

"Oh, by the way, we had another shelter call in from Texas and they have about fourteen dogs that they are bringing in for shelter because they are all filled to capacity over there on the Texas coast. I believe these are coming from Galveston and the surrounding area."

"Where are they now?"

"Well, the shelter called me at ten o'clock this morning and said that their van had left late last night and were heading this way. They had seen our Web site that we set up for networking and immediately sent them out and said that they would call us in the morning since it was late and we were closed. They called first thing this morning and said that they were in route and that the van left last night."

"Okay! So where are they now?"

"They're already here."

"Really!"

"Yep! Arrived several hours ago with an exhausted driver who couldn't wait to get the dogs out of his van, who said they gave him a migraine headache from all the barking they had done, not to mention also needed a bath. He smelled like one of the dogs and smelled really bad. He must have driven straight through. So I got the dogs kenneled with the help of the staff here and sent him up the street to the hotel between Pine Island and University on the left side on Commercial Blvd. There are two hotels side by side. I told him we would pick up the expense for the room since he was up all night driving, trying to bring these dogs down here.

"Besides, I kind of felt bad for him smelling awful as he did and having a migraine. It was the least I could do."

"I have no problem with that," replied Donald. "I knew that was another reason why I hired you. You have a big heart! And that's another reason why I wanted you to work for me."

"I took care of his room bill and put it on the company expense card."

"Not a problem whatsoever. I would have done the same," Donald said. "I have to go now and sign the papers for the van. I'll call you later to make sure everything is okay with our guest."

"Okay," she replied. "It's all under control, just take your time." As they said good-bye to each other and hung up from their cell phones, Donald walked over to the salesman's office and proceeded to sign the papers on a brand-new van, but not before he brought out his checkbook and wrote a check for the total amount including the sales tax, tags, and license. It was nice to have money. Ms. Kitty on the other hand was trying to get Freeway and Sheba into their kennel with both of them not wanting to go in. It was as if they sensed something was wrong and wanted nothing to do whatsoever with getting into the kennel. Finally she was able to get them both into the kennel with help from her staff, and a little coaxing with a treat. She was able to get them into the kennel together since they must be caged together. If it hadn't been for Steve mentioning that, to please keep them caged together so they wouldn't be separated from each other, they would have been separated into their own kennels.

Unaware to Derek, Freeway and Sheba were now in Florida because the shelter he had entrusted them with was overwhelmed with more than they could handle and that they were moved out of state to someplace else for safety. He himself was on the road heading north as far as possible away from hurricane Alden. He was going back for the two of them once the storm had passed the New Orleans area.

Ms. Kitty now had all twenty-one dogs from both Texas and New Orleans getting settled into their cages and resting comfortably. Fresh water and a meal were on the way to each and every one of them with the help of two of the shelter's staff who volunteered to stay behind to help her out and get them settled in.

The remaining staff headed home to get ready for a long night of questionable weather if the rains or winds picked up any from the hurricane in the Gulf.

Ms. Kitty had canines from Texas and Louisiana in her care that ranged from the two border collies—one named Freeway and his companion Sheba—that were in kennel number twenty at the very end of the row of cages, which belonged to Derek, a trucker driver from New Orleans, the beginning of the list on her letter-size pad as they were being kenneled up.

The list would be some kind of record of how many canines were in their care, from the names of each one to the breed of them as well as color or any specific markings that could identify them, and also their size and gender. Ms. Kitty wanted to have something to go by to identify them since they came into the shelter with no manila files or records on them or their owners, just a name tag with a first name attached to a dog collar that she was going to use to make her list from as they were getting kenneled up. It was for reference in case something decided to go wrong in the day ahead while the canines were in their care at the Freeway Shelter.

The list she had made up started with, from kennel number one, Sissy, a black-and-white Dalmatian from Texas City, #1; Winston, a black cocker spaniel from Metairie, Louisiana, #2; Juanita, an older blonde cocker spaniel, from Houston, Texas, #3; Duke, a tan Labrador from Sugar Land, Texas, #4; Bailey, a black and brown beagle from Humble, Texas, #5; Clayton, a golden doodle from Freeport, Texas, #6; Gina, a blonde Chow also from Freeport, Texas, #7; Bentley, a boxer from New Orleans, #8; Roscoe, also a boxer from Bay City, Texas, #9; Jesus, a Doberman from New Orleans, #10; Lucas, a golden retriever from Missouri City, Texas, #11; Clifford, a St. Bernard from Galveston Texas, #12; Angela, a reddish-colored Chihuahua from Humble, Texas, #13; Alfie, a white

Bichon from New Orleans, #14; Antoinette, a blonde Afghan hound from the French Quarter in New Orleans, #15; Kingston, a Shar-Pei from Galveston, Texas, #16; Lolita, another Chihuahua from Freeport, Texas, #17; Austin, a miniature schnauzer from Houston, Texas, #18; Bella, a long-haired Chihuahua from Houston, Texas, #19; and last, Freeway and Sheba, the border collies from New Orleans, #20.

Their owners who also had to evacuate to shelters of their own were not able to bring their dogs along with them. It was just as hard for them having to be separated from those that depended on them as they greeted them at the front door when they came home from work. The canines would take a bad day and turn it around if you had one. They had put smiles on their faces as they spent just a few moments of their time with them at the end of a bad day. They brought joy, and all they wanted in return was to be loved and cared for as they jumped up and down or climbed in your lap. Some might have dragged out their toys from wherever they had laid them and wanted to play at that very moment.

They took away the stress of a rough day and kept your blood pressure low from just looking into their eyes as they looked back at you as if to say, "It's okay, I'm here and you can relax," as they cuddle up to you and give you a lick on the nose or even just by placing their head into their owner's lap.

That companionship was gone, as they, too, were seeking shelter of their own from Mother Nature. And they only hoped that the outcome would end up with little or no damage to their home whatsoever as Mother Nature unleashed her wrath, knowing their dog was safe and not scared as they were that very moment.

After something like a hurricane, a lot of animals that were brought into shelters because of the laws that varied in different communities don't end up getting reunited with their owners. More were abandoned because they were left behind, for unknown reasons—like when the owner's home was destroyed, and they had no place to go back to. Or maybe worse, the owners never survived the storm and lost their lives, and the canines were left orphaned or homeless, needing to be cared for by some stranger.

This is why there are so many cries for help within the humane society, needing assistance in reuniting pets with their owners after a major disaster. Something was needed to be done to allow those pets to be able to go with their owners when an evacuation notice is issued. After all, they have become part of the family from the day the owner brought them into their home or until the day the canines leave them when they have had a full life of love and pleasure from being their friend and then one day move on to a better place and play with all the other animals who went before them.

After Ms. Kitty reviewed her list, she did a final walk through, starting with the first kennel cage and putting a check mark next to their name.

She then walked back to her office and called Donald on his cell phone to let him know that the dogs were here and kenneled up and fed and tucked in for the night, and she was getting ready to lock up the shelter and head home.

Donald was glad to hear all was taken care of, and he, too, was just leaving the dealership with the new van that he had purchased and was taking it home with him tonight. Donald mentioned that he was going to leave his BMW at the dealership till the morning and that he would need her to bring him down there in the morning to pick it up.

She said it would not be a problem as long as the roads were safe and clear from any debris from the winds or rain that would hamper them from getting it.

He also agreed. Donald once again thanked her for covering for him today and wished her a good night and told her to be safe. She said that's what she was here for, to assist him at the shelter, and added for him to be safe and if he wanted to talk to her later as the night progressed and the storm could be felt over Florida that they would call one another to check in. He said that he would. So with that they both said good night and went on their separate ways, Donald now heading home, in between the raindrops, from the dealership in a new van as Ms. Kitty was heading home in between the raindrops as well.

As the overhead fluorescent lights that hung above the cages swayed a bit over the kennels that had been left on for them, Freeway and Sheba as well as the other canines that had joined them in the kennel area were not going to be in complete darkness for the evening unless the power had gone out.

It was just then that Freeway was pacing back and forth like a caged tiger in a cage at the zoo. Sheba who was his kennel companion would not stop barking as she joined in a chorus with all the other barking and whimpering sounds coming from the other cages just next to them. They weren't the only ones that were scared; so were the other canines. It was the roaring winds as well as the pounding rains hitting the rooftop just above their heads. Freeway was pacing from the inside kennel to the outside kennel run that was separated by a doggie door that was built into each of the kennels.

It was built for the comfort of the dogs so they could come inside or go outside anytime they wanted to but yet be confined to the cages they were kenneled up in, which just happened to face the access road to I-75 just below the mural on the building of the shelter were all the dogs painted on the wall could be seen as you exited off to get on to Commercial Blvd. The winds were just a-howling away as well as the dogs that were inside the kennel that wanted nothing to do with the outside kennel area whatsoever due to the howling of the rain and winds. Freeway was not comfortable being caged up, and neither was Sheba from her barking. Freeway sniffed his way to the back of the outside kennel in which he started to dig at a big piece of broken concrete from the slab that the kennel had been on, which fenced them in.

Freeway had now dug himself a space big enough for him to slip out from under the fence of the kennel and make a run for it, unaware to Sheba who had calmed down a bit and was now lying down on her stomach, stretched out with her nose between her paws, whimpering instead of barking as her eyes kept looking up at the hanging florescent lights just swaying in the air above her. Unaware to her was that she was about to be left behind on the inside kennel as Freeway was making a run for it from the outside kennel in the middle of a stormy night ahead.

CHAPTER SIXTEEN

Over on the other side of town over at the Dixie Arms, a crazy and a bit freaking out Ms. Honeycutt was driving LaVonda nuts with her ranting and raving about the world coming to an end and that all the fires and floods and tornados and wicked weather across the country was finally approaching.

LaVonda was just minutes away from bitch slapping Ms. Honeycutt and telling her to get a grip on herself and that it was just a storm and that the world was not coming to an end. LaVonda's cell phone rang, which stopped her from whaling on Ms. Honeycutt; it was Mario, who was now on duty and heading over to the interstate of IH-75 and was going to be west of the county for the remainder of the evening, staking out under the overpass at Commercial and I-75 from the rains. He was just checking in and wanted to make sure all was okay at the shelter and to see if any more homeless people had showed up for cover tonight since it could be a messy night on the streets for them.

"No!" she replied. "But I do have one person whom I would love to throw out on the porch like a cat for the evening and see if she has nine lives to make it through the night."

"Oh my God!" he replied, as he started to laugh out loud. "Let me guess. Ms. Honeycutt giving you a hard time?" he asked.

She couldn't say much with Ms. Honeycutt standing only a few feet away from her but said, "Yes!"

"You can't talk now, can you?" Mario asked.

"No! Hang on just one moment, okay?"

Mario said, "Okay!"

"Gloria"—Ms. Honeycutt's first name as LaVonda sometimes calls her—"would you be a dear and go into the kitchen and bring me a glass of wine since I'm going to be on the phone for a few minutes."

Ms. Honeycutt said she didn't mind as she kept mumbling to herself, "The world is going to end, the world is going to . . ." as she walked away from LaVonda and headed toward the kitchen for the glass of wine that she had asked for.

"Mario, are you still there?"

"Yes!"

"She's gone for a few minutes. She's driving me crazy tonight with the nonsense of the world coming to an end." Mario told LaVonda to have patience with her and that she, too, was probably just as scared with the news coverage of this hurricane out there in the Gulf. "Yeah you're probably right. I'll just pour a little booze down her throat tonight and she'll sleep through it till the morning."

"You would do that to her?" Mario asked.

"Hell yeah if it shuts her up for the night."

Mario didn't know what to say back to her on that comment. She told him she had everything under control but Gloria and was fine and that no one has shown up for shelter tonight off the streets. The windows were covered up, and they had plenty of food and water. Flashlights and lanterns were ready if the power went out and a battery-operated, portable television and radio. "Sounds to me like you have it under control," Mario told her.

"Yep! I got it under control," she said as Gloria or Ms. Honeycutt came back from the kitchen with LaVonda's glass of wine.

"Thank you!" LaVonda said.

"You're welcome," Gloria said back. "Oh, is that Officer CHILD PLEASE on the phone?" she asked as Mario was quietly trying to hear in on the conversation with the rain that was coming down around him from his patrol car. He chuckled and asked LaVonda to give her cell phone to Ms. Honeycutt.

"Here! It's for you!"

"Me! Who would be calling me on your cell phone? Is it Philip?"

"No! It's not Philip. Speaking of, where is he tonight?"

"He's, well, he's kind of sleeping at the moment."

"Where is he?" LaVonda asked.

"Uh. He's in my room!"

"He's in your room?"

"Yes, ma'am! He's in my room!" Confused, LaVonda took a swig of the glass of wine as she handed her cell phone over to Gloria. "HELLO!"

"Hi, Gloria, it's me Mario. Are you okay tonight staying at the Dixie Arms?"

"Yes! I feel safe here."

"Okay then. What's this I hear, you going around saying the world is coming to an end?"

"Oh, I think I might have got mixed signals."

"What are you talking about?"

"See"—she whispered into the phone—"I just had a little s-e-x a while ago with Philip up in my room and he said to me that he wanted to rock my world. So I took it as the world was coming to the end. If it rocks, wouldn't that mean the world would break up then?" Mario was about to piss his pants from laughing so hard in his patrol car.

"Good night, Gloria," and he told her to go to bed and get a good night's sleep and that everything would be okay. "Give the phone back to LaVonda," who now was holding the bottle of wine and guzzling from the bottle instead of the glass. She had heard Gloria's part of the conversation and was dumbfounded.

"Here! He wants to talk to you again," Ms. Honeycutt said as she gave LaVonda back the phone with this crazy look in LaVonda's eyes like she wanted to say, "You crazy bitch!"

"Good night! I'm going to bed."

"Good night! Oh, by the way, make sure you change the sheets in your bed tomorrow. I'm not touching them!"

"I will!" Ms. Honeycutt said as she walked out of the room.

Mario was still trying to keep from wetting himself. "Can you believe that? She has been driving me crazy all night and it was because she thought the world was coming to an end. And it was because she got lucky tonight! For real! Mario replied, we need to talk about her when I see you next time."

"We will," Mario said. And he added that he had to hang up the phone, but not before he said, "Good night!"

"Good night to you too," LaVonda replied back as they both hung up at the same time. Mario had to hang up the phone because he had seen what looked like a dog running up by the side of his patrol car from the side mirror. He rolled down his window to stick his head out, and for sure it was a dog; it was Freeway.

"Hey, fellow." Freeway approached the patrol car. "What are you doing out on a night like tonight loose on the street?" Freeway jumped up on his hind legs with his front paws on the door, trying to get into the patrol car and out of the rain. "Oh hell. You're soaking wet." He kept jumping up and down on his hind legs, trying to get into the patrol car. "Hold on. Let me get you in here and into the backseat where you can dry off. I think I have a blanket on the floorboard that you can lie on." Mario then got out of his seat belt and helped to get Freeway into the patrol car, and once he was inside, he closed the window and opened the door and stepped out and closed the door so that the dog wouldn't escape. Once he was safe inside the patrol car, Mario stepped out of the patrol car and then opened the back door and looked for the blanket that was all folded up on the floorboard and not in the trunk where he had first looked. Now that he had the blanket, he climbed back into the front seat and tried to wrap it around the dog that was shaking water all over the front seat by now. Mario was not amused but was concerned for the well-being of this dog and did his best to get him a little dryer.

While he looked at him more and more as he was drying him off, he couldn't help but recognize him as maybe the dog from a few months ago that he had seen on the highway that was being taken out of a red BMW, and he had arrested the driver for animal cruelty and DUI. Could this be the same dog?

Mario was looking for a dog collar or a license tag and couldn't find one on Freeway. So now what was he supposed to do with him for the night? Freeway climbed down onto the floorboard of the passenger's side of the patrol car. Mario folded up the blanket the best he could from the sitting position and laid it out next to him on the front seat for Freeway to lie on, which he did immediately.

Mario had company for a while tonight, but he was going to have to find a place for him in the morning before he went back to the sheriff's office to turn in his patrol car and get his car. It was getting late, and it was dark and windy and drizzling, but not to the point that he couldn't drive; he was getting a bit hungry and was going to drive over to the hamburger stand just up the road on Commercial Blvd. and grab himself a couple of burgers and French fries he was craving for. Actually he wanted the French fries, and the burgers were for the dog. He had a soft spot for this dog and didn't know when the last time the dog ate something. "Hold on, boy. We're going for a little drive just up the road." Freeway looked over at him from the passenger seat as they drove off from under the overpass into the drizzling rain for burgers and fries.

Donald was at home and comfortably lying on his bed, watching the weather, when he couldn't help but have a gut feeling that Freeway was somewhere close; but it was just a gut feeling because he had those feelings before when he was doing community service at the shelter, and those never amounted to anything either. It was just a feeling he had, and he was going to place a call to Ms. Kitty and see how she was holding on tonight and that he was going to hopefully see her in the morning if the roads were passable. Ms. Kitty was snuggled up on her couch and reading a romance novel and was content as could be and very appreciative of Donald checking in; she said she was fine and told him to good night.

Donald, feeling better that he checked in on Ms. Kitty, decided to watch a bit more of the weather channel, But not before he dozed off completely to hear that hurricane Alden was going to make landfall in a few hours over New Orleans and that Florida was only going to get some winds and continuous rains till the late morning hours once it made landfall as a category two. "Thank God! We dodged another bullet," he said as he slowly closed his eyes and fell asleep.

Over at the Dixie Arms, a crazed Ms. Honeycutt was sound asleep in her bedroom with Philip, her new beau, who was snoring like a buzz saw just a few feet away as he lay next to her. LaVonda on the other hand passed out on the sofa downstairs in her office with an empty bottle of wine at her side on the floor. She was in a middle of a dream that had something to do with why she was let go from her job with the IRS and her deceased husband, Earl; it was a mixed-up dream that had her tossing and turning until she finally fell off the sofa and onto the floor and saying, "OH HELL NO!" She then got up from off the floor and headed to her own bedroom upstairs to hopefully pick up from where she had left off in that messed-up dream she had just been tragically awakened from.

Meanwhile, Mario was the only patron sitting in the parking lot of the burger joint, enjoying his French fries and Coke as well as the complimentary burgers from the burger joint that were in the process of closing down for the night when he drove through the drive-through. It was just about an hour ago from the time they drove through the window, and the girl working the window had noticed Freeway sitting beside Mario, who was just cute—if not cuter than the one sitting next to him. They were given free food as long as Mario agreed to sit outside in his patrol car until they locked the doors so they wouldn't be afraid of any nut jobs coming in, or worse, a robbery to take place. Mario agreed, and they all were winners this night. Now what was Mario going to do with this dog—after they ate and before he would have to turn the patrol car in? I know Let's go to my part-time job. It's a house, a big house, with lots of room and places to run around in and food to eat until I can figure out what to do with you till then. Hope you enjoyed that burger because now we are going for another

drive but a bit farther so just lie down and be a good boy and we'll be there
before you know it." Just before he could finish that sentence, Freeway
was already nodding off on the front seat on a full stomach from the two
burgers and few French fries he just ate. "Okay, boy, you just sleep and we'll
be there before you know it." As the lights in the burger joint went out,
so did Freeway; they were closed for the night. Both the night manager on
duty and the girl from the drive-through waved good night to Mario as
they walked to their cars in the parking lot; Mario was sitting in his patrol
car and just flashed his headlights on and off to let them know it was his
way of saying good night to them. As he followed them out of the parking
lot, Mario headed east towards I-95 and then was going to head south to
the downtown district area exit, which then would bring him closer to the
Dixie Arms. The burger joint employees headed west on Commercial Blvd,
while Freeway was already out like a light himself next to him in the front
seat, letting a bit of gas out of him from the burgers he just ate. It was so
bad that Mario had to roll down the windows for fresh air before he put
his own foot on the gas pedal. Once he was on the interstate, he had his
flashing red lights from the rooftop of the patrol car, alerting other drivers
that he had the right of way as he was approaching from behind, which
told them they needed to pull over to the side of the road.

However, tonight was an exceptional night. Broward County had no
one on the 95 Interstate whatsoever. It was going to be a safe drive down,
and within ten minutes he was already downtown and heading in the
direction of the Dixie Arms just minutes away through the drizzling rain
and flashing yellow downtown streetlights. As Mario pulled up in front of
the Dixie Arms, he couldn't help but notice the sign in the front yard that
he had put out there several days ago, which had a glow from the yard light
below, which read, "Dixie Arms, a Place for the Homeless. No One Will Be
Turned Away. All in Need of Shelter Is Welcome. Please Ring Bell by the
Front Door for Assistance."

"Well, boy, I guess we'll be okay to go on in," Mario said as Freeway
woke up from his nap and sat up and looked around and then looked over
at him as he undid his seat belt and shut off the patrol car. "Come on, boy,
I'll carry you in since you don't have a collar or a leash. I wouldn't want
you to run away from me all the way down here in the downtown area."
Freeway watched Mario get out from the front seat and waited for his call
to jump into his arms as Mario kicked his patrol car door closed with his
foot and carried Freeway up the path to the front porch and rang the bell
for assistance. He knew the drill many times since he has brought several

people here for shelter, but in this case it was a dog, and was LaVonda going to turn him away?

Once Mario reached the front door, he pushed the doorbell several times, and finally he had seen a shadow approaching from behind the beveled glass door. To his surprise, it was Ms. Honeycutt who was up and about early this morning, waiting to see if she would or would not have to report to work. Well, she was restless and couldn't wait to find out the outcome of the weather and decided to get up and get a glass of milk and pace the floors, only to find out from Mario that there was no hurricane warning being issued after she let him in and that she was going to have to get up and take the bus to work unless she could find another way in—she was dropping hints for a ride in the patrol car with him. "Oh! Goodness, what have we here?"

"Oh, this is a stray that I picked up on the interstate just north of here tonight. He really seems to be a well-behaved dog. I have had him with me most of the night and I got to spend some time with him and he was pretty good and very friendly. I have to bring my patrol car into the station in a couple of hours and I cannot show up with him. So I knew that LaVonda a few weeks ago mentioned to me that she was thinking of getting a dog so she wouldn't feel alone at night here in this big house at times. I thought since he needed a home until we can find his home and since my apartment does not allow pets I cannot take him home with me. So here I am. Do you know if LaVonda's up yet?"

"I couldn't say. I haven't seen her for several hours since I spoke to you on the phone. I guess she's up in her room asleep. You could go up and knock on her door. I don't think she'd mind. She pretty much has been a light sleeper these days with all the people that have been coming and going lately."

"Yeah, I know what that's like these days." Mario put Freeway down on the floor and said to him to sit, which he followed instructions at that moment and sat by his side on the floor. "Good boy," Mario spoke to him. "I'll just run upstairs and see if it will be okay to leave him here."

"You know the way there," Ms. Honeycutt said as she bent over to pat Freeway on the head.

"You stay right there. I'll be right back. Stay!" Mario commanded to Freeway as he moved away from him and headed up the staircase to LaVonda's bedroom. Freeway watched him climb the staircase without moving an inch. Until Mario hit the second floor and turned the corner and was out of sight from Freeway, he dashed up the staircase and went looking for him. Ms. Honeycutt had turned away for just a split second and looked away, and there was no dog in sight.

"What the hell! Oh shit, where did he go?" She started walking around the first floor of the Dixie, calling out, "Here, doggie! Here, doggie!" unaware to her and Mario that he was slowly creeping up behind him as he was about to enter LaVonda's bedroom with the door just about opened when he was knocked over by Freeway who knocked him down, entering LaVonda's bedroom, which happened to wake her up along with the help of Freeway who was at the time already in her bed and licking her face.

"Get down from there!" Mario called out.

"What's all the racket? And what the hell is this dog doing in my bed and in my face ?"

"This is a dog that I found on the interstate." And as he went into the story on how he found him, Freeway was already lying next to LaVonda with his head on her guest pillow, just looking up at her and Mario who was standing by her bedside, talking to her.

"Okay, it will be fine with me," LaVonda told Mario. "This is only temporary until we can find it another home." Mario agreed with until they found him a home. LaVonda looked over at Freeway and patted his coat and looked into his eyes and had this strange feeling about this dog. This dog was really friendly with which she told Mario that usually all the dogs she came in contact with growled and tried to bite her. She was not comfortable with dogs at all. But this one was different.

Just after that comment was made, entered Ms. Honeycutt calling out, "Here, doggie."

Freeway sat up and looked over at her and barked, as if he was saying, "Here I am" to her. With that, since LaVonda was already up, she offered Mario a cup of coffee before he headed back out into the wet night and said, "Besides, we can talk about you know who!" Ms. Honeycutt then said to them that she was going back to bed for another hour or so before she had to get up ready for work and asked LaVonda to please wake her up if she oversleeps.

"Damn! I was hoping I had a day off and with pay too."

"Sorry!" LaVonda told her.

"YEAH! YEAH! YEAH!" Ms. Honeycutt said as she left the bedroom and headed to her bedroom down the hall where Philip was still snoring away like a buzz saw.

"So what flavored coffee suits you this time of morning?" LaVonda asked Mario. She glanced over at her alarm clock that was on her nightstand, which was flashing four thirty in the morning, and said that she was going to have a long day ahead of her and that at least one of them, Mario, was going to be able to get some decent sleep in a just few hours when he gets off duty, just before he had to come back to the Dixie Arms to work his part-time job for her; and he now had another job as well, which was to watch this dog!

"Come on, let's get some coffee," LaVonda said to Mario.

He replied back with, "Hazelnut sounds good this morning."

"It sure does, doesn't it?" And they both called out to the dog at the same time to get him down from off the bed, who was going to join them for a bowl of water as they drank their coffee and discussed Ms. Honeycutt and what they were going to do with her and how they needed to find her a place of her own, before Mario had to leave and head back to the station to get off duty and head home to bed for some well-needed sleep.

CHAPTER SEVENTEEN

The alarm clock was beeping continuously before Donald realized it was going off from a hard night's sleep. He glanced over and saw it flashing 7:00 AM in bright red numbers on the nightstand he than rolled over to shut off the buzzer. He was not ready to get up this morning since he had very little sleep last night because of the weather that was over South Florida last night due to hurricane Alden. But like the rest of the working world, it was just part of life, and he had to face another day as an owner of a new business for it wasn't going to run itself without him checking in on a daily basis or showing up like everyone else who had to go to work whether they liked it or not. In his case, he was wealthy enough not have to work, but he chose to because he wanted to make a difference in those that could not fend for themselves and needed a good home and love and companionship and for those who adopted them wanted the same in their lives. So he jumped out of bed and headed to the kitchen for a glass of apple juice and to make a pot of coffee as he tried to wake up before having to get ready for work. He glanced outside through his patio doors and saw that the rain was just sprinkles and that the winds were no longer blowing as hard as last night.

He turned and walked over to his television and turned it on to see what the local weather channel was reporting on the weather. And to Donald's eyes, it seems that most of the local news stations were reporting the same information that the weather was dissipating over South Florida as other channels were reporting that the Gulf Coast has sustained some rough weather last night.

Reports of flooding in several communities were being reported in to local news stations as far as the Texas coast, all the way over to the panhandle of Florida and with minimum damage as of this time of morning. It was now six o'clock in the morning on the Gulf Coast States, and as soon as they could, they would send in more local news reporters and crews to survey the damage, if any, with which they would keep the public updated as it came in.

Now that Donald had watched the weather updates, he was ready for his first cup of coffee of the day before he jumped into the shower. He said to himself, "I think I'll head to the shelter a bit earlier today to drop off the new van and wait for Ms. Kitty to show up and to take me down to pick up my BMW that I left at the dealership overnight," hoping that it was all right and had no damage done to it. On top of that, he was anxious to see the dogs that came in from Texas and New Orleans to see how they survived the night in their new surroundings. Just as he was about to jump into the shower, his phone rang, it was Ms. Kitty who also was up at the crack of dawn and was wondering what the weather was like over on his side of town and if he survived okay in his townhome. Donald said to her that he survived it just fine as well as his town house and that he was just about to jump into the shower and that he was going to head in to the shelter within an hour.

"That's great. I was just thinking the same thing. I want to check on the dogs that were brought in yesterday and want to make sure they were okay."

"It sounds like we'll be there about the same time then." And Donald reminded her that he was going to need a lift to the dealership later to get his car. She said she had not forgotten and that she'd see him shortly as he said good-bye, then hung up the phone, and headed to the shower, but not before he finally had his first sip of coffee of the day.

The rest of South Florida was waking up to the same news that they had dodged another bullet this year with hurricanes, and there were signs of relief; some prepared to go into work, and others stayed home. School was going to be open, so traffic was going to be back to normal for those who had to commute to work. All businesses and government offices will be open today, so it seems like just another drizzly day in South Florida with yet signs of sunshine later in the morning, breaking as the feeder bands from hurricane Alden disappear overhead in the skies above.

Donald arrived at the shelter within the hour like he told Ms. Kitty who was ten minutes ahead of him and was already walking around the shelter and kennel areas to make sure that everything was fine and that no damage was done to the shelter.

When she was about to enter the kennel area, she heard Donald call her name out and said, "Good morning!"

She turned around and replied back, "Good morning to you too."

"So how'd we survive last night?" Donald asked.

"So far so good. I'm heading out to the kennel area now to check on the dogs. You care to join me?" she asked him.

"Yeah Just give me a couple of minutes. I want to run to my office and check a few appointments I have today and call the dealership to see if they are open so you can run me down there to pick up my car."

"Okay, I'll follow you then and this way I can finish turning the lights on for the rest of the area in the shelter and I'll stop by your office on the way back to see if you're ready to come meet our guests then."

"Sounds good to me," Donald told her. "I'll see you shortly then." He went to his office, and she went around, turning on the remainder of the shelter's lights. Donald checked his appointment book on his desk and had one appointment set up for eleven o'clock with a veterinarian who was new in the area and looking for work and two later in the day—a driver for the van as well as an animal control officer to help rescue the dogs loose on the streets and to shuttle dogs back and forth from the south shelter from time to time. And his last appointment of the day was with someone that was representing a local shelter who was trying to find jobs for the homeless that were released from their care and was ready to go back out into society and work and make a difference in their lives as well as others. Just as he was looking over his appointment book, his cell phone rang; it was the dealership for the van, who told him that his request for a special license plate for the van could be done and that it'd take about ten days before he could pick it up.

"That's great. I look forward to hearing from you once it comes in. Just give me a call me and I'll come pick it up then. Oh, by the way, is the dealership now open?" Donald asked.

"Yes! We always open at six o'clock for the service center for those needing to bring in their vehicles for maintenance.

"Great, I'll be down shortly and pick up my car that I left there yesterday while purchasing the van."

"No problem, it's here in front of the building. I remember it very well. I can see it from my office window. It is a red BMW, right?"

"Yes," Donald replied back.

"It's fine," the salesman said. "Nothing happened to it during the storm last night."

"I'm glad to hear that."

"I'll see you soon then."

"See you soon and again thank you for calling me on the license plate request."

"You're very welcome," the salesman said as he hung up the phone with Donald.

Knock! Knock! "Come in!"

"You ready for the walk through the kennel with me to meet our guests?" Ms. Kitty asked.

"Oh! We're going to have to do that when we get back."

"Back, back from where?" Ms. Kitty asked.

"The dealership just called me about the license plate for the van that I specially ordered for the shelter that's going to say '4 MY FRWY.' It's short for 'For My Freeway' in honor of the dog that I built this shelter for."

"That's a nice thing to do," Ms. Kitty replied. "Well, let me just lock up but I'm going to leave the lights all on since we're going to be gone only a short while. No need to shut everything down."

"Yeah, that will be fine," Donald told her as they walked toward the entrance of the building and headed out.

"So where is this dealership at?"

"It's just up the interstate on Sunrise. So we'll jump on the interstate right outside of here and hang a left at the stop sign and head south and we'll be there in about eight minutes. That's if there's no traffic backing up."

"Wow! That really is close," Ms. Kitty said.

"That's why I picked out the land that the shelter was built on. It is convenient to everything." So with small talk about last night's weather and the van purchase, they were just moments away from the dealership where Donald could see his red BMW from Sunrise Blvd. just ahead as if it was just calling out to him to take it home. He loved that car; it was his pride and joy from the day he purchased it with his savings from his job. He took good care of it, and it ran nice with no problems whatsoever.

Ms. Kitty asked, "Would you like me to wait for you?"

"No! It's fine. I'm Just going to jump in and head back to the shelter."

"Okay then," she said to him. "Oh, I'm going to make a stop at the supermarket on the way back to the shelter if that's okay with you, Donald."

"No problem. You need any money?"

"No, I got the company card. I'm going to pick up some donuts and Danish for the staff and supplies for the break room and coffee creamer and sugar as well as a few other things we need to put in the refrigerator for the staff."

"Okay! Not a problem, take your time," Donald told her.

I'm going directly back to the shelter and I'll check in on the dogs in the kennel area that we're boarding while you're running to the market."

"Sounds good to me!" she replied.

"Then I will see you shortly," he replied as she drove off in her car, and he jumped into his car as they both left the dealership's parking lot.

On the other side of town over at the Dixie Arms, LaVonda was enjoying her new boarder, Freeway, which she still had no clue as to his name and who was just following her from room to room and wouldn't leave her side. When she stopped, he stopped. He was not letting her out of his sight. She played fetch and gave him chicken tenders as a treat. The both of them then headed out on the veranda where LaVonda drank her third cup of hazelnut coffee of the morning as Freeway lay down by her feet and looked out onto the pathway from the veranda to the sidewalk and wondering if Mario was coming back to see him, whom was sound asleep in his very own bed from a long night of baby-sitting him.

LaVonda, enjoying her coffee, was enjoying the very little breeze that there was from the storm last night. Mario had left him a few hours ago to head to the sheriff's office to clock off duty and to head home to grab a few hours' sleep before he came back to the shelter to his part-time job. Freeway just looked up at her from where he was lying at her feet, but not before LaVonda told him, "Mario will be back a little later if that is who you are looking for to walk up that path." Then he resumed his position, with his head lying between his front paws, staring out off the veranda.

A few seconds later, the front door of the shelter opened up, and there was Ms. Honeycutt in all her glory with Philip by her side as he was walking her to the bus stop that was just out in front of the shelter. She was not thrilled about having to go to work because the answering service that she was instructed to call to see if she had to report to work stated when she called that all employees were to report to work today as scheduled. That's all she had to hear as she was rushing around to get dressed quickly to meet the bus out in front of the shelter to make it to work on time if she caught her transfer buses on time to get her to Weston.

She could not complain; she needed the money because she was making car payments, unbeknown to LaVonda, with part of her paychecks for some time. She had put down several payments on a yellow 1970 Volkswagen convertible that was in mint condition with a new engine that one of her coworkers had inherited from a relative that passed away and has been sitting in his garage for a long time and needed to get rid of it. Therefore, he made her a sweet deal, and she took it.

She just had to pay him one hundred dollars a week from her paycheck; he gave her a receipt each time, and when she had paid him six hundred dollars, it was hers. She was only a couple of payments away from owning an automobile and a few screws loose if she thought she could drive a stick shift in Florida traffic.

She had no choice but to go to work today as she had another surprise for LaVonda at the same time when she told her about her car. She and Philip, who was in the final stage of him getting a job that has been in the works for several weeks, were going to get a place of their own together once he got himself established with that job. He had been offered a job at a new locally owned barbershop downtown that was opening up very soon.

He just needed to pass a few test required by the state, and that's where he was heading this morning after he walked her to the bus stop. It was going to be a great day for LaVonda when Ms. Honeycutt broke that news to her. So all around, a night of wicked weather turned out to be a great night for everyone, including Freeway.

As Ms. Honeycutt came out onto the veranda, heading to catch her bus, she stopped a moment to say, "Good morning, LaVonda," and made a comment to her as she saw Freeway lying at her feet. "I see you're picking up strays these days."

Freeway who was lying at her feet lifted up his head from in between his paws and looked up at her and let out four loud barks at Ms. Honeycutt. Did she startle him with her choice of outfit she was wearing today? Or was he just talking back to her by saying, "Hey, I'm not a stray!"

LaVonda chuckled and said, "Have a nice day, Gloria," as she stepped down of the veranda with the back of her gold skirt tucked into her panty hose and a mini purple waist jacket that looked like it was beaded by a first-time Bedazzler. She was wearing a hat that looked like one of Carmen Miranda's hats that had little fruits dangling along the edge of the entire hat. No way in hell was LaVonda going to tell her that she was showing some booty!

LaVonda was going to keep her mouth shut and was going to let her get on the bus looking like that, hoping that she wouldn't notice it or that someone would and bring it to her attention. It was the start of a great day as she sipped her coffee with a big grin on her face as the bus pulled away, and Philip crossed the street to go wherever he was going after spending the night at the Dixie Arms.

CHAPTER EIGHTEEN

The local news channels throughout the Gulf Coast were now updating the residents in the surrounding communities that the back end of hurricane Alden was now over them and it was starting to dissipate as it was leaving the area and to expect feeder bands and some rains for the next few hours as it exited out to the north.

Derek, the truck driver from New Orleans who was the owner of Freeway as well as Sheba's, was listening to the news from his radio in the cab of his tractor trailer that he had parked in a rest area just one hundred and fifty miles outside of Louisiana for the night. He wasn't alone; there must have been at least a dozen other truckers who refused to drive any farther due to the heavy rains and winds and who pulled over at the first rest area they had come to. It was not wise to drive any farther, and they, one by one, started to pull over and stop and pray that they would survive the night in their cabs with Alden blowing winds in their direction.

Derek was thrilled to hear the news over his radio and made a quick decision to turn around and head back to New Orleans in the little bit of rain that he was enduring outside his cab and get back home and to his beloved dogs that he had sheltered, only to find out once he returned back to New Orleans that his two dogs were evacuated to Florida because the shelter he had placed them in was overcrowded. They had made a decision without his consent and had relocated them. There was an overwhelming number of people bringing in their pets and other canines as they, too, had to seek shelter of their own since they were not comfortable with this storm or the residence they were in since a lot of the homes were very old and not hurricane proof. Derek also found out first that his own home had sustained major damage because of the winds and rains. The roof was three-quarters torn off from the house, and the rains that had poured into the house destroyed all of his belongings.

"My home!" he screamed out as he drove up the road and saw all the destruction in the neighborhood and drove up to his house. With tears in his eyes and heartache in his chest, he was just glad that he left and did not stay behind. Sadness was not the only emotion he was feeling—anger as well, soon to be followed with frustration as he had to make a choice whether to rebuild or not to rebuild his home.

Derek climbed out of his cab and headed into the destruction in front of him and started picking up anything in sight that was salvageable and threw it into the back of his cab and finally threw his arms up and said, "The hell with it," followed with shaking his head back and forth and saying, "I'm not going to rebuild it. I'm going to get Freeway and Sheba and move to Dallas"—to be closer to his sister and where he would feel more safe than living on the Gulf Coast. He would contact his insurance company as soon as possible, knowing it would take several weeks or more before he hears or sees any money from them.

It was a devastating day for him; at least he was alive and had his truck, which he depended on to make money with. His dogs were going to be returned in a few days; at least that's what he was told, as he went to pick them up, by one of the staff from the shelter. He said he'd be in touch with them to see when they would be on their way back from Florida. Otherwise, he would be contacting an attorney for this mistake they had made if he does not get them back. Being upset as he left the shelter, heading back to his cab, he grabbed his chest in the parking lot and collapsed.

Derek was found several minutes later by a person who was also leaving the shelter with their pet and noticed this man lying in the parking lot clutching his chest. By the time the paramedics arrived, it was too late; Derek had died in the parking lot of the shelter, only to be taken away to the morgue where the next of kin would be notified of his passing.

Donald was now back at the shelter while Ms. Kitty was at the market buying food and supplies, and he decided to check on the dogs in the kennel, who were his guests from Texas and Louisiana.

One by one, Donald personally met each and every one of them; he gave them fresh food and water, starting with the first kennel to the last kennel. However, Donald decided not to lock the cage door entirely. Donald recalled his fear of being locked behind bars for his DUI, and it was scary as hell.

Once he stepped out of their kennels from feeding them fresh food and water, he stepped out of the cage and left the doors ajar.

After looking into each and every one of the dogs' eyes while meeting each one of them, he knew he could trust them and told them that they would be safe and taken care of and that it was only temporary. He trusted them not to escape from their cages. And even if they did escape, they wouldn't get too far because they would have to go through the main entrance of the shelter, the only way in and the only way out.

As Donald got down to the last kennel where Freeway and Sheba had been kenneled, he saw Sheba just lying there on the concrete, not barking like the rest of them for food or attention. He went into her kennel and introduced himself and left food and water in which she had no interest in at all—didn't faze her a bit. He said to her that it was okay. "You'll eat when you are hungry. I know you are still upset because you miss your owner but you'll see them soon."

Donald did not know that she was sad because Freeway, her buddy and companion, had escaped during the night while the wicked weather was blowing through. She was staying inside where she felt safe. Donald just missed having Freeway back in his life by several hours; they could have been reunited once again.

Donald walked back to the main building and into the break room where he saw Ms. Kitty who was unpacking supplies from her trip to the market and was putting away the supplies. He mentioned to her as he walked over to the sink to wash his hands from feeding and petting the dogs from out of town that they were all fed and taken care of and how friendly they were to him and how they varied from size to breed; it was interesting because he wondered if it was true like the saying went, "Man's best friend always looked like their master." He was imagining what some of the owners looked liked from meeting the dogs he just met as he mentioned it to Ms. Kitty as he was heading back to his office.

As the day progressed, Donald had met with several of his appointments and hired on a new veterinarian to come on board at the shelter as well as a new driver for the van that he had just purchased waiting to be broken in. Ms. Kitty also had a fulfilling day with training more of the staff on the process of adoptions as well as pricing and putting away new merchandise for the gift shop. Then there were a few new canines that were brought into the shelter to be adopted out because their owners were relocating out of state, or they were not able to take care of them anymore due to an illness that had overcome them financially, so they had to give up their dog.

More and more senior citizens had to give up their best friends or companions that kept them active and kept them company because they were lonely at one time and wanted a little companionship. What better than a canine! So the years had gone by, waiting for that monthly social security check to arrive once a month, which would no longer go far. They then realized they could no longer afford the food and upkeep of having them because the money was now going toward health care and medicine that Medicare would not cover and had to come from their own pockets.

That was hard for her, having to see an elderly person who had so much love for their best friend having to break that bond and be separated because they could no longer have time for them with constant medical care around the corner that some would endure down the road. Then were the trips to see their physicians and leaving them home alone for hours at a time, and sometimes days at a time if hospitalized.

They walked out of the shelter in tears, hoping the shelter would find them another good home. That was the only bitch of the job she did not like. She would have to reassure those owners as they brought their pets in that they would be going to a new home and to always remember, "You did your best for as long as you could and that they, too, knew that you loved them very much and had no choice but to give them up." It was time for them to find a new home that could give them as much love as they had brought them, the owners, along with the joy and memories of the times spent together, to their lives as they did with theirs.

While saying this, she was reminding them that they will always hold a special place in the owners' hearts, never to be forgotten, as they say good-bye. "And thank them for making your life a little more complete as you did for them from the very start for having taken care of them for as long as you possibly could and that they will be okay,"

As for the shelter, only being open a few days, it was already getting a good response from the public with people coming in looking to adopt while others came to see the vets for checkups and shots. Others took advantage of the grooming and baths specials, and then there were those seeking to use the boarding facilities, as they get ready to travel or go on vacations. It looked like the shelter was a big hit after all in the northern part of Broward County, with Donald on the phone with vendors and placing orders for supplies that they'll need around the shelter as well as the office supplies for copy paper, toners, and pens, just to name a few things. His final call of the day was to the Weston supplier where he bought things for the grand opening day on a quick moment. He had browsed through the catalog that he was given from that crazy woman named Ms. Honeycutt, and he grinned because he knew he would no doubt be speaking to her again in the near future or at least run into her again once he got there to pick up his order in the will-call area. He looked for the credit application he had filled out and faxed in several days later and was going to see if his account was open now to go ahead and charge the goods and pay the bill at the end of the month. Donald dialed the number, and after a few rings, a pleasant voice had answered the phone, answering, "Good afternoon, Everything Canine Inc. Ms. Honeycutt speaking. How may I help you?"

"Good afternoon, Ms. Honeycutt. Don't know if you remember me but I was in there a few days ago and placed an order and waited for it and you had given me a catalog for future orders as well as an application to open an account." The voice sounds familiar. "My name is Donald."

"Oh sure, you are, the cute gentleman that was opening up the shelter down on Commercial Blvd. and I-75."

"Yes! That's me. I would like to see if my account was approved and place another order if possible."

"Just one moment," she replied as she put her hand over the mouthpiece and yelled over to Theresa, one of the temps in the office that was only working there part-time while she went to school in the mornings.

"It's that CHILD PLEASE I told you about. He's on the phone and would like to place an order and see if his account has been opened yet."

"Oh my God !" Theresa yelled back. "Can he hear you?"

"No, I've covered the mouthpiece of the phone. I don't think so!"

"Put him on hold and I'll pick up your extension and take the call."

"Okay!" Ms. Honeycutt replied, not knowing that Donald could hear the entire conversation while waiting for her to come back to the phone and was turning beet red. He could hear everything and was grinning from cheek to cheek. Ms. Honeycutt came back to him and said, "Donald, I'm going to transfer you to Theresa and she will be glad to assist you."

"Thank you!" Donald replied back.

"You're more than welcome."

"Have a nice evening," Donald told her.

And she said, "The same to you," as she put him on hold, and Theresa was ready to take his call.

"Hello! This is Theresa. How may I help you?"

"Hello, Theresa," he said as he introduced himself to her and told her where he was calling from and gave her all the information she needed to pull up his account and see if it was open.

"Oh yes, sir, it is open and you can use your account today to place an order," she said as she noticed he had a high credit limit and could go ahead and shop till his heart was content. As she was getting ready to place the order, she asked if it was going to be delivered or picked up. He said he would pick it up later this evening if that was possible, around six o'clock. Theresa said that that wouldn't be a problem. He was obliged and thanked her. "So what can I get for you today?" she asked.

"Let start with this," he said as he thumbed through the catalog where he had placed colored Post-it notes on the page in the catalog with the item number of each item he was ordering. Theresa gave him an invoice number for his pickup and told him where to go and pick it up, and he said that he had been there once before and was helped with the assistance of Ms. Honeycutt, who was very interesting!

"Oh, you know her then?" Theresa asked.

"Not really. It was my first time doing business with your company. She was a very colorful person when I first met her," Donald said.

"Oh! That she is!" Theresa told him. "I could tell you stories but that would not be nice of me to talk about a coworker that way, at least not till I get to know you better." Donald chuckled back. "Just let me say she is a wonderful woman with a heart of gold, but the woman has some issues as I gather you saw when you first met her."

"Oh yes, I saw! She was a train wreck with me. I almost pissed my pants from laughing so hard."

"Then you know!"

"Well, it was a pleasure speaking with you and hopefully one day we can meet in person."

"That would be nice," Theresa told him as they said good-bye to each other.

Ms. Honeycutt looked up and noticed that Theresa was off the phone with him and said, "Well?"

"Well, what?"

"Did you find him interesting?" Ms. Honeycutt asked her.

"Yes! He was very pleasant to talk to."

"That is all you can say?" Ms. Honeycutt asked her.

"Yes!"

"Well, you're a damn fool if that's all you can say."

"He has a sexy voice," she added as she grinned, trying to avoid a long-drawn-out conversation with Ms. Honeycutt about him.

"Girl, you should stick around and wait for him to come and pick up his order and his call and then just go out there like you're looking for a package and check out his!"

"Oh, you are a mess!" Theresa busted into laughter. I can't believe you said that," Theresa said to her.

"I may be old but I'm not dead yet, honey," was Ms. Honeycutt's reply back to her. "As long as I can work and dress myself," she added as Theresa was still laughing, because in her mind this woman must shop at the Crazy Are We Boutique and Accessories and should not be bragging about her dressing herself with some of the outfits she has seen on her. But that's cool because she makes this part-time job more interesting each day, not knowing what she will see next and getting paid for it at the same time.

"No! I cannot wait until then because I have a test first thing in the morning and need to get out of here on time so I can head home and study all night."

"Suit yourself," Ms. Honeycutt said as she walked by her cubicle. And she told her, "You don't know what you're missing!" She was on the way to the ladies' room to fix herself up, hoping to run into Donald again, as Theresa couldn't help but laugh once more.

Meanwhile Donald was finishing up some last-minute things in his office as Ms. Kitty popped her head into his office and asked if he would like to join her for a drink and a bite to eat after work, and he said he would love to but had to take a rain check because he was going to take the van and head up to Weston and pick up the supplies and leave them in the van at his home tonight and bring them in the morning when he comes in to work. But if she liked, he would let her take his BMW home with her and baby-sit it as long as she was careful.

"Sure, I'd be glad to drive that home. Beats the clunker I have."

"Well then, just lock up your car after you close up tonight, and park it by the entranceway and take my car keys," Donald said as he took them off his key ring and gave them to her.

"Thanks!" she said.

"No! Thank you!" Donald told her.

His red BMW was his pride and joy, and though he had so much money he could buy anything he wanted, he loved that car. And entrusting it in Ms. Kitty's care for the evening was better than leaving it out in the parking lot all night, and God knows if someone was going to steal a car tonight in Broward County, it was not going to be his.

CHAPTER NINETEEN

On the other side of town over at the Dixie Arms, a very relaxed and calm LaVonda was enjoying the peace and quiet of the house for a change. She couldn't recall the last time it was like that since she opened up the shelter. It was nice for a change, and she was going to take advantage of it the best way she could, and that was to let Mario start taking over some of her duties in the office and spend more time with the new houseguest, Freeway, which she still did not know that was his name.

They played in the backyard and she took him for a drive along the beachfront in her car with his head hanging out the window, taking in the salt air from the ocean breezes.

They stopped for soft ice cream on Las Olas Blvd., as they sat on a park bench and watched the tourists just walk by them as they were enjoying their ice cream—she had a soft swirled chocolate ice cream cone, and Freeway was enjoying his very own cup of soft swirled vanilla ice cream that she held in the other hand.

It was as if they had known each other for years and not as complete strangers since they have only known each other for one day. Just as she was finishing up her ice cream cone, her cell phone rang, and it was Mario who was wondering when she was going to be heading back to the shelter.

"Oh," she said, "I'm just around the corner on Las Olas and we'll be back there shortly. Is everything okay?"

"Oh yeah, it's just that I have to get ready to go into work at the sheriff's office, you know, my main job."

"Oh Hell! I completely forgot about the time. I have had such a great day and spending it with this dog you brought over last night."

"Glad to see you bonded so well."

"I'm on my way. I'm so sorry!" she told Mario as she hung up her phone and looked over at Freeway and said there's no more ice cream as he kept sniffing the cup. And she said, "Come on, fellow we have to go home so Mario can go to his other job right now!"

Freeway jumped off the bench and looked up at her as if to say, "I'm ready, let's go then!" She could not believe how well mannered and behaved this dog was as they headed back to her car that was parked up the street on the side of the road.

The Dixie Arms was just a hop and skip and a block or two away from the ice cream stand. Mario, who was standing on the veranda, waiting for her as she drove up, had just a minute to tell her what he had done today and that he would call her later and hated to run but he had to get ready and get to work for highway patrol duty tonight. She apologized and said that she would make it up to him somehow for making him late if he doesn't get to work on time tonight.

"It's a deal. I will collect it from you later," he said as she laughed and sent him on his way.

"We'll talk later," she said as he dashed down the path to the street to get into his car that was parked out front, but not before he heard several barks from Freeway who was sitting next to LaVonda, barking at him as he walked away from them.

Mario glanced back at the both of them on the veranda as he was getting ready to jump into his car and noticed that Freeway was sitting next to LaVonda and was raising his right paw up in front of him as dogs normally do when you train them to shake your hand. It was as if he was waving good-bye to him. It struck him odd, but he had no time to figure that out as he yelled back and said, "I'll see you later, fellow," as he jumped into his car and drove away.

"Bye!" LaVonda yelled out as she, too, was waving good-bye to Mario and then turned and looked down at Freeway who was still shaking his paw out to her and seemed like he was waving good-bye. "What are you doing, fellow?" she asked as she looked at him. "Are you saying good-bye to Mario?"

He let out a loud bark like, "Yeah!"

"Come on, let's go in and see what's on the television tonight and we can eat popcorn while we watch the television," she said as they both entered the front door to go inside. LaVonda said to the dog, "Let's go to my office first and see what Mario had accomplished today and check my voice messages on the answering machine."

As they approached the office, Freeway jumped up into her chair and looked at the computer screen, only to see his reflection on the glass. He tilted his head from side to side, just looking into this dark screen with his reflection from the glass looking back at him, and started barking. "What's the matter, boy?" LaVonda asked him. He looked at her and looked back at the computer screen. "It's okay. It's just a computer screen. Nothing to worry about," she said as she listened to her messages.

There were only two calls for her, and one was from her son in North Carolina that said, "Just checking in to make sure you're okay, Ma. I see you're not in so I'll try back later. Not an emergency just wanted to say hello." And the other was for Ms. Honeycutt. It was Philip leaving her a voice message on the Dixie Arms' answering machine.

"Hey, darlin'," it started out. And it said, "I got good news. We can celebrate tonight. Call me at this number and let me know what time you can be ready for me to come over. Philip."

"Oh hell no! This will ruin my night along with yours," LaVonda said as she looked at Freeway. "I'm not going to deal with both of them tonight. Last night was enough. Not doing it two nights in a row." She hit the delete button on the answering machine as if she never had gotten the message. "That's just between you and me, okay?" she said as she looked at Freeway. And she added, "She'll never know. Let's go get something to drink in the kitchen and see what's on the tube tonight, okay?" Just then Freeway jumped down from the chair and started to follow LaVonda to the kitchen and stopped for a moment and looked back at the computer sitting on the top of her desk and then turned and walked away.

Now back at the Everything Canine Inc. in Weston, Ms. Honeycutt was hanging around the time clock, waiting for it to hit five o'clock so she could clock out and begin her journey back to the shelter in the wicked traffic that was starting to pile up on the interstates of Broward County. It was just another day for her in the working world, and she was wondering why she had not heard from Philip today on his test to go to work at the Barbara Shop downtown.

"It's odd. I know I gave him the phone number to my office to call me this morning while I was rushing around trying to get out of the shelter on time to meet my bus. Or maybe I didn't. I'll just wait and see if he shows up tonight at the shelter. That's what I'll do, just sit up in my room and wait and see if he comes over."

As she was leaving the front of the building and crossing the street to meet her bus, she glanced and noticed the van that was pulling into the parking lot with temporary signs that read "The Freeway Shelter for Canines and Other Pets" along with the address and phone number. "Oh hell, if I only hung around a bit longer at the time clock I would have seen CHILD PLEASE! Who was picking up his order in the back of the building. Till next time, you handsome devil," just as her bus ride pulled up in front of her, and the doors automatically opened up as she climbed the three steps to reach the landing and pulled out her bus pass from her handbag to show the driver.

"Good evening, ma'am."

"Good evening, sir," Ms. Honeycutt replied as he stamped her bus pass and waited for her to take a seat before he could pull away from the curb as she stumbled her way to find a seat toward the middle of the bus for her long journey back to the shelter.

The sun was sinking in the west, and the shelter was getting ready to close when Ms. Kitty instructed three of her staff workers—one was to feed the boarded dogs and the other was to feed the dogs up for adoption and the last one was to feed the dogs from Texas and Louisiana and to report back to her as soon as they were through so they could lock up for the night. The first two staffers reported back to her within half an hour, and the last one came back an hour later. That's because he had more to feed as he took his time because he was too busy listening to his brand-new iPod and not paying attention. He, like Donald, just opened the door, placed the food and water, and closed the cage door but did not lock it completely, just kept it ajar like he found it. It was now eight o'clock in the evening, and it was a long day for Ms. Kitty as she went to move her car to the front entranceway and take Donald's car home for the evening; she noticed a helicopter with searchlights flying around in circles over the everglades just west of the shelter on the other side of the access road near the shelter. It was pretty clear something was happing close to the shelter. Was it someone lost out there? Could they have been looking for a robber hiding out there? Whatever it was, she knew she'd see it in the news later tonight because several news channels were parked along the access road with the high towers that record everything and report it back to the station for editing and then release it to the public. She was exhausted and just wanted to head home and grab a bite to eat, but not before cruising down Commercial Blvd., looking for some fast food to take home because she was in no mood to cook.

Mario was now on duty at the sheriff's office and was heading out on highway patrol at his usual location and decided to call LaVonda to see how the dog was doing with her and to report on what he had done for her today while she was out enjoying a day off. All was well at the shelter. Ms. Honeycutt was just coming in from work, complaining of her day and in the kitchen making soup and grilled cheese sandwiches. LaVonda was not going to deal with another night of her craziness. I'm heading up to my room to watch a movie and the dog is just sleeping on the floor next to my feet. "I must have worn him out with all the fresh air and walking today."

He said, "You must have if he's already a sleep. He was up with me all last night in the police cruiser. It was a long day for him too. Well, if you need me for anything just call my cell phone. I'm out west at my usual patrolling area. Have a nice night, enjoy your movie, and if I don't hear from you later tonight, I'll see you in the morning then."

"You too, please be careful on the roads tonight and I'll see you in the morning." They said good night to each other and hung up the phones. "Come on, boy," she called out to Freeway to wake him up to head upstairs to watch a movie. Freeway opened his eyes the minute he heard her voice and got up and followed her to the staircase, and up he went already on the first landing, watching LaVonda climb the stairs to meet him at the top.

Donald was home, paying a few bills that were due like his cable, electric and water bill, phone bill, and charge cards and finishing his laundry and was ready for bed as well. It was a busy day for him too, but he enjoyed it; it was worth every minute of the day, doing what he truly enjoyed.

Tacos and burritos were the choice of meals tonight for Ms. Kitty who was eating very late, watching a television reality show just as the commercial break had a sneak peek on the news that would be coming up at ten o'clock. "Watch how local environmentalists are going to continue to fight with the power company over an old building structure in the everglades that was causing the waters in the everglades to be contaminated." She said to herself, "Maybe that's why the helicopter with the floodlights and news crews were close to the shelter earlier tonight." Hoping to make it till then to catch the local news was not going to be easy. She could hardly keep her eyes open much longer. On a full stomach, her eyes started to close, and before she knew it, she was out like a light. She was now spending the night on the sofa instead of her bed.

Donald's cell phone rang; it was about ten thirty in the evening when he said, "Who'd be calling me at ten thirty at night?" It was not a number that he recognized. It was Steve, the van driver from New Orleans, calling him with bad news that the shelter in New Orleans had sustained lots of damage and that some of the dogs, survived the hurricane, and others ran away. "Oh No! What can I do to help?" Donald asked. He had the means of helping out and offered to send assistance to them if they needed it.

"Seems like we are going to have to start from scratch and rebuild.

"Let me help," Donald told him. "I'll talk to my assistant and make arrangements to fly her out to you and I'll call my vendors and order supplies to help get you on your feet and in the meantime have someone start looking for a new building and keep me posted on a daily basis of the progress."

"Great!"

"I'll call you tomorrow after I talk to Ms. Kitty and let you know what we're doing."

"That would be great!"

"So in the meantime don't worry about the dogs here. We'll take care of them as long as needed and if the owners come looking for them, have them call my office and we'll make arrangements to get them back even if I have to fly them home one by one if need be so that they can be with their owners."

Steve said, "We'll talk tomorrow and keep you posted."

"Thank you for calling and again I'm here if you need anything else," Donald told Steve.

"Thanks," Steve replied as they hung up. It was going to get busier in Donald's life, helping out with their disaster and running his own shelter. The adrenaline was flowing. Now Donald couldn't sleep; he was making a list of plans to get the ball rolling first thing in the morning after he broke the news to Ms. Kitty that she was going on a trip for several weeks, and he needed to find her replacement while she was gone, or would he be able to handle running the shelter, or should he get assistance or go himself? This was something he was going to have to ponder for the remainder of the evening.

CHAPTER TWENTY

As the night fell, you could hear the crickets and the bullfrogs among many places in Broward County, but more so in the undeveloped areas out west of the turnpike as you drove west toward I-75. They became noticeable even for Sheba, Freeway's buddy and companion, as she ventured outside of her kennel to the outside and found out that Freeway was no longer on the other side of the wall that she thought he was on because she did not like the sounds of the automobiles exiting to get onto Commercial Blvd.

She was one Border collie that was terrified of cars; the slightest sound made her run for shelter. So this evening she was very lonely and stuck her nose through the doggie door that separated the outside kennel from the inside to only discover that her buddy Freeway was gone. She sniffed her way to the front of the kennel on the outside portion of it and discovered a very large hole that was dug up, and this was the way Freeway had gotten out and the cause why she hadn't seen him since last night.

She used her scent to go and find Freeway as she dug her way out of the kennel to only come across the broken collar that had fallen off Freeway as he escaped. She sniffed and sniffed until she got a good scent and slowly walked away from the kennel toward the access road of I-75, when she heard a car coming down the road toward Commercial Blvd., she made a dash looking for shelter where she would feel safe. No way in hell was she going back to the kennel. She was going to find Freeway as she looked around, and only a few feet away was this huge drainpipe that went under the access road to Commercial Blvd. She made a dash for it to get away from the approaching car she heard coming. It was Officer Mario taking his usual place of stakeout like he normally does on the nights—just about the same location that he and Freeway met last evening.

She sat at the edge of the drainpipe and listened to make sure the car was gone, turned around, and slowly started walking through the drainpipe, not knowing what was in there or where it may end. As she slowly crawled into the darkness, she could feel that her paws were stepping on something wet and stopped for a moment to figure out what it was.

It felt like water and tasted like water but a little funny than drinking water as she continued to crawl ahead, when she had felt this sensation over her and stopped. Sheba was not feeling good and decided it was time to turn around and go back the way she came, when she blacked out for several minutes and had awoken into human form. She was no longer a border collie! What the hell happened to her? She looked around in a daze and saw fingers and toes and other body parts that were new to her; she even had longer hair now!

The moonlight glistened on the other end of the drainpipe in the direction she was heading to look for Freeway; she continued to crawl through the drainpipe until she got to the other end and saw the moon shining down on her. She was covered with dirty water and had an awful smell. She needed to get out of there in a hurry! But where would she go? She was completely naked and had no identification on her except for nine numbers tattooed on her belly. Once she was on her feet, she crawled back up the embankment toward the road to see where she was.

She could see the Freeway Shelter just on the other side of the access road in the distance because of the streetlights reflecting down on the mural that was painted on the side of the building. The streetlights and power lines along the edge of the road were very visible to her, but it was complete darkness as far as she could see directly behind her as she listened to the sounds of the crickets chirping and bullfrogs croaking just behind her. "What happened to me?" She then noticed a huge Windmill Palm tree just a few feet away from her and crawled over to it and broke off several palm fronds to cover her new body parts to get across the access road to get back to the shelter.

The minute she stepped onto the access road, Officer Mario noticed her crossing the street directly in front of his patrol car and turned on his high beam light to see what was crossing in front of his patrol car. The look on this poor woman's face was as if she was a deer caught in headlights! "What the hell!" Mario said to himself as he stepped out of his patrol car and yelled, "Freeze!" She stood there frozen in place at that very moment, in shock and horrified. She started babbling on to Mario and ranting and raving as he approached her. He noticed an awful smell reeking from this woman as he approached her, which caused him to stop in his footprints. He asked her, "Ma'am, what are you doing out here?" He asked her several times the same question, "What are you doing out here?" All she could do was babble, and he couldn't make any sense of what she was trying to say. He asked her several more questions, and then the final question he asked was, "Have you been drinking?" Sheba, still in shock, had stopped babbling and just stood there, staring directly at him with the headlights still in her face. "Ma'am, let me help you," he said as he took her by the arm and escorted her over to his patrol car and opened the back door and helped her, trying to avoid an eyeful since she only had palm fronds covering the parts that she wanted to hide, while Mario figured out what to do with her next. She wasn't injured; there were no signs of violence or bruises on her.

He did notice several numbers that were tattooed on her stomach that he found rather odd. Here was this naked woman in the backseat of the patrol car, covered with palm fronds and smelling awful. Mario was bewildered on how this woman could have ended out here. Was she a kidnap victim who was possibly raped and then dumped out here, leaving her for dead? Was she drunk when she first came out here?

There was one person that knew how to deal with situations like this possibly a homeless person. Mario started up the patrol car and was heading south on I-75 toward the downtown area; he was going to bring her to the Dixie Arms. Mario felt that he could trust her in the care of LaVonda, who knew how to handle situations like this since she deals with the homeless people on a daily basis.

Sheba started babbling once again as they drove off. Mario wanted to give LaVonda a heads-up on this one, so he called her from his cell phone en route to her place. He wasn't going to drop her there like he did with Freeway the night before.

As he was placing his call to LaVonda he glanced up and looked up into his rearview mirror to check on this woman who was actually Sheba, a canine, which he didn't know, who was still babbling on in the backseat and was also sniffing the blanket that he had wrapped her in, which was used on Freeway from the night before. Thank God he had placed it back into the trunk of the patrol car before he had taken it out to wash it.

It was either this, or LaVonda was going to meet Eve, the other half of Adam and Eve very shortly. Oh well, a little dog scent wasn't so bad compared to the aroma that this woman was giving off. It really didn't matter to him at this point, just as long as she was covered and not completely naked; anything was better than palm fronds, and most importantly, she was out of harm's way, being left out on the street in the condition she was in. There were no signs of abuse or injuries on her; it was not an emergency case where she would have to be taken to the hospital for observation, and it was something that he would not normally do, due to being outside of standard procedures, without calling it into the sheriff's station first. Who would know? Beside him and his passenger in the backseat who was in no condition to be talking to anyone at this point. He took a chance and went with his gut feeling that LaVonda would be able to help her.

"Hey, you!" said LaVonda as she recognized his cell phone number on her phone ID. "What's up?" she asked him.

"Well, I have this urgent situation at this moment and I could use your assistance on this one. I'll fill you in when I get there. I'll tell you one thing now! I found this woman off the highway, alone and frightened, and I'm on my way to your place with her right now. I think she could use your assistance in the shelter. I'll see you soon."

"Not a problem. That's why I'm here," LaVonda told him, "to help those in need. I'll see you in a few minutes." And she hung up the phone and looked over at Freeway who was lying next to her on the bed sound asleep, making strange noises as if he was dreaming. As she reached over to pat him and tell him she was going downstairs, he opened his eyes and looked at her like he understood and got up and followed her downstairs.

"You know, Mario's on his way over here right now and he's bringing someone with him who will be staying with us tonight." He walked down the hallway beside her as they were heading toward the staircase to go downstairs to wait for him. "But first we're going to put on a pot of coffee in the kitchen because I think our quiet night at home has just ended and we're going to need it." Freeway continued to stay by her side and followed her into the kitchen and headed directly to his water bowl that was on the floor in the kitchen area.

"What am I doing? Have I finally lost it? I'm talking to a dog and telling him we are having company tonight." Freeway lifted his head from the water bowl and looked up at her as if he knew exactly what she was saying. "Well, the coffee's on and we'll just wait a few minutes," she said as she walked over to the refrigerator, looking for something to snack on, when she saw Freeway fly out of the kitchen, heading toward the foyer toward the front door where he let out a loud bark. "Wow! That was quick," she said as she, too, headed toward the front door to meet Mario and her houseguest for the night. "Hey, boy, what is it? Is it Mario? Is he here already?" She opened the front door and looked out onto the street in front of the shelter and saw Mario's patrol car parked out front with Mario helping this woman get out from the backseat.

As he made his way up the walkway toward the front porch, Freeway made a run toward him to greet him as he said, "Hello, boy! How are you?" In the meantime, this woman he had by the arm was digging her fingers into his arm as he was helping her up the stairs onto the porch and into the shelter where LaVonda was waiting for him at the door.

"Come on, boy!" LaVonda told the dog. "Give Mario a second to get settled in and then you can go see him as long as you want." The four of them headed toward the parlor. Freeway was sniffing this woman up and down as she was being led into the parlor by Mario who was still holding on to her arm as she continued to hold on to Mario for dear life.

Mario sat down on the sofa with Sheba in tow right next to him as LaVonda sat down on the other side of her. "So where did you find her?" LaVonda asked Mario. He told her how she walked out onto the road on the access road to Commercial Blvd.

"This is the way she was, but holding palm fronds to cover her private parts. I had this blanket in the truck and put this on her to cover her up. I couldn't let her sit butt naked in my patrol car. I should be following protocol and called this into the station but my gut feeling told me to bring her to you because you are used to helping out the homeless."

"I don't think she's homeless, Mario. She doesn't have the signs like I saw with Ms. Honeycutt. Dirty hair, she doesn't look unnourished, and she seems healthy. She looks like she's in shock by the way she's babbling on. Do you remember the boy in the movie that was with Susan Sarandon that was filmed in New Orleans where the boy had witnessed a murder and then went into shock and was hospitalized where he was babbling like she is doing now?"

"Oh, the John Grisham movie made from his book. It was *The Client.*"

"Yes, that's one! First what we need to do is get her cleaned up because she smells awful, like she's been rolling around in dog shit."

"That's what I smelled. I couldn't figure out what that smell was. It just smelled horrible."

"Then I'll get her some clean clothes from the store upstairs. I'm sure we have plenty of clothes to fit her and then something for her to sleep in tonight. We'll put her to bed in one of the other bedrooms upstairs and keep an eye on her till the morning and see if she comes out of the shock she is in. I'll try talking to her to get more information while she is here tonight and you can go back to work and when I see you later in the morning when you come into work, we'll discuss what we can do with her then. For now we'll get her cleaned up and into a comfortable bed." LaVonda stood up and extended her hand out to Sheba and asked her, "Please take my hand and I will help you. You are safe now and no one is going to hurt you."

Sheba took her hand and stood up, when all of a sudden Freeway made a dash for Sheba and started humping her legs.

Mario yelled, "NO! Get down!" And he tried to push Freeway away from her legs.

LaVonda also yelled, "No! Bad dog!" Mario stood up from the sofa and took Freeway by the back of his neck and walked him into the kitchen and separated them.

It was funny to both Mario and LaVonda at that moment when Freeway did what he did to this poor woman. They both had to hold back from bursting out into laughter in front of this poor woman who had been through enough for one night.

LaVonda escorted this woman up the staircase. She was still in the blanket she came into the shelter with from Mario's trunk, and she looked down over the side of the railing on the staircase, looking for the dog with tears in her eyes for she had remembered the dog. It was Freeway, her buddy and friend, but she couldn't speak to anyone that she knew him because she, too, was a dog who had now become a human being and was no longer a canine. Mario had Freeway with him in the kitchen while he poured himself a cup of coffee while he waited for LaVonda to get back to him after she got this woman settled into the shelter for the night. Freeway was barking up a storm in the kitchen; he wanted to get out and go find Sheba and LaVonda, and Mario yelled at him to stop barking.

"What has gotten into you tonight?" he asked. "You weren't like this last night or all day today. What got your tail all in a knot?"

Meanwhile LaVonda had drawn a bath for this woman and got her settled in the tub as she told her that she would be in good hands and that everything would be okay. She had calmed down and stopped babbling. It was a good sign that she was coming around. "You just soak in this warm water for a few minutes and I will be right back with something for you to wear for the night and we'll deal with getting you more clothes tomorrow."

LaVonda ran down the hall to the women's boutique and found a housecoat and robe for her and a pair of slippers for her feet and headed back to the bathroom where Sheba was rubbing her fingers over her stomach on the numbers that were tattooed on her belly. LaVonda noticed the numbers and memorized them as quickly as she could, then looked around for something to write them down with when she noticed something up on the bathroom vanity that would work.

"This will work just fine." She had found a tube of Ms. Honeycutt's red lipstick on the counter by the sink and wrote the numbers on the mirror in the bathroom only to retrieve them later once she had a pad and a pen. "God, I hope Gloria doesn't see this and wash it off by the time I get back. She'll have a coe once she sees that her lipstick is all used up and on the mirror instead of her face! Now let's get you out of this tub and dried off and into some bedclothes," After several minutes of getting her cleaned up, LaVonda asked her if she would like something to drink before she went to bed. Sheba shook her head like a dog would to get water for them, which LaVonda took as a no! So off they went to the guest bedroom where Sheba was tucked into bed and again reminded by LaVonda that she was safe and that she should get a good night's rest and that she was going downstairs to say good night to Mario who was waiting downstairs with Freeway.

Once LaVonda left the bedroom, Sheba buried herself under the covers like a dog would who was going to bed for the night, with her head heading for the foot of the bed under the sheets and bed linens instead of where it should be up at the head of the bed.

LaVonda stopped by her bedroom and grabbed a pen and a notebook that she had lying on the nightstand where she kept notes on things that she needed to do as they popped into her head that she wanted to do the next day. She headed to the bathroom and wrote down the numbers she had scribbled on the mirror with lipstick and wiped them off the mirror before Ms. Honeycutt saw them and freaked out. With her notebook in hand, she headed downstairs where Mario was on his second cup of coffee in the kitchen with Freeway sitting by his side on the floor until he saw that LaVonda had entered the kitchen alone and not accompanied by Sheba. Freeway immediately ran past her and escaped from being held hostage in the kitchen by Mario and flew up the staircase to the guest room where Sheba was asleep.

The bedroom door was ajar just enough for him to nudge it open, and he jumped up on the bed and lay down next to her. They had reunited once again but in a different form this time.

"So I see you found the coffee. Okay?" LaVonda asked Mario.

And he replied, "Yes, and it's just what I need to get me through the rest of the night."

"How is she?" Mario asked.

"She's all cleaned up and tucked in the guest bedroom upstairs where I gather Freeway is heading this very moment by the way he dashed by me just a second ago."

"I'll go get him!" Mario told her.

"No! Let him go. He'll be fine. It's okay. He's just curious so let him be. I'm not worried about him going upstairs. He has free rein of the shelter."

"Oh, really!"

"Yes, really," LaVonda told him with a grin on her face.

"You got attached to him, didn't you? You only had him a day from the time I brought him by last night."

"He's a very smart dog and a lot of fun to have around and not to mention I enjoyed his company today when we spent some time together. I have a soft spot for him in my heart. There is something about him that has me puzzled and I have not pinpointed it yet, but I will. I'll check on him when I go back upstairs to check on her and try to get a little shut-eye before dawn."

"Speaking of dawn, I need to get out of here and get back to work. Thanks for the coffee and thanks for taking her into the shelter tonight. We'll see if we can get some information out of her when I come back later. It sounds like you got it covered here so I'll get out of your hair so you can get some shut-eye," Mario said as he took his last sip of coffee as they said their good nights to one another. Mario said that he would see himself out so that LaVonda could get some shut-eye before the sun came up. LaVonda, being the gracious hostess, walked Mario to the front door to make sure he got back into his patrol car and went back to work, and she made a short detour to her office with the notebook in hand instead of heading to her bedroom upstairs.

She went directly to her desk and turned on her computer as she sat down and opened up the notebook to the page where she had jotted down the nine numbers that she wrote down from the mirror in the bathroom upstairs.

She went directly onto the Internet and typed in the IRS Web site and did some unethical hacking into the files for which she was fired years ago. She hacked into files of social security numbers and did a search using the nine numbers from the notebook that she wrote down, and within seconds up came a file on a deceased Ms. Lucy Applegate from Metairie, Louisiana, that had passed away eight years ago in an auto accident.

The file had information regarding Ms. Applegate's past income, her wages for the years that she was employed and reported over the years to the IRS, as well as any payments she had to pay back to them.

LaVonda wrote all this information down under the nine digits in her notebook and called it a night and shut down her computer and took the notebook and headed upstairs to bed, but not before she peeked in on her houseguest. She noticed Freeway was lying up on the bed, and right next to him was a huge lump under the sheets. They were both fine as she said good night to them, unaware they were being looked in on, and she went directly to her bedroom for a few hours of shut-eye just after she put away the notebook in the top drawer of her nightstand. What on earth was she going to do with that information? LaVonda then turned toward the bed and lay down and within minutes was off to sleep for it had been a long day and evening for her; after a few hours of napping, she looked up and noticed her alarm clock was flashing sixty thirty in the morning. She struggled to get up to face another day, which just now was facing her. There was now going to be another houseguest to look after and find out more about and if she couldn't she would have to use the information in her notebook. This information was going to be used as the identity on this woman who was sleeping in the guest room with Freeway. It would help her find a job and give her a name. Was she prepared to take in another boarder just like her other boarder, Ms. Honeycutt, who she heard singing a happy tune as she was walking by her bedroom on the way to the bathroom, which she assumed was to get ready for work.

LaVonda yelled out, "Gloria! Gloria!" as she walked by.

"Yes! LaVonda, you yelled?" She peeked her head into LaVonda's bedroom. "Isn't it a bit early for you to be screaming first thing in the morning?" Ms. Honeycutt said to her as she found her lying on the bed, struggling to get up.

"I'm not screaming, just wanted to say good morning and see how you were, and how are things going with Philip?"

"Oh, what's the interest in my life all of a sudden?" Ms. Honeycutt asked her.

"I just wanted to see how you are doing. There's no harm in me asking that, is there?"

"No! I'm sorry I snapped back at you. I just didn't have a good night's sleep last night."

"Oh?" LaVonda asked.

"I heard voices last night that kept me tossing and turning and then I have other things on my mind, which I will talk to you about later, but I have to get ready for work to meet the bus on time or I'll be late for work."

"I'll get up and make us some fresh coffee so when you come downstairs after getting dressed you can have some before you leave for work."

"That would be nice. I overslept this morning so I'm running behind. Thank you," Gloria told her as she headed on her way again toward the bathroom. LaVonda then realized that the voices she must have heard was her and Mario downstairs, yelling at the dog who had been trying to hump the woman in the guest bedroom; it was what she must have heard, or she was losing her mind if she heard voices then. She pulled herself up and got out of bed and headed toward the door to head downstairs to make fresh pot of coffee for her and Ms. Honeycutt.

CHAPTER TWENTY-ONE

It was just another restless night as dawn was approaching for Donald because he had so much on his mind; therefore another good night's rest just wasn't in the cards for him since becoming a wealthy millionaire. He tossed and turned, thinking of ways to help the New Orleans shelter what with what devastating news he had received the night before from Steve. He wanted to do more besides sending Ms. Kitty down there. He wanted to be involved and have more hands on in the rebuilding of the shelter.

He was going to join her on this trip as well to see for himself the devastation. It was the least he could do to help out. What was the purpose of having all this money and not being able to share it toward a worthy cause like this?

They may have financial expenses that the insurance company would not cover like food and other supplies that they would need right away for them to rebuild. Once Donald finished getting ready for work, he was going to head to the shelter and look into the earliest flight possible to New Orleans; hopefully something would be available for later in the day.

Once Donald arrived at the shelter, he headed for his office and jumped online on his computer and started looking for flights; hopefully he could find a direct flight. "Bingo!" he said to himself as he just located a flight leaving at three o'clock in the afternoon from the Ft. Lauderdale Airport directly to New Orleans Airport nonstop.

Donald pulled out his company credit card and booked the flight immediately for two seats—one for him and the other for Ms. Kitty. Now he had to call Ms. Kitty and tell her to pack a suitcase and to be in the shelter by eleven o'clock for she was going with him on a trip later today.

As he glanced at the clock on the wall in his office, it read 8:45 AM, so he thought it'd be safe to call her and break the news. As he waited for her to answer the phone after several rings, he heard a soft whisper say, "Good morning," as she finally picked it up and answered.

"Did I wake you?" Donald asked.

"No! I have been up for the past two hours just dozing on and off on the sofa."

"I have some news for you that might get the adrenaline flowing."

"What?" Ms. Kitty asked.

"I just booked two airline tickets to New Orleans to go down and help rebuild the shelter and you're coming with me."

Ms. Kitty's eyes were wide open by then, and she was so excited, she got up of the sofa and did a jig and said, "I'm honored to go along with you on this trip to be of any assistance I can." Donald told her that the flight was at three o'clock this afternoon and that he was already at the shelter just wrapping up some last-minute things that he had on his desk before he left for this trip. It just dawned on him that it would be better if he picked her up at her place instead of having her come into the shelter.

"Please be ready by eleven o'clock and I'll swing by there and pick you up on the way to the airport. Just give me your address and I'll Google it on the computer and print out a map from my place to yours. I'm going to leave my car parked in the long-term parking garage at the airport. First thing I need you to do before anything else," Donald asked her, "is to call one or two of the staff that you would trust and find reliable to look over the shelter while we are gone for a few days to oversee the shelter in our absence."

"I have two in mind already and I'll do that right now and call them before I get ready and pack."

'Tell them they need to be at the shelter on time if not earlier so I can go home and pack a suitcase as well. I'll leave my set of keys to the shelter to whomever shows up first to lock up nights. I will trust your judgment on this one, so do not let me down!"

"I won't," she told him. "I won't"

"Well then, I'll see you in an hour or so."

"It sounds like a plan." And they both hung up from the phone. Ms. Kitty then called Jessie and Martin whom she chose to be in charge and oversee the shelter in her absence. One was going to oversee the care and feeding of the dogs as well as oversee the adoptions out of the shelter; the other was to oversee the other areas of the shelter and any issues if any other when and if they came up. She was only just a phone call away if they had any questions or problems they couldn't handle on their own.

Ms. Kitty had no idea that Donald had spoken to Steve, the van driver, just last night and that he had offered to fly out the boarded canines from New Orleans and Texas at Donald's expense to the owners if they came looking for them at the destroyed shelter and wanted them back so they would be together again.

She was going to be filled in on this information when they got together later on this morning if Donald didn't forget to tell her. Ms. Kitty chose to give the feeding and adoption process duties to Martin for he was more in touch with the animals than Jessie was.

Jessie was more interested in the office and administration part of the shelter and would be more suited for that position in her absence. Martin on the other hand was more suitable for handling the adoptions and feeding of the canines since he was like a kid with a new puppy, very attentive and the caring kind, like a younger version of Donald when she had first met him. Unless he was too busy playing his new iPod that he was listening to all the time when he was out in the kennel area feeding the dogs. So that was her plan for the both of them.

Donald, who was on his way to another part of the shelter, was walking through the lobby or entrance of the shelter from his office and noticed Jessie, one of his staffers, who was approaching the front door of the shelter; Donald then unlocked the front door and let him in.

"Good morning!" Donald said to Jessie.

"Good morning to you, sir. I just got off the phone with Ms. Kitty and she told me that you both would be heading out of town for a few days and I rushed over so you can go pack since I only live down the street a few lights down off Commercial."

"Great! Here are the keys to the shelter. You will be in charge of locking up the shelter at night, as well as a few other special request that I'm going to give you to handle if the phone calls arrive. I will need you to make arrangements to fly any one of the dogs in the back that are kenneled up from the New Orleans and Texas shelters back to the owners if they call looking for their dog. They will be instructed to call this shelter if they show up at the shelter looking for the dogs down there.

"Because of the overcrowding down there in the shelter in New Orleans, we have been asked to assist them by taking in the overflow from down there. So here is a company credit card to book airline tickets for them to get them home to their owners and it is not to be used for anything else than that unless instructed by me or her when we call here to check in on things while we are gone. You will be in charge of getting them from here back to their owners."

"I can handle that, sir. It's not going to be a problem, sir!"

"First thing, Jessie, please call me Donald. Sir makes me feel old."

"Yes! Donald," Jessie replied back.

"Good. Now we are on the same track."

Unaware to Ms. Kitty that this was happening, she had put Martin in charge of the canines out back for feedings and overseeing the adoptions and had no clue that Jessie was put in charge of that with Donald and sending them back to their rightful owners when needed to be. As the morning progressed, Donald was all packed and heading to pick up Ms. Kitty at her home who was all packed, ready, and just waiting for Donald to pick her up on the way to the airport. They both were on schedule, and on the way to the airport, they talked about the plans once they got there, when they both realized that they needed to find a place to stay while there.

"Shit! I forgot to make those arrangements," Donald told her. "It didn't dawn on me at the time while making the flight arrangements we would need a place to stay. What was I thinking?" Donald asked Ms. Kitty to do him a favor and reach back there into the backseat and get his laptop case and pull out his laptop that was fully charged and look into a hotel in the area close to this address that he pulled from his shirt pocket, which was the address of the shelter in which they were going down to assist in getting back to normal, as normal as could be if the hurricane hadn't taken everything.

"I've located several that were in the area," she said as she wrote down the phone numbers one by one and then called from her cell phone one by one; they were either filled up, or the phone just kept on ringing as if they were not open, or the phone lines might have been down. The last call she made was a mom-and-pop inn just blocks away. "Not looking so good, Donald," she said as she was making the calls and he was driving them to the airport. "This is the last phone number I'm calling, so cross your fingers that this one will have something available."

Donald crossed his fingers as he was exiting the interstate and heading in the airport grounds looking for the long-term parking sign to exit off of without having to circle around again through the drop-off and unloading areas of passengers leaving Fort Lauderdale on the curbside at their airlines terminals for boarding flights. As Donald pulled into the first available parking place and parked his car, Ms. Kitty was pulling out her company credit card from her handbag to reserve the only room that was available. He looked at her as if to say, "What!"

Ms. Kitty was thanking the other person on the other end of her cell phone. "Thank you so much! We'll see you in a few hours then."

"So I gather from that conversation you got a room and not two rooms?" Donald asked.

"Well, because of the situation down in New Orleans, there is nothing available and this was a miracle because just ten minutes ago the people who had booked it weeks ago just canceled."

"Boy, that was good timing if I hadn't seen it myself," Donald told her.

"Only thing is they have a single bed but they have a roll-away bed that they can bring into the room once we get there."

"So, we'll flip a coin on who gets the bed and who gets the rollaway or we can do this," Donald suggested. "We can alternate nights and both get the chance to sleep on a bed."

"That works for me," Ms. Kitty agreed.

"This way we both can try to get a good night's sleep in between bed-hopping and not in the good way either," Donald told her as they both exited the car and locked it up and headed toward the entrance of their airline that was taking them on an interesting trip.

Once inside the airport terminal, they received their boarding passes, and since they each had just one suitcase, they chose to carry it on with them and placed it in the overhead compartment above their seats. Once they got down to the terminal, Ms. Kitty decided to place a call to the shelter and check in and see if all was okay there with Martin and Jessie.

"While you do that," Donald said, "I'm going to run over here to the gift shop/snack bar/newsstand and get us a drink since we still have time before they start boarding."

"Oh, bring me back a surprise for the flight, will you please? Since we won't be eating anything on this flight, a snack would be nice for later on in the flight."

"A surprise it will be," Donald replied as he walked away from the terminal as she made her phone call to check in at the shelter. Donald returned back to the terminal carrying two drinks and a paper bag with her surprise. It was a bagful of goodies for her to snack on during the flight. He had several chocolate bars, some with and some without nuts, malted milk balls, peppermint patties, chips, licorice, and a bottle of antacid if she needed it after eating all that stuff in the bag before the plane landed in New Orleans.

"Why'd you get so much?" she asked him.

"Well, I didn't know what you liked and besides I was in the mood for the malted milk balls and the rest was right in front of me so I grabbed it because I wasn't sure what you would like. So, surprise!" She laughed as they sat down at the terminal and watched the rest of the passengers arrive at the terminal. There really weren't as many people going in that direction. Maybe a couple of dozen people at the most by the time they started calling seats to board the plane, starting from the front of the plane to the back.

"If were lucking maybe they will let us sit anywhere on the plane since it didn't look like a full flight."

"Maybe, we'll just have to wait and see," Donald told her when all of a sudden the airline attendant started calling passengers from row one to fifteen to start boarding and to please have their airlines tickets available to give the flight attendant upon boarding the airplane. With that said, Donald and Ms. Kitty, both picked up their carry-on bag and pulled out their airline tickets and headed toward the gate. Donald asked, "Was everything under control at the shelter with Jessie and Martin?"

"They said they had it under control and that it was slow this afternoon but everyone was busy in their areas from grooming to two boarders coming in for a few days while the owners went out of town for a few days."

"Glad to see that everything is going good for them," Donald replied back. "We'll just have to see how the remainder of the week goes for them, won't we? Just be sure you check in on them and keep me posted on a daily basis and let me know what's going on with the shelter."

"I will keep you posted," Ms. Kitty replied as they gave their boarding passes to the flight attendant and headed down the ramp to the plane that was about to take them to the unknown and the devastation ahead of them.

CHAPTER TWENTY-TWO

Martin and Jessie had everything under control for the first day with no issues whatsoever with running the shelter on their first day of being in charge, until they received the first phone call into the shelter the following day from one of the owners looking into the status of their dog that was here from New Orleans and Texas. Well, Jessie took the call and arranged to fly the dog back to the owner the following morning. It was not as bad as he thought it would be to arrange to send the dog back to their rightful owner. With the help from several of the coworkers at the shelter, which consisted of the van driver that Donald had just hired and one other from the staff who took the canine to the airport and personally processed him through right down to the gate before he was handed over to the airline steward to head home.

Martin, not aware of this, wasn't paying much attention to the canines and had assumed that most of them were being flown back to their owners one by one as the days went by, and he didn't know that there was less for him to feed because they were actually escaping, and neither one of them knew it. There was a definite communication problem going on between the both of them; they did not have even the slightest clue that they all had been escaping and not going home via airplane.

One by one over several nights, they all had escaped from their cages and ran down to the cage that once housed Freeway and Sheba who first escaped from the shelter through the outdoor kennel area where the cracked slab of concrete was and Freeway had dug a huge hole to escape. The scent of Sheba led them into the same direction she headed. One by one they all went through the drainpipe near the access road and blacked out and awoke in human form, dazed and confused as they approached the other side of the drainpipe near the everglades, completely naked with nine numbers tattooed across their stomachs on each and every one of them. Mario, who was on duty all of the nights they had escaped, continued to bring them one by one each and every time down to the Dixie Arms instead of the police station. They were now under the watchful eyes of LaVonda who had taken them all in due to Officer Mario's watchful eyes while on night duty; he brought them to the Dixie Shelter, and one by one LaVonda gave them all new identities like she did with Sheba, who is now Ms. Applegate, using the tattooed numbers found on her stomach as well as all the others she took in and found jobs for, which she used as she continued to access the IRS database and gave them all new names and identifications from the list of deceased people that was on file. They all had one thing in common, and it was that they all had tattooed numbers across their stomachs, but she had no friggin' clue why! It was like a scene from the movie *The Pod People*, where they were all cloned and let out into society to take over.

Ms. Lucy Applegate was a former receptionist for a law firm in New Orleans when she passed away. She would get this same position to the new Ms. Applegate, at the Everything Canine Inc. in Weston.

She would clothe them all, feed them, and even find them jobs. As they all lived under the roof of the Dixie Arms, she had to expand several of the floors into sleeping quarters to accommodate them. She separated the men from the women on different floors.

The bus ride into work was now a bit more enjoyable for Ms. Honeycutt, who now had plenty of company to join her. They all have been hired on as well at the Everything Canine Inc. where Ms. Honeycutt was employed thanks to the help of LaVonda who had gotten them all jobs working out there together. There were several job openings in various departments within the company that was posted in the local newspaper for numerous positions since the company was expanding.

They had positions in different areas for warehouse work that was for order pulling, shelf-stocking positions, inventory, and even in the shipping and receiving area. They had two positions open. Customer service had a few positions posted, and even in management they had several positions that were also listed.

With the new identities given to them by the help of LaVonda who often hacked into the IRS Web site and used the tattooed numbers as a social security number and found them identifications of people who have passed away, each and every one of them had a place to work within the Everything Canine Inc. LaVonda took part of their income to cover expenses of the shelter food as well as room and board in exchange. Who knew that the pet products would be so lucrative with so many positions open in just one company? She watched them all go off to work each morning to their new jobs that she had found for them at Everything Canine Inc.

She would then make sure their sleeping and boarding spaces were all cleaned and that a hot meal was on the dinner table for them when they came back to the shelter from work. Most of them worked in Weston with the exception of a couple she took in. Winston Johnson from Metairie, Louisiana, was a hotel manager in the French Quarters when he passed away, so she found a position open in the hospitality industry in Fort Lauderdale for him from his records she hacked into from the IRS database. She also found a position with the postal service for one Sissy Bagcheck, from Texas City, who worked for the post office for fifteen years as a delivery lady for mail. And then there was a Jesus Garcia from New Orleans who worked for a nationwide delivery company for six years before a terrible accident. He was driving on the Kenner Freeway when a bad rainstorm caused him to roll and flip due to hydroplaning across the highway.

LaVonda placed him with a local delivery company, which by the way happens to be the delivery company for Everything Canine Inc. that's used on a daily basis to make deliveries to their customers.

Ms. Honeycutt had plenty of company on her ride into work with her fellow roommates from the shelter; it was never a dull moment for any of them on the bus ride into work from downtown Fort Lauderdale. She had to deal with them more as coworkers. There was Juanita Morales from Houston Texas, her new identity was now the new office manager along with the following positions also filled at Everything Canine Inc.: Duke Ryder from Sugar Land, Texas, as the general manager; Bailey Hickley from Humble, Texas, as assistant general manager; Clayton Legg, from Freeport, Texas, as operational manager; Gina Glickmore from Freeport, Texas, as the Shipping Manager; Bentley Armstrong from New Orleans as an order puller; Roscoe Hernandez as a receiving clerk, from Bay City, Texas; Lucas Balistar from Missouri City, as the receiving manager; Clifford Bernard from Galveston, Texas, as an inventory clerk; Angela Marcos from Humble, Texas, as a customer service rep; Alfie Churchhill from New Orleans, also was customer service rep; Antoinette Bustling as HR from the French Quarter, in New Orleans; Kingston Ming from Galveston, Texas, as inventory control clerk; Lolita Jersey from Freeport, Texas, inventory control clerk; Austin Daniels from Houston, Texas, also working as an inventory clerk; and Bella Lopez from Houston, Texas, was customer service rep.

Every morning they would all leave together from the Dixie Arms just around six thirty in the morning straight out the front door and across the porch down the walkway and out to the street corner. They looked like a pack of dogs with the tallest leading the way. There was Clayton, and following was Antoinette, Clifford, Kingston, Duke, Sissy, Gina, Bentley, Lucy, Roscoe, Lucas, Juanita, Austin, Bailey, Angela, Alfie, Lolita, Bella, and at the end of the pack was Ms. Honeycutt.

LaVonda found this odd as she watched them leave the shelter as she was sitting at her desk in her office downstairs with Freeway by her side lying on the floor next to her. The minute he heard them coming down the staircase, he sat up and watched them leave the shelter one by one in the odd formation as well. But the only difference was that when Ms. Applegate (Sheba) walked out the door, he would start barking and run to the window, stand on his hind legs with his two front paws on the window ledge, and continued to bark until Ms. Applegate(Sheba) got on the bus and was out of his sight.

LaVonda was getting more and more curious on why Freeway acted like this every morning as they left for work. It was out of his normal behavior to act out like this. It started the day they all got hired on at Everything Canine Inc. This was something she needed to pay more attention to with him, and if it continued, she would have to find out what was causing this behavior and soon.

He started acting out the day Ms. Applegate came to the shelter from the very moment he started humping her legs and Mario had to separate him from her.

Once aboard the bus and seated, they all opened the bus windows and hung their heads out the window as if they were enjoying the breeze as the bus pulled off and headed to their next stop, with the exception of Ms. Honeycutt who sat in the first seat across from the driver. She would be the first person off the bus at the next bus stop and the first person on the bus until they reached their final destination in Weston.

Sometimes the ride would be a hoot for Ms. Honeycutt as she sat back quietly and observed her new roommates on the bus act like a bunch of animals. The bus driver would have to yell at Clifford, Roscoe, Clayton, Kingston, and Duke to sit down because they would be yelling out the windows at passing cars. The bus driver has more than once threatened to pull over to the side of the road and throw them off the bus if they did not stop.

Antoinette, Juanita, Gina, and Lolita would sit together and smell each other's hair and talk about the wardrobe they put on that day and sometimes exchanged their accessories before getting off the bus. Angela and Bella sat together and just talked all the way into work in Spanish, and Ms. Honeycutt had no clue on what they were talking about, which she found to be very rude but was okay as long as they were not talking about her.

Alfie always chose to sit by herself and buried her face in this book that she carried everywhere. The book was hidden by a book jacket she made one evening at the shelter. A few of the girls wondered what she was reading. All they knew was that it must have been something good, for her not to look up until it was time to change buses. They were determined to find out what she was reading in a matter of time.

Alfie was always wearing the most interesting pillbox hats. As so did Ms. Honeycutt, which reminded folks of a Kentucky Derby. Ms. Honeycutt just wanted to get her hands on them and snatch them right from her head for she was the queen of the hat collection and wanted to be the only one on the bus wearing one.

Sometimes the guys would take the hat off of Alfie's head and tear them apart by chewing on the rim as if they were shredding toilet paper from the bathroom roll. Alfie, being proper and ladylike as she was, said nothing and just sat back and watch these crazy folks do whatever they wanted for she would eventually get even with them if they didn't give her hat back. She would put salt in their coffee cups when they were not looking at break time. Once she accidently tossed a cup of cold water on Clayton's trousers near the crotch area and made it look like he wet himself by accidently slipping or losing her balance. Harassing her fellow coworkers was her way to get back at them for messing with her hats.

The day usually started out once they punched the time clock with the ID badges that had a photo of them and identified them as employees by Everything Canine Inc. Some would come early and sit in the break room until the start of their shift and drink coffee or eat some breakfast if they brought it with them and watched the television that was in the break room to catch up on current news and events. Others chatted about their evening's events once they left for the day, while others just hung out in the office, chatting with the girls in customer service.

Antoinette was watching her weight because of a dress she found back at the shelter on a rack the day she turned up at the shelter when she was brought by Mario who found her wondering the street. It was a designer dress that she just snatched off the rack and brought to her room before someone else had seen it.

She was determined to fit into it. So her diet began, drinking plenty of water and eating celery and carrots and plenty of leafy greens just to try to fit into this dress, when several of her coworkers—Sissy, Bella, Austin, and Bailey—noticed her sitting in the break room, watching this television commercial for dog food, and she yelled out, "OMG! This dieting is killing me. I am sitting here drooling while watching a dog food commercial."

As the employees looked on and laughed, Bailey walked over to the paper towel roll dispenser near the sink; he brought her a sheet so she could wipe the drool off her face.

Thank you said Antoinette!

No problem This not the first time this has happened "Oh!" she replied back.

"Yeah, it seems that whenever this commercial comes on the television, other associates seem to have the same reaction. It's rather amusing. By the way," he asked Antoinette, "could you please place an order for several more cases of paper towels because we seem to have some fellow associates who think they're funny by rolling the paper towels, throwing them out in the warehouse in the very back of the building, and then shredding it up and when I find out who's doing it, they will be getting a written warning."

"No problem. I am heading back to my office right now and I'll call it in so it will be here by the morning unless we are completely out and then I will see if they can rush it over this afternoon."

"No, we'll be just fine until the morning. Thank you!" Bailey told her.

"You're welcome!" she replied back as she got up from her seat and headed back to her office with her celery in hand.

Just then Clayton came into the break room and told Bailey that he was just told by Duke that he wanted him to make an announcement over the intercom that they would be testing the fire alarms and that no one needed to leave the building; it was only a test.

Since there was a phone hanging on the break room wall, he walked over to it and picked it up and made the announcement over the intercom, and within seconds the alarms went off, and all the associates from the office to the warehouse started howling and continued until the alarms stopped going off.

Then again another round of the testing started, and it happened again; all the associates throughout the building started howling again until the alarms finally stopped. It was a sight to see, the entire building from management to associates howling all at the same time. The alarms must have pierced their ears like the noise of fingers scratching across a chalkboard. It was unbearable to their ears.

Management agreed while standing around chatting that this was not going to be done again anytime soon as they stood there shaking their heads from side to side as if they were trying to shake the ringing sound out of their heads. Within moments after testing of the alarms, there was a mad rush to the restrooms by warehouse associates who started to drink from the toilets in the stalls, all of them parched from howling, and they soon returned to their job duties with the exception of Clifford who stayed behind and drank a bit more.

A truck driver who was having his freight unloaded on the dock needed to use the restroom and walked in on him and caught him drinking from the toilet. Shocked and horrified, the driver dashed out of the restroom across the dock area to his empty truck that had just finishing unloading the last pallet of dog food and jumped into his cab and peeled out of the parking lot.

Meanwhile in the front of the building, two local fire trucks that had been dispatched had a Dalmatian named Sparky on one of them, who was the fire station's mascot. He was a gift to a fireman from that station from a couple whose home was saved by the fireman when a spark from a firecracker landed on the roof of their home last Fourth of July and ignited the shingles on the roof. They wanted to show their appreciation to the fire station for how grateful they were for saving their home.

Three of the firefighters that were on the same ladder truck with Sparky entered the building while the fourth one stayed behind. They entered the building, wanting to speak to the management who had forgotten to call ahead to the alarm company to let them know that they were going to be testing the alarms.

As Ms. Honeycutt looked up from her cubicle and noticed them coming into the building, she called out to the other girls in the office and yelled out to them, "Hey, you BITCHES, get up here now!"

Juanita sprung out from behind her desk from her office just across from Ms. Honeycutt's cubicle with a dirty look and said, "I don't ever want to hear that coming out of your mouth again," as she rushed over to the firemen as well.

Lolita, who was talking to Angela and Alfie, and Bella also rushed over to the firefighters who were now standing in the lobby side by side in the front of the office. All the girls from within the office had surrounded the firemen and started sniffing them one by one, up one side and down the other.

It was amusing as hell to watch, but once Duke, Bailey, and Clayton came out of their offices and saw the ruckus going on up front with the girls and the firemen, they were not amused. Duke told Bailey to handle the matter as he backed up into his office as Clayton entered Duke's office and closed the door. Bailey told the girls to get back to work as they backed off one by one and headed back to their desks.

Bailey introduced himself and apologized for not calling the alarm company and informed them that everything was fine in the building. Just that it was the annual testing of the alarms and they were getting ready to go in for a staff meeting, and it slipped their minds and forgot to call it in. The three firefighters stood there with shock on their faces because they had just been violated by these women from this office.

Bailey assured the firefighters that they would call ahead of time before they tested the alarms, and even though they were still somewhat in shock, they understood and told him to please make sure to call ahead next time before they ran the test.

Bailey said he would see to it. As the fireman turned to leave the building, Bailey, too, had taken a liking to the last fireman as he sniffed him from behind his neck as they left the building. Bailey then headed to Duke's office to prepare for the staff meeting with Clayton who already had gone in and had a head start on it. Bailey then scratched at the door to let them know he was on his way into the meeting as well.

It was the scent of Sparky on the firefighters that had everyone in the office in an uproar, but the firemen didn't know that. They just assumed it was brought on because they were recognized from the calendar benefit that they just held over the weekend at a local mall. The three "child please" firemen climbed back into the fire truck and headed out of the parking lot, followed by the second fire truck just behind them.

CHAPTER TWENTY-THREE

While Donald and Ms. Kitty remained in New Orleans, working hard and diligently on reopening a new shelter from day one when they first arrived, they had first rented a storage container and put everything that they could salvage from the old shelter into it since the shelter had become a total loss due to the hurricane.

They found temporary shelter for the animals with the help of volunteers who came forward to assist them with the pets that had remained in the crumbled building when the storm hit. While others in the shelter's care who had escaped from the building as it started to crumble and fall apart were out there somewhere on the streets, running scared and hungry and hopefully safe and taken care of by someone who cared.

Donald was updated daily on his shelter when he found some time to call in and check up on everything to make sure everything was under control and that they had no problems while they were away. He was told that everything was running smoothly and for him not to worry, and was informed that all the dogs from the New Orleans shelter were sent home to their rightful owners, unaware that there was a major communication problem between, Jessie and Martin, and in fact they had all really escaped from their pens and not sent home to their owners via airline.

Donald and Ms. Kitty had found temporary living arrangements that were satisfactory. They had a large room at a mom-and-pop motel that was very clean under the circumstances in which it had just escaped the hurricane and had minimum damage to the motel; it was just blocks away from the French Quarter that was within walking distance to the shelter.

They ate out every night in the restaurants that were open and not damaged by the hurricane. They then drank coffee and ate beignets on the way to the shelter every morning. Donald would buy a dozen or so beignets and bring them back to the shelter, which he would share with the other volunteers who were working with them diligently side by side to reopen a new shelter.

Even though the city barely missed the brunt of a major hurricane, the locals pulled together and helped one another out through these tough times. It was visible to both Donald and Ms. Kitty that the people of New Orleans came together and helped one another.

Even complete strangers who never met one another bonded in a time of need. These were people who had come together to rebuild a community that had their livelihood destroyed, which they once took for granted on a daily basis, going to work or business that was no longer there for them.

Donald and Ms. Kitty figured out they had at least two more weeks in New Orleans to finish up what they came to do, and with Donald's finances and connections, they'd be heading back to Florida before they knew it.

Throughout his day, Donald would have moments where he would have thoughts of Freeway that crossed his mind, and he hoped that he was okay and being taken care of by someone who might have found him after he ran off and disappeared into the bushes on the expressway back in Florida. Donald knew in his heart that he could never make up for that night to him, but he would find a way if they ever crossed paths again.

Back in Fort Lauderdale at the Dixie Arms, Freeway was playing fetch with a Frisbee in the backyard with Mario as LaVonda watched them both from the kitchen window. She wondered about Freeway's behavior this morning as her boarders left for work and more so on the way he reacted when he saw Ms. Applegate leave the shelter and head to the bus stop with his barking constantly. Did he know her from somewhere? What was their connection? She was going to have to pursue this a bit more, but she had to get ready for an appointment on the other side of town in just an hour.

She tapped her long manicured nails up against the glass window to get Mario's attention to call him in so she could give him instructions on what she wanted him to do while she was away.

"Come on, boy, playtime is over. Got to go in and see what LaVonda needs. We'll play again later, okay?" Freeway let out a loud bark as if to say okay.

They walked side by side up the stairs and into the back door into the kitchen where LaVonda was standing at the sink, finishing her cup of coffee.

"So what's on the agenda for today?" Mario asked.

"Well, I have an appointment on the other side of town off of Commercial Blvd. with a supplier for linens and then I'm heading west of there to a consignment shop that called and has several items they want to donate to the shelter if I was interested to stop by and see what they had to give us.

"I shouldn't be gone more than a couple of hours unless the traffic is horrific, and since it's going on noon, I'll no doubt hit some with everyone going to lunch on the road or running errands on their lunch hour.

"I would like you to take an inventory of the closets upstairs and put it on a spreadsheet for me on my computer so I can see what I have up there since our boarders have taken most of the clothes for their work attire. I received a call from someone who has lots of women's clothes and few men's that they would like to drop off for the shelter after they got off work around five o'clock. She was going to be in the area meeting some friends for dinner on the riverfront. I told her I'd call her later this afternoon if we had the room and she said that would be just fine."

"Okay then, I'll just grab a pad out of your desk in the office and head up so I can get started and hopefully have a majority of it down before you get back.

"Come on, boy, you can join me as long as you behave yourself and not destroy any of the shoes up there."

"Well then, I'm off!" she said. "I will see you in a few hours. I'll have my cell phone with me if you need anything."

"We will be just fine, right boy?" And he let out a loud bark and followed behind Mario as they left the kitchen in the direction of the office.

Mario heard the front door close a few minutes later and waited for LaVonda to drive off so he could get into her computer and follow up on what he saw much earlier with the information on the IRS site he saw. "I'll have a few hours to kill before she returned from her appointments." Freeway just cuddled up on the sofa across from the desk in the office and watched him from a distance as he started snooping thru her computer.

Mario came across the Web site and was able to hack in using her children's names, and he tried Matthew, no luck, Scott, no luck, and finally Savannah and yes! He was in! As Donald scrolled through her computer, he found a file that consisted of names of deceased people whose identities were next to social security numbers that he had found scratched on a pad in her desk as he searched for a pad. This was very interesting, as the list was exact as the names of the people staying at the shelter that he had brought in over the past few weeks while on traffic duty, which he had found naked and confused off Commercial Blvd. and I-75. What in hell was she doing?

Who was this woman that he had admired and come to like and was now working for too. Was he now going to become an accomplice to this sham she was playing? What was she to gain from all of this?

This was not a good thing; what was he to do with the information he just found on her computer? Mario, stunned by his findings, looked over at Freeway who was watching him from across the desk on the sofa and said, "What would you do?" as he raised his head from between his paws and barked. "Great! Now I'm losing it. I just asked a dog for his input. Come on, let's go do the inventory like we're supposed to do," he said as he closed down the computer and decided to deal with it one day at a time.

"I'll just have to keep a closer eye on her to see what this is all about." His heart had just fallen to a million pieces, finding this information and knowing that she was doing something illegal, and eventually he would have to tell his superior and bring her in for questioning.

This was not going to be easy because he was so fond of her, and they were just becoming good friends. He stepped away from the desk and said "Come on, boy, let's go upstairs and get this inventory done before she gets back and I'll worry about this later." Freeway jumped down from the sofa and followed Mario to the foyer and then up the staircase to take inventory of the closets.

Meantime, LaVonda was just exiting off at the Commercial Blvd. off of I-95 and was sitting at the red light when she remembered she was supposed to send a fax over to Winston, who was staying at the shelter, of a list of names of employers she had on her Rolodex sitting on the top of her desk. This would help him with some cold-calling for potential business for the hotel he was managing.

She called the shelter, and after numerous rings, Mario finally answered the phone, and she asked him to please fax the list to Winston, and he said he would take care of it. She asked how it was going with the inventory, and he said it was going fine, but she noticed a hesitation in his voice because he was not his cheerful, friendly self. Maybe he was deep into the inventory, and having to run from upstairs to the office downstairs to answer the phone interrupting him, and he was frustrated.

She just blew it off because she was turning left onto Commercial Blvd. and had to get off the phone since there was a police officer behind her, and she didn't want to get caught on the cell phone since they just passed a no-cell phone law in Broward County while driving. She said she'd catch up with him later, and he hung up the phone and started going through her Rolodex for the names and numbers to fax over to Winston.

The list was completed, and he called ahead to let Winston know to be on the lookout for the fax he was sending now, who said he was actually standing by the fax machine and when it started ringing would watch it come through.

"Got it! Thanks for sending it over," Winston said.

"You're welcome," Mario said as they hung up the phone.

Winston noticed that the name of Everything Canine Inc. was on the list as he remembered that his fellow housemates from the shelter worked out there. He walked over to Parker and asked him, "Don't you have a dental appointment in Weston this afternoon?"

"Yes, I do," he said.

"If it's all right with you, I'd like to catch a ride with you and make a cold call while you're at your appointment. What time are you leaving?" he asked.

Parker looked up at the wall clock behind the front desk and said, "In about an hour."

"Great!" Winston said.

"Shit!" Parker mumbled to himself. "I was hoping to make a few side trips on the way back from the dentist for some personal errands but that's now shot to hell since he's coming along."

"It will not be a problem for you if I ride in with you, will it?"

"No!" Parker said. What could he say? Winston was his boss; he could not do that.

"You could just drop me off and pick me up on the way back after your appointment. There's a company I want to check out for potential business and besides that, my roommates, most of them, work there and I'd like to surprise them and see what they do for work."

On the other side of town, LaVonda was just finishing up with her appointments off Commercial Blvd. and was heading west with no clue on where she was going since she rarely came this far north of the county. She noticed a huge sign that read I-75 with an arrow turning to the left that would take her toward Miami or I-75 to the right that would go toward West Palm Beach. Well, she knew she did not want to go to Palm Beach, and she was not sure if there was going to be an exit closer to downtown that would get her back to the shelter.

Not sure what to do, she decided to pull over to the right before she had no choice but to exit onto I-75 in either direction. She pulled off the side of the road into a parking lot of a strip mall and noticed to the left of that a huge building facing the access road of I-75 that turn around and head east back on Commercial Blvd. toward I-95.

What she noticed was the Freeway Shelter for adoptions, pet supplies, grooming, boarding, and more. She pulled into a parking space just out front and shut off her car and got out and walked in to the shelter, heading toward the pet supply section. She remembered that, the dog with her, was just about out of dog food and wanted to get him some chew toys to keep him from chewing on the expensive designer shoes in the shelter's closets that were donated and were for her boarders.

She looked around and was impressed with what she saw from where she stood in the middle of the gift store. The shelter was one of the most state-of-the-art shelters that she had ever seen, and she was very impressed. It was very clean, and the staff was very professional and seemed to cover a lot of services for canine lovers. LaVonda glanced down at her watch and realized what time it was and that she needed to get out of there and head back to the Dixie Arms so she could avoid the afternoon traffic on I-95 before the four o'clock rush hour. She wanted to make sure that Mario had done the inventory as well as the spreadsheet so she could see if she had room for donations possibly coming in later today.

While paying for her dog food and chew toys, she noticed several flyers on the counter with information about the shelter and what services it offered. Now that she had a dog staying on with her at the Dixie, she could always use their services sooner or later. *Why not*, she thought, as she took one of them and then noticed another flyer on the counter that particularly caught her eye. There was going to be a volunteer charity event to raise money for the medical expenses for the canines that were injured by hurricane Alden on the Gulf Coast where their owners could not afford to take care of them financially and needed assistance. She also took one of them as well.

It wouldn't hurt to attend, where she could possibly network with other people in the community who would maybe come to one of her events at the shelter to raise money for the Dixie. Besides, she needed to make an appointment soon for the dog to be groomed and have his anal glands squeezed. He had a habit of scooting across the kitchen floor while she was preparing breakfast for everyone at the shelter before they headed out to work; she did night find that amusing at all.

She was done for the day, running her errands up north, and needed to head back to the Dixie as she pulled out onto Commercial Blvd. and headed east, backtracking the way she came in. She knew for sure it was a guarantee to get back to the shelter with time to kill before rush hour began on the IH.

CHAPTER TWENTY-FOUR

Over in Weston, Parker was en route to his dentist appointment, and Winston was at the Everything Canine Inc., hoping to get some potential business for the hotel. He wanted to see and surprise his roommates and see where they worked, when he ran into Ms. Honeycutt who was standing by the mailbox, getting ready to go back into the building, when she turned around and saw Winston coming up from behind her and asked, "What on earth are you doing way out here?"

"Oh, potential business, and besides, I wanted to see what you and the rest of the gang do out here."

"Come on in and I'll show you around," she said as they entered the office area of the business. Winston saw an office with about a dozen cubicles going down this long room, and there were several offices along the wall. He noticed Antoinette sitting in the first office, snacking on celery sticks while on the computer doing work, and he popped his head in her doorway and said hello! With a surprise on her face, she stood up from behind her desk and walked over to him and gave him a snuggle and a lick on the face.

"What are you doing way out here?" she asked.

Winston told her he caught a ride into Weston with his assistant who was up the street at the dentist. "I wanted to surprise everyone and to give the person in charge of handling overnight stays for salesmen or vendors looking for a place to stay overnight while in Fort Lauderdale some literature on the hotel and its services offered with rates."

Antoinette said she'd be the one who would handle that and to leave it with her. "I'll pass the information on. That's what friends are for, to help one another when they need it." He gave her a snuggle and licked her back.

Ms. Honeycutt, who was waiting for him to give him the grand tour of the building, was freaking out on how they greeted one another with licks.

What in hell nationality does that? Rubbing noses, she heard of, a kiss on both cheeks, she heard of, but licking each other across the face? That was one for the books, and she found it to be rather interesting and was going to have to try that greeting with other next dates or sooner, whichever opportunity came first, hopefully sooner.

"So let me give you the grand tour of the building," she said as she strolled by his side and lead the way. "This is the customer service area where Angela, Bella, Alfie, and I work.

"These cubicles back here are where Lolita, Austin, Kingston, and Clifford from the inventory department all work. The offices along the wall are where Duke, Bailey, Clayton, and Juanita all work and this long desk back here behind inventory is where Gina works. They're all in a staff meeting in the training room right now and the girls from customer service are around here somewhere," she said as she took him through the door in the back of the office area to the break room. "Here they all are!" Lolita was talking to Angela in Spanish once again, just talking a mile a minute, and Ms. Honeycutt could not understand a word they were saying.

Bella was talking to the gentleman who comes once a week to refill the snack machine and was begging him to put more bacon-flavored snacks, as well as more peanut butter-flavored treats, those were her favorites. They noticed Winston immediately and ran over to him and gave him a snuggle and licked him across his face as well. This was it. Ms. Honeycutt couldn't deal with it anymore and said, "Screw it." She walked over to the vending machine and said, "Excuse me, Bella," grabbed the gentleman, and licked his face. The gentleman was horrified and didn't know what to do; he was stunned as Bella looked on and watched Ms. Honeycutt do this. Ms. Honeycutt yelled out, "Yuk, he tastes like anchovies!"

"What did you expect him to taste like?" Bella asked.

"I don't know. You all seem to greet each other in this manner and I thought I'd give it a shot. I don't know what to expect but it was not anchovies! Yuk!"

Bella whispered into her ear and said, "Honey, he's been driving around in the ninety-degree heat in and out of a truck, carrying heavy boxes and sweating. Yeah, he would taste like anchovies!"

The vending supply gentleman quickly locked up the machines, grabbed his hand truck, and dashed out of the break room through the back door that led to the warehouse to his truck on the loading dock and left.

Winston, being a gentleman, got Ms. Honeycutt a glass of water to wash her mouth out, and she said, "I don't know what you all taste when you lick one another's face, but I will never do that again." Now that she got rid of the bad taste in her mouth, she continued with the tour by escorting Winston through the back door of the break room to the warehouse area. Here, she explained to him, was where all the products—from pet beds, cages, and water bowls to leashes and several lines of food products as well as a new line of chewable toys, not to mention several lines of clothing brought in from the West Coast—all are going to be shipped to pet stores and shelters across the country.

"Wow! What a big warehouse," he said. And as he was walking through the warehouse area, he saw Alfie talking to Lucas, in charge of receiving, who was looking for a shipment to come in that needed to be flagged and shipped directly out to a customer in West Palm Beach as soon as it hit the dock. She, too, gave Winston a snuggle and also a lick across his face as Ms. Honeycutt looked on and thought to herself as she shook her head, *I don't get it, I really don't, but whatever floats their boats, more power to them.* Farther back toward the warehouse was the returns area where merchandise is returned to the building from the customers who either cancelled their orders or found damaged or defective products and returned it back for credit on their account.

Austin, who was talking to Bentley and Roscoe as Lucas approached them to see what they were doing in the returns area, looked up and saw Winston heading his way with Ms. Honeycutt and did a full ninety-degree turn for he had seen Winston at the shelter where they both were boarders and rarely spoke because he was shy. He had a crush on Winston and wanted to know more about him but couldn't find the courage to speak to him without turning all the colors in the gay flag. Austin was back there in the returns area being sniffed up one side and down the other by Roscoe as Bentley and Lucas walked by them and told them that they were crossing the line when it came to work ethics and to leave Austin alone and get back to work immediately.

Just then Jesus pulled up in his twenty-foot delivery truck and brought the shipment that Alfie was looking for and helped Lucas unload the shipment and signed for the delivery. Jesus then thanked Lucas for his assistance with helping him, and Lucas commented on how fit he looked and how great he looked in his uniform and wondered if he would be interested in joining his newly formed soccer team he was putting together. Jesus said he didn't play soccer and thanked him for asking. But if Lucas ever had interest in starting a softball team, he could count him in since he liked playing with the bats and balls and catching the fly balls and running around the field so to count him in. "See, that's how I keep in shape," he said to let him know.

"Sure, I'll keep you in mind if ever we decide to make a team together," Lucas said.

"I'll see you around," Jesus said as he headed back to his truck to continue on with making his deliveries.

Lucas headed up to the front office to see Alfie to let her know the shipment had just came in so she could call the rush courier service to come and get the packages that he will put in the will-call area waiting for them and take it to West Palm Beach before five o'clock.

Austin, in the meantime, was trying to get away from Roscoe and Bentley so he could approach Winston and Ms. Honeycutt and sniff him out while trying not to turn into the colors of the gay flag.

Winston was determined to face the facts that he had a crush on Austin as well and wanted to get to know him just as well. Austin had an outgoing personality and was friendly with everyone in the shelter that had his back literally! As Winston nodded his head as he passed Austin heading in the opposite direction, Ms. Honeycutt could pick up on the vibes between them two; after all, she lived in New Orleans and was married to a hairdresser who had plenty of gay clientele, and she suggested that they take it slow and see what happens. "If you two are meant to be together, it would all happen when the time is right."

When they were paged to the front office, Parker was in the lobby, waiting to take Winston back to the hotel.

Mario was just completing the spreadsheet when LaVonda came back into the shelter, carrying several bags with her as she placed them on the sofa next to Freeway who started snooping through the bags because he could smell the dog food and came up with a chew toy. Both Mario and LaVonda chuckled as they watched on. He was so friggin' cute to watch. "Well, how did you make out with the inventory?" she asked.

"Great!" Mario replied. "There's plenty of room in the closets for more clothes."

Just then her cell phone rang, and it was the woman who wanted to check in and see if she was still interested in accepting her donations. LaVonda told her that it'd be fine for her to stop by on her way downtown this evening and that she'd be there all night and to take her time. LaVonda thanked the woman and told her that she looked forward to meeting her this evening.

Mario said that he needed to leave because he had someplace to go before he reported to the sheriff 's office later for his shift and asked if she was fine with the spreadsheet he just put up on her computer. She looked over his shoulder and said, "It looks perfect! Great job! Now get out of here so you can run your errand. Go!"

"Thanks!" Mario replied as he walked over and patted the dog on the head, who was in heaven with the new chew toy he just received. "I'll see you later," he said as Freeway stopped for a moment from chewing his new toy and let out a loud bark as if to say good-bye to him back. Mario said good night to LaVonda, but in the back of his mind, he couldn't forget what he had found on her computer and wondered what she was up to.

"Mario, by the way, before you go, I want to run something by you," she said as he was getting ready to go out the front door.

"What?"

"I picked up this flyer from where I got the dog his food and chew toy"—she handed it to Mario—"and was wondering if you would like to join me when they have this charity event in a few weeks for a good cause, and besides, we could network at the same time for possible contacts to raise money for the Dixie Arms."

"Wow!"

"What?" she asked him. Mario said that this was right near the place he stakes out at night on duty and in the vicinity where he found the dog as he looked over at Freeway who was enjoying his new toy from LaVonda, which sent off a light bulb in LaVonda's head who now had the first piece of the puzzle on why he has been acting the way he was when around Ms. Applegate each morning. Could he have come from that shelter? Did he escape from there?

"Sure, I'll go with you. It should be fun," he told her. Mario knew that he needed to spend more time with her, so what better way than to spend more time with her as possible so he could look into what she was up to with the information he discovered on her computer.

"We can take the dog with us!" LaVonda said. They both held a grin on their faces, for now they both had a mystery on their hands to solve.

CHAPTER TWENTY-FIVE

They day finally arrived for the volunteer charity event at the Freeway Shelter.

LaVonda was sipping her coffee in her office and writing out a check for five hundred dollars to donate to the shelter while waiting for Mario to come in from getting off his shift from the sheriff's department.

Mario was at the sheriff's office in the middle of an intense conversation with a fellow officer coming on duty about possibly knowing information on someone who had committed identity theft and fraud, and he was told by his fellow officer that he needed to do the right thing and bring them in for questioning and to face the consequences to their actions if they are true.

This put a knot in Mario's stomach like he never felt before. He was going to be sick if he goes through with bringing this person in because he was fond of her and couldn't believe this was happing right under his eyes. This was not going to be an easy decision to make first thing this morning; he just wanted to end his shift and forget he ever brought this up with a fellow officer.

He was expected to be at the Dixie Arms within three hours to meet up with LaVonda and the dog and go with them to the Freeway Shelter to do some volunteer work this morning and at the same time do some networking for the Dixie Arms.

Mario thanked his fellow officer for his advice and told him he would take it into consideration regarding the matter and would keep him posted on what he was going to do.

Just then Mario's cell phone started to ring as he was saying good-bye to his fellow officer, and he wished him a nice day when he answered his phone and heard LaVonda's cheery voice on the other end say, "Good morning."

"Good morning to you!" he replied back.

"I thought I'd check in and see if you were on your way over to the Dixie Arms to go with me to the Freeway Shelter to do our volunteer work this morning and do some networking at the same time."

"Yeah I'm just leaving the station now and I'll need to stop by my place first for a quick shower and change clothes and I should be there within the hour."

"Great! I'll see you soon then," LaVonda told him as they both hung up their phones at the same time. LaVonda heard a bit of a commotion coming from the foyer and stood up from behind her desk to see what was going on. She called out to Ms. Applegate, "HEY! HEY! HEY! What's going on out there?" It was Freeway trying to hump Ms. Applegate's legs again, and he tore a hole in her panty hose, and Ms. Honeycutt was laughing at her and Freeway and did nothing to assist her; she just stood there laughing at them both to the point that she laughed so hard, she wet herself, and there was no time to go back upstairs to change into fresh panties, or she would miss her bus to work. She was going to have to ride the bus all wet.

As the table turned, it was Ms. Applegate laughing now because Freeway took his attention away from her and toward Ms. Honeycutt who was now the center of Freeway's attention, and she was not amused at all. Freeway was trying to stick his head up her dress because of the smell of pee. LaVonda screamed at Freeway and told him to come into her office where she was standing and said, "Get over here right now or you won't be going for a ride with me later." He looked at her with his brown eyes and got down on his four paws and put his head between his front paws as if to say "I'm sorry." This put a smile on LaVonda's face because she couldn't resist how adorable he was.

By now all the houseguests from the Dixie had all filed out one by one like they do daily to catch the bus on the corner, and once again Freeway dashed over to the window and stood on his hind legs and started barking until Ms. Applegate was out of sight. This really baffled LaVonda, and she wanted to know more on why he behaved this way. She wasn't the only one with a secret. Freeway had one of his own too. She only had to figure it out.

Well, just as the bus turned the corner, Mario was parking out front of the Dixie Arms, and Freeway saw him and continued to bark as he jumped down from the window sill and dashed to the front door to meet him. "Hey boy,. how are you today?" Mario said as he patted Freeway on the head as he jumped up and down on Mario's legs as if to say hi and to greet him.

"Good morning," LaVonda said as she came around the corner to see what caused Freeway to dash out of the office. "I thought you were heading home first to change?" she asked him.

"Yeah, I thought about it but decided to come right from work. I had a backpack in my truck with some jeans and polo shirts for emergencies in case I get asked to go for drinks with anyone from the station after our shift."

"Great then," she replied. "You can go upstairs and change and if like can take a shower."

"No shower, I'll be fine."

"Would you like me to get you some coffee and some breakfast before we head out?" LaVonda asked.

"No breakfast, just coffee please."

"Will hazelnut be okay?"

"That's fine, sounds perfect," he replied as he headed upstairs to change out of his uniform with Freeway in tow.

Meantime the crew were on the bus on the way to work in Weston as Juanita reminded Bailey that they had the volunteer charity at the Freeway Shelter today, and he had forgotten to tell everyone that they would be all going together in a shuttle bus from the shelter.

Donald made a call back to the shelter from the New Orleans Airport, letting his staff know that he was on his way back from helping rebuild the shelter down there and asked that someone from the shelter take care of getting volunteers to the charity event by picking them up and bringing them back, which he made prior to today's charity event when he called Duke and made the arrangements to see if the associates from Everything Canine Inc. would be interested.

Just then Bailey stood up in the aisle of the bus and made an announcement to the group from the Dixie Arms about the event as they all listened to him. He said, "It was just brought to my attention by Juanita, which I had forgotten about that today was going to be the day of the charity event at the Freeway Shelter and you were all volunteering your time to this for a few hours or so depending on the turnout they receive at the shelter." As the bus rounded the corner near the building, there was the shuttle bus just parked out in front of the building, waiting to take them to the charity event. "Just give me a few minutes," Bailey asked the shuttle driver who was Martin from the shelter, who was the designated driver of the shuttle bus that would be in charge of taking them back after the event. Bailey said to Martin, "Just give me a few minutes to run and check on everything in the building and then we can leave." There was going to be a skeleton crew working today, and he wanted to make sure that all was covered.

He then pulled Ms. Honeycutt out of the line from them boarding the shuttle bus and asked her to go inside and take care of that smell that was coming from her. "Great!" Ms. Honeycutt had time to run into the office and try to get rid of the smell she had been dragging along with her from the time she left the Dixie Arms. He could see why now; she was sitting all by herself in front of the bus with the seats all around her as far back as three rows empty. She smiled and waddled into the building with Bailey holding the door open for her as well as his nose for it was unbearable to deal with.

Just as Ms. Honeycutt reached the office and Bailey just ahead of her heading to his office, she noticed a broken bag of cat litter that was in the hallway near the ladies' room used to absorb liquid spills in the warehouse when something breaks, to soak up the liquid and smell since it was pine scented. She grabbed the bag and snuck into the ladies' room where she grabbed a handful of cat litter and lifted up her skirt and put it into her panties, but not before she realized it was a clumping formula and made it worse. She heard Bailey call out to her from the other side of the ladies' room door to let her know that the shuttle bus was leaving and she needed to step on it or wouldn't be able to go. "Oh hell!" she said as she fumbled around, trying to get it out of her panties, which now was worse than before. She jumped up and down to get rid of it and decided to slip her panties off and throw them in the trash can and go commando with the pine scent now reeking from her instead of pee. She yelled out to Bailey, "Just a minute!"

"Okay," he replied back. "We'll be on the shuttle bus and leaving in a couple of minutes with or without you," he said as she was washing her hands and grabbing a paper towel to wipe them. She waddled back out to the shuttle worse than she came off the bus as. Everyone was aboard and waiting for Ms. Honeycutt when Gina noticed her coming down the walkway toward the shuttle walking funny.

"There she is!" Gina yelled out. Those sitting next to the window looked out and saw this fox peeking out from the bushes from in front of the building, which run over and attacked Ms. Honeycutt; it has been seen living on the grounds and seen numerous times in the early mornings running across the parking lot toward the field out back. She screamed; as Martin saw this, he immediately jumped out of the driver's seat of the shuttle bus and came to her rescue.

"God bless you!" she said to Martin as he tried to kick the fox away from her, and he got her onto the shuttle bus without a scratch whatsoever. Ms. Applegate and Juanita asked if she was okay as the rest of the group looked on from their seats. Most of them were stunned because they just witnessed the attack of Ms. Honeycutt by a fox. What on earth just happened? And several of them came up to her from their seats to see if she was okay, and they could smell the pine scent coming from her who-who!

"Damn, you need to take care of that as soon as we get to the shelter because that scent on you is what caused the attack of the fox."

"I will do that first thing when I get off this bus," she said as they all sat back down in their seats, laughing their butts off.

"Welcome to Fort Lauderdale" was the first sign that Donald and Ms. Kitty saw as they came through the airport terminal from their gate after landing.

"Home," Donald said out loud.

"Thank God," came from Ms. Kitty's mouth as they walked up the ramp together to the main airport, looking for the closest exit for the parking garage. They just wanted to get the car and head away from the airport since it was a nightmare with all the new construction going on out there.

They couldn't wait to get back to normal on home turf after spending weeks away from the Freeway Shelter and at the same time make sure that everything they had planned for the charity event, which was done by phone weeks ago by Donald and Ms. Kitty, was on schedule. They planned it as they were finishing up things in New Orleans, getting the shelter up and running again, bigger and better than before. It was going to be a long day for them both, but it was going to be well worth it. Once they found their car from the parking garage, they hoped that it would start because it sat so long in the long-term parking without ever running for weeks and it would not be a good sign.

Ms. Kitty crossed her fingers as Donald put his car keys into the ignition, and with a few turns, it started right up. Both of them at the same time let out a sigh of relief as they pulled out of the parking garage and went down the ramp toward the gate to pay the charges for long-term parking before they hit the highway just outside of the airport.

Donald turned on the car radio so he could hear what the traffic report was for this time of morning since it was just approaching rush hour in the morning for people going to work, and he needed to drive about forty-five minutes to get to the shelter, which was on the other side of town and north. The radio station said there was a steady drive going north on 95 and a little slow going west on the 595, where he needed to go due to construction but if he took the access road to the 595 could miss it, which was his plans.

The weather report was just coming on after the traffic report, and it was going to reach the mid eighties today, and there was no sign of rain in the forecast. It was going to be a nice day for the charity event, which was going to start at 10:00 AM, and it was now 8:45 AM by his watch. And he said, "Thank God for early flights"; otherwise, they would have missed the start of the event and wouldn't have been there to welcome the volunteers and make sure everything was in place and ready to go.

As they exited off 95, heading west on the 595, Donald asked Ms. Kitty to keep a lookout for breaking taillights from cars that would give them a heads-up on the construction area they would be approaching, which they heard about on the radio. Then he could avoid that construction area and look for the next exit and get on and head north, which would take them to the Freeway Shelter, which could be seen from I-75 at the Commercial Blvd. exit.

Just then Ms. Kitty said, "I see break lights ahead up our way." So Donald who was looking for the next exit and noticed Nob Hill exit coming up on the 595 decided to exit off there. He knew he only had about half a mile to go because it would then turn into I-75 just minutes away, and by his watch they made it in good timing; it was now 9:10 AM.

"Only took twenty-five minutes from the airport to get here so we should be at the shelter by nine thirty," he told Ms. Kitty, "and we'll still have a half an hour to go to the actual start of the charity event."

"Great driving!" she complimented Donald on his driving.

"Not a problem. I'm used to this area. I know it like the back of my hands with shortcuts and all." As they turned onto the I-75 heading north, they both noticed three different local television crew trucks heading south past them one behind the other.

Both wondered out loud if they had come from that area across the access road just outside the shelter and on Commercial Blvd. It was all over the news that there was a run-down and falling apart old power plant that was uninhabitable, and the environmentalists were boycotting and picketing to have it torn down and removed from there to protect the wildlife out there in the everglades. "It was all over the news prior to us going to New Orleans," Ms. Kitty said as she reached into the backseat and pulled out her laptop and looked for the three television stations online to see if any of them had information on why they were out this way.

"Good idea," Donald told her. She turned on her laptop and searched the Internet, found one of the televisions' Web sites, and pulled it up on her laptop, which when it downloaded to her laptop had flashing across the Web site, "Breaking News: Everglades Power Plant Ordered to Be Removed!"

She clicked on the news article that produced a short paragraph; it said, "The condemned power plant in west Broward in the everglades will be torn down by the county in a matter of weeks. Due to the picket lines and boycotting over at the new power plant in Port Everglades, this has caused the county and state agencies to take notice of the situation and decide to have it removed soon. More news to follow on this decision at five o'clock."

"Well, looks like that was it after all."

Donald mentioned, "I'm glad to hear that because all the news that was covering that situation and it being so close to the shelter kind of concerned me a bit."

"Why?" Ms. Kitty asked.

"Well, with it being so close to the Freeway Shelter and people not wanting to get involved would have kept the community from coming out to this side of town and away from the shelter and cause less adoptions and not to mention boarding, and the other services we offer at the shelter."

"Yeah, you do have a point," Ms. Kitty said, "but on the other hand, it could also be good."

"What do you mean?" Donald asked.

"Well, those folks that did come out this way to see what the commotion was about with the power plant would stumble across the shelter as they exited off and onto the I-75 and would then see the shelter and stop in and check it out. It could be one of those fifty-fifty chances if you look at it that way."

"You're right too!" Donald replied back as he also mentioned in the same breath, "I see the Commercial Blvd. exit just ahead. We're almost there!"

Mean while, Mario, LaVonda, and Freeway—who by the way had his head sticking out the sunroof of LaVonda's car as she held on to him with Mario in the driver's seat—were on their way to the shelter. He offered to drive his car, but LaVonda was not comfortable riding in a patrol car, which brought back memories from her past of being in one and handcuffed and which was now parked in front of the Dixie Arms.

It was nice having someone else drive for a change so she could sit back and enjoy the ride for once instead of driving someone else around, but having to hold on to this dogs hindquarter as he hung his head out of the sunroof of her car, enjoying the warm breeze and exhaust from the traffic, which was not as bad as she thought. She just loved being around him no matter how crazy she thought he was. After all, she had a houseful of crazies these days staying with her, so what was one more, but at least this one didn't talk back.

Mario told her to get the dog down from the sunroof now that the traffic was moving quicker and that he was going to be picking up the pace and exiting soon onto I-75 north. So with that in mind, LaVonda said to Freeway, "Come on down here," as she tugged on his hindquarter and mentioned she had a treat for him. The word "TREAT" brought him down as she directed him to the backseat and pulled out a dog bone from her purse and threw it on the backseat for him to chew on.

"We should be there in about fifteen minutes," Mario said to LaVonda.

"That quick?" she said.

"See this stretch of I-75 that we're on right now? I work this area nightly and just up ahead on Commercial Blvd. is where we will be getting off. This area is where I found this dog," he said as he pointed into the backseat with his thumb. "He was wondering the access road up here late at night, not to mention all those other folks now staying with you at the shelter that I brought downtown to the Dixie Arms. Each one of them came from this area as well, naked and disoriented. You know the ones that you found jobs for and located their identities." She just sat still, staring out the passenger's side window, busting into sweat in her seat and just about to pee herself, hoping he would change the subject. She thought to herself, *Oh shit! I think he's on to me. Think fast! Think fast!*

LaVonda just then heard the dog in the backseat coughing and turned away from the window and looked into to the backseat, trying to avoid Mario, and called the dog to her lap and talked to him and asked him as she patted him down if he was okay.

"Well, here we are," Mario said as they pulled into the parking lot of the Freeway Shelter. *Saved by the bell*, LaVonda said to herself as she undid her seat belt.

Mario shut the car off and undid his seat belt and opened the car door just about ready to step out when Freeway leaped out from LaVonda's lap and dashed across his lap and out of the car. Freeway ran over to the shuttle bus parked a few spaces away and started sniffing around the bus and then dashed up to the front door of the shelter and started to bark as if to say, "Let me in! Let me in!"

Mario ran over to him and put his leash on him with LaVonda only a few feet behind him, wiping the sweat off her face from a laced handkerchief she pulled from her purse from avoiding a sticky situation she was going to be in if she hadn't turned her attention to the dog coughing in the backseat. She reached Mario who had just finished putting the leash on Freeway, waiting for her so they could all go in together for the charity event and opening the front door and holding Freeway by his side and opening the door for LaVonda to go ahead of him, being the gentleman that he was. Mario had almost fell on top of LaVonda as she walked past him because Freeway ran past her with his leash toward the left side of the shelter sniffing his way toward two double doors; with Mario in tow right behind him.

LaVonda walked over to the front desk and asked the young lady working behind the desk where everyone who was volunteering for today's charity was to go. She was directed to go to the right of the building through the two double doors to the courtyard for further instructions from the owner of the shelter who was sponsoring the charity event, which was Donald. She also asked for directions to the women's room to freshen up and was directed to the left side of the building where Mario and Freeway were already standing by the double doors just on the right side. "You will see it," said the receptionist. She thanked her and headed over that way.

Mario was still trying to calm Freeway down, who was jumping up and down at the double doors and barking. LaVonda asked Mario as she approached him what was going on with the dog, and he said, "I have no clue. It must be these doors."

"Great! We'll soon find out because I have to go to the ladies' room and it's just beyond these doors so we'll see what's got him in an uproar." Mario, being a gentleman, opened one of the double doors for her, at the same time holding even tighter on to the leash. LaVonda thanked him as she walked just past him as he then followed behind her with Freeway in tow, and went went directly to the ladies' room door as well. Freeway came to a complete stop and started sniffing the door; then the barking began.

"What is up with this dog?" Mario asked.

"Let me have the leash," LaVonda asked him. "I'll take him in with me to the ladies' room. You just wait right here and I'll be back shortly," she told him as they entered the ladies' room.

"What is it with this ladies' room that has this dog so worked up?" Mario asked himself.

CHAPTER TWENTY-SIX

Over in the courtyard on the other side of the building, the volunteers stood around chatting with each other, waiting to hear from the sponsor of the event to speak, who was just minutes away from speaking as he was freshening up in his office just doors away from the ladies' room on the other side of the shelter. Donald had just stepped off of a plane and wanted to brush his teeth and change shirts before meeting everyone who was volunteering for today's event and who were waiting for him in the courtyard.

He just wanted a moment to himself to enjoy a decent cup of coffee—because the cup of coffee he got on the airplane was weak—before meeting all the volunteers who turned out this morning.

Donald's moment was just about to end as he took his last sip of coffee and proceeded out of his office and down the hall, passing Mario who had his back toward him and was speaking to a volunteer. Mario was killing time, waiting for LaVonda to exit the ladies' room with Freeway. Mario was the arresting officer who had put Donald in jail some time ago for animal abuse and DUI.

Mario would soon find out that he would be volunteering for the same guy who totally changed his life around by building this shelter. Ms. Kitty was in the front office area, talking to a volunteer who had questions on what she would be doing today, and noticed Donald walk past the receptionist's desk toward the courtyard, who looked preoccupied with something on his mind. She politely excused herself away from the volunteer and politely asked one of the staff members to assist this volunteer by getting her to set up behind the table out front in the lobby area and have her give out the raffle tickets for a trip to Orlando for two and five hundred dollars cash spending money and to please make sure everyone signs the guest book.

Ms. Kitty called out to Donald as he turned around before entering the courtyard, and he looked in her direction as she approached him and said, "It looks like it's going to be a good turnout after all and it hasn't even started yet."

"Yes, it's going to be a good day I can feel it. Are you all right?" Ms. Kitty asked.

"Yes!" he replied. "Just a bit nervous. This is my first time addressing a crowd of people."

"Would you like me to stand by you and start off with thanking everyone for coming and a brief speech on why we are doing this today and turn it over to you to finish off from there?"

"You would do that for me?" Donald asked.

"Of course!" she replied. "I have public speaking under my belt and it won't be a problem at all. Now do you feel a little better?"

"Much better," he replied. "Thank you for doing this for me."

"No problem. We are a team and we will work together and make this a day you will not forget." As they took center court together, Ms. Kitty took the microphone first and thanked everyone for volunteering their time to come out to the shelter to raise money for a good cause. She then introduced Donald as the event sponsor and owner of the shelter as she passed the microphone over to him who was still a bit nervous by the cracking of his voice but was able to pull it together within minutes and was fine.

Donald went on to say why he held this charity event and what it stood for by helping all the canines with medical attention, food, and rebuilding shelters. He went into a brief scenario of his and Ms. Kitty's recent trip to New Orleans and getting back this very morning, describing what they saw and how bad it was over there due to the hurricane and ending with them leaving there knowing it was much better than before. The applause from the courtyard could be heard as far as the parking lot, and everyone gathered after the applause around Donald and Ms. Kitty and said it was a wonderful thing that they've done and wished more people would be as caring as they were and that being here today volunteering would hopefully change all that.

With that, Donald made an announcement to the volunteers: "Would everyone please go to your stations that we have set up throughout the shelter and do your very best to be as informative as you can be by handing out the pamphlets that are at each station describing the areas they are in and the purpose for it. Try to collect as much or as little money they can give you or something, cash or check, into the donation boxes we have set up at each one so we can help those in need on the Gulf Coast."

Mean while, Mario was still waiting outside the ladies' room for LaVonda who seemed to have gotten lost in the ladies' room and had not come out yet. He politely asked the woman he was speaking to if she could pop in there and see if a woman wearing a purple sweater and jeans with a black-and-white Border collie on a leash was still in there. She said she would be obliged to check and would be right out. As the woman entered the ladies' room, she saw LaVonda talking to an elderly woman who smelled like pine scent trying to wash the smell off of her with a roll of paper towels and soap in a stall, and the dog was just peeking his head under all the other stalls to see who was in there.

She came out and reported this to Mario who looked more confused than ever hearing that. He opened the door slightly and yelled into the ladies' room, "LaVonda, what are you doing in there?"

She yelled back, "I am in here with Ms. Honeycutt who rather got herself in a bit of a jam and I am trying to help her." With that bit of information, he could not wait to hear the rest of the story. Ms. Honeycutt was a hoot in the first place; who knew what kind of mess she had gotten herself into. Within seconds, they both came out from the ladies' room.

Ms. Honeycutt was trying to be all proper but kept fidgeting with her skirt with just a hint of pine scent coming from her as she said hello and walked right past him. Mario had no clue how really crazy she was until he got the long version from LaVonda about the cat litter and the fox, and he just busted out laughing so hard that several people looked over at them as he turned beet red from embarrassment.

"That's way too funny," he said as he envisioned the fox attacking her. He looked down to see where the dog was, when he noticed he was not with them as they left the ladies' room.

"Oh hell! I forgot the dog. I will be right back," LaVonda said as she went back into the ladies' room to retrieve him and found him crouched on his stomach with his head under the last stall, looking up at someone occupying the stall. She walked over to him, grabbed him by his leash, and dragged him out of there. She then gave the leash to Mario, who was waiting outside, and said, "You take him!" while mentioning in the same sentence that he was being naughty and bothering someone in the stall. The three of them stepped away from the ladies' room door and began to walk around the shelter to see what part they could do to help raise money and do some networking of their own, with Freeway in tow who kept looking back at the ladies' room door every chance he could until it was out of sight. Just at that moment, the bathroom stall opened, and out came Ms. Applegate who was the one who was occupying that stall that had kept all of Freeway's attention.

She walked over to the bathroom sink to wash her hands and within seconds from washing her hands started feeling a bit funny, a little light-headed; her vision became blurry, and then everything that once was colored had turned to black and white.

She rubbed her eyes a few times to focus; when she looked into the mirror, she saw that her hands started to grow fur and shrank. Within seconds, she had turned back into the Border r collie Sheba, Freeway's friend and companion from Texas.

Sheba was now on all four paws and was running around in circles, yapping in the ladies' room. Ms. Kitty who just had to make a pit stop to the ladies' room came upon this border collie alone and crying and picked her up and carried her out and brought her over to Donald and said, "Look what I just found in the ladies' room."

"What?" he asked.

"This!" she said as she stood there cuddling the Border collie in her arms.

With amazement written all over his face, he said, "Is she from here? Did someone just abandon her in the ladies' room?"

"I do not know but I am going to check with the staff to see if anyone recalls seeing anyone coming in with a border collie today."

"Okay, let me take her." She passed her to him. "I'll just put her in my office till later and in the meantime we'll keep our eyes and ears open in case someone lost her and we'll both take turns checking in on her to make sure she's okay." And he headed toward his office to get her settled in and gave her a bowl of fresh water and dog treat.

The charity event was going well; within hours they had a packed shelter, the donation boxes seem to be filling up, and even some folks who stopped by ended up adopting some of the canines that were on property that had been there for weeks.

People were enjoying the free hot dogs and burgers, and the kids loved the face painting and the clowns and magic shows. Then Mario started asking LaVonda about her houseguests that he noticed were all scattered throughout the shelter, which she had just found out when she ran into Ms. (Pine Scent) Honeycutt in the women's room.

They were volunteering their time as a group from the Everything Canine Inc. office in Weston, which the shelter offered to pick them up and shuttle them back when it was over. "Okay! That explains them being here. Now explain how they got their identities."

She stood frozen. She did not know what to do or what to say as she tried to walk away, avoiding the subject. As he reached out to grab her by her arm, someone stepped in between him and her and spilled their cold drink all over him. The person was no other than Ms. Honeycutt who stumbled across them, not paying attention on where she was going, and who apologized for the accident. Mario accepted her apology and asked her to take the leash that he was holding with Freeway until he came back from the men's room from wiping up the spill on him. Saved by the bell once again!

LaVonda said to Ms. Honeycutt, "I'm going over to the other side of the shelter if he asks when he gets back. You stay here with the dog"—who was sniffing her skirt—"until then and stay out of trouble if you can."

Oh, how much trouble can I get into here, she thought to herself, trying to shoo the dog away from her skirt sniffing. Mario who was in the men's room trying to remove the stain from his shirt had company shortly in there with him. One by one the stalls were filling up, and he couldn't help but notice that it was the guys from the Dixie Arms, the same guys he brought down to the shelter over a period of time to LaVonda, whom he found wondering the street just outside the shelter on the access road. That's odd.

He listened in on the conversation between the stalls and realized that they all had eaten hot dogs and hamburgers and it did not agree with them. *Holy shit, I'm not going to be eating any of the culinary from here*, he thought, as he dashed out of the men's room quickly, running into Ms. Honeycutt who was standing just outside, fighting off Freeway who was still sniffing her skirt.

"Looks like you got most of the stain out of your shirt," she said as he grabbed the leash from her and took the dog who just kept on poking her skirt with his nose.

"Yes, I was able to get most of it out," he told her. Mario wanted to know if she had eaten any of the hot dogs or hamburgers they were serving at the event.

"No, but lunch does sound good about right now." At the same time they were chatting, the guys who were vacating the men's room stalls left the stalls one by one, and they walked over to the sink and began washing their hands. Every one of the guys had gotten the same reaction as did Ms. Applegate in the ladies' room.

Within seconds after washing their hands, the guys, too, started feeling a bit funny, a little light-headed at first; then their vision became blurry, and everything that was colored to them turned black and white. Each one did the same as Ms. Applegate and rubbed their eyes to see what was causing the blurry vision and noticed, too, from the mirror they were standing in front of that their hands started to grow fur and shrank as well. They, too, had turned back into canines.

Puzzled by Mario's question if she had eaten any of hot dogs or hamburgers, Ms. Honeycutt wanted to know why he would ask her that question.

"Well, it's a long story," he told her, "but trust me, don't eat the meat." Then all of a sudden, this horrific smell started to come down the hall from around the men's room area, and everyone that was standing in the hallway made a mad dash for the courtyard area or closest exit outside.

"What is that smell?" Ms. Honeycutt asked Mario.

"Well, let's put it this way. If you eat the hot dogs or hamburgers here, you will have more problems to deal with other than that pine scent which is more refreshing right now," he answered as he made a quick dash out to the courtyard with Freeway in tow. Mario had mentioned to Jessie that he overheard a conversation from within the men's room about the food and it concerned him and wanted Jessie to check it out as the smell came down the hallway toward them.

"Thanks for the heads-up!" And Mario continued his way to the courtyard with Freeway.

"Oh Hell No!" Jessie said to himself. "I'm not going to deal with the men's room. It's bad enough I have to deal with dog shit from time to time but men's shit, no way!" And he looked around for Donald to deal with it since it was his shelter. Jessie spotted Donald standing by the grooming area of the shelter, talking to a guest, and he noticed Jessie pointing at him with his finger to come see him. Donald excused himself from the guest he was speaking to and walked over to Jessie who told him about the commotion. "I hope you don't mind but you're coming too!" As they reached the men's room, they both heard a lot of barking coming from the other side of the door.

They both looked at each other, puzzled, and went in, with Donald leading the way. There was a faint smell in the air, but that was to be expected coming from a men's room. They checked all the stalls; they were fine. As they went around the corner to check the other side, they found eleven canines huddled in a corner; some were barking, and some were whining. "What on earth!" Donald said out loud.

Jessie bent down to see them all, and they all got up and jumped on him and started licking him. It was a moment that Donald enjoyed seeing, the canines giving affection to Jessie by trying to lick him. There was a mixture of breeds in that corner of the men's room, which consisted of a black cocker spaniel, a tan Labrador, a black and brown beagle, a golden doodle, two boxers, a St. Bernard, a Shar-Pei, a Doberman, a golden retriever, and finally a salt-and-pepper miniature schnauzer.

"This is pretty freaky," Donald mentioned to Jessie who was trying to get up from the floor of the men's room while dogs were all over him. "Well, it seems like this is the second time today that we found a canine in a restroom."

"What?" Jessie asked.

"Ms. Kitty found a black-and-white Border collie in the ladies' room earlier which is in my office right now. I'll go get some leashes from the back room," Donald said, "and then we can bring them over to the boarding area until we can find out how they got in here. Just stay in here with them and I'll be right back." Jessie was being pummeled by dogs of all sizes in the men's room.

"I'm not going anywhere especially with this St. Bernard on my chest."

Meanwhile LaVonda was playing hide-and-seek around the shelter trying to avoid Mario and his questions about the boarders staying on at the Dixie Arms and their identities. "I need to go figure out what to say to him before he's on to me. I have been able to avoid that conversation twice this morning but the third time is out for me, and I will no doubt be going down and probably downtown as well.

"Hello girls! How are you today?" LaVonda asked.

"Oh, I am doing just fine," replied Juanita, as she was walking by with Gina, Alfie, and Antoinette who were looking for the ladies' room. "Do you happen to know where it is?"

"Yes, I'll walk you over there. I was there earlier and found Ms. Pine Scent in there freshening up." And they held back the smirk on their faces.

"Oh, you mean Foxy," Gina said as she laughed.

"You're mean," said Alfie. "That was not nice, Gina. You'll pay for that remark one day."

"Just ignore her, Gina," said Antoinette. "She's just mad because she had to come here today and she's leaving here smelling like a dog!"

And Juanita busted into laughter. "Be nice, be nice. This is a charity event for canines not cats!"

"Well, there's the ladies' room. It's just over yonder on the right-hand side."

"Thank you, LaVonda, for showing us the way," Juanita replied.

"You're welcome," she replied back. And the girls went in to the ladies' room, and just as they went in as women, they would be coming out as canines just like Ms. Applegate, now Sheba. Within seconds from washing their hands, they started feeling a bit funny, a little light-headed; then their visions went blurry, and then everything that used to be colored had now turned to black and white. And as they rubbed their eyes, they also noticed that they, too, were growing fur on their hands as they shrank. Juanita was now an older blonde cocker spaniel, Gina was a blonde Chow Chow, Alfie had become a white Bichon frise, and Antoinette was now a blonde Afghan hound. As Gina, Alfie, and Juanita lay on the floor in the ladies' room, waiting for someone to come, Antoinette went from stall to stall, drinking toilet water for she was very thirsty.

"Eww," said Alfie. "That's disgusting."

"Oh, shut up. It's not like you didn't drink from a toilet bowl before. And don't try to hide it."

"Quiet," said Juanita. "I hear voices coming from the other side of the ladies' room from that other entrance on the other side."

"Look," said Gina. "It's Lolita, Bella, and Angela heading our way."

"OH my god!" said Angela. "They have dogs in the ladies' room."

Lolita said, "I don't think they belong in here," and they went over to the counter and brushed their hair.

Antoinette heard their voices and came out from one of the stalls where she was still drinking toilet water and noticed the three of them standing by the sink. She decided to jump up on Lolita first to keep her from turning on the faucet and then she jumped up on Bella and finally Angela. The three of them yelled at Antoinette to get down, in the process of being jumped on by her who had gotten wet paw prints all over their blouses. One by one they turned on the water faucet in front of them to dampen the towels lying on the counter to try to wash off the wet paw prints off their blouses. Gina, Alfie, and Juanita who were shaking in the corner covered their eyes with their paws and then heard little yaps seconds later.

"Oh my god" said Antoinette. "Look they turned into Chihuahuas, two short-haired ones and one long-haired one. Now what are we going to do to try to get out of here? These three little rats aren't going to be able to help get us out of here now."

"Who you calling rats?" said Lolita.

"I have an idea," said Gina. "We can flush them down the toilet and they can cause a flood in the ladies' room and then someone would come when they saw the water coming out from under the door."

"Oh no, I don't like water," said Lolita.

"I can't swim," said Bella. "I had to ride over on my cousin's back to get here from Mexico."

Angela said, "I'm not afraid. I will do whatever it takes to get us out of here."

"God bless you," said Alfie.

"Bless this," said Angela as she turned around for Alfie to see her butt. "I don't see you doing anything, to try to get us out of here."

"I never!"

"Yeah, and it shows," says Gina, "because if you did you wouldn't be so uppity."

"Just because you're a hussy doesn't mean we all have to be," Alfie replied back.

"Did she just call me a husky or hussy?" Gina asked.

All at once they said, "Husky!" even though they all looked at each other and knew she said "hussy."

"Girls, girls," said Juanita, "we have to all get along. We need to find a way out of here. No more fighting please."

Gina replied, "Oh shut up, you old drunk."

"Who are you calling a drunk?" Alfie asked.

"Juanita," said Gina. "I know you are too. Don't even bother hiding it now."

"What are you talking about?"

"That book you're always carrying around which you say is your holy book has a hole in it that's hiding that flask filled with Jim Beam."

"How do you know that?" Alfie asked.

"We have our sources but I'll give you a clue," Gina said. "She has a new nickname and it's called Foxy!"

"Oh, that miserable old goat couldn't keep a secret if her life depended on it," Alfie said.

"Enough is enough," said Antoinette. "We need to find a way out of here. Enough with the bickering. Concentrate. What can we do?"

Just then Ms. Kitty was making her rounds to make sure that there were no more dogs in the restrooms. She had heard about the eleven in the men's room and decided to check and see if it had happened again. As she checked the ladies' room once again, she found seven more dogs in the ladies' room. "How can this be happening?" she asked herself. She then told the canines to stay as they rushed to her. "Stay! I'll be right back," she said as they looked at her and tilted their heads to the side. Ms. Kitty turned around and headed back out of the ladies' room, hoping to flag down a volunteer in the hallway to come and to stand guard by the door while she went for help. "Do not let anyone in or anything out here," she said as she ran down the hall, looking for Donald who was somewhere within the shelter.

Donald was just about to enter his office to check on the Border collie when he received a tap on his shoulder from Mario who said, "Excuse me, but are you Donald?"

He turned around to see who it was tapping him on the shoulder. "Yes, I am," he said.

"Well, do you remember me?" Mario asked.

"Yes, how could I forget? You're the arresting officer that had taken me in a while back for DUI and animal abuse."

"Yes, I am," Mario replied. "I thought that I recognized you earlier and wanted to find you because I believe we have some unfinished business."

"Hang on just a moment. What unfinished business are you talking about?" Donald asked. "Let me tell you something," Donald told Officer Mario. "I have none whatsoever unfinished business with the sheriff's department after going through that night, which I would very much like to forget.

"I first have cleaned up my act with the drinking under control as for; the animal abuse charge that was brought against me, it was covered by me serving community service at the pound. Since that awful ordeal, I came into a large amount of money and built this shelter, which you are standing in right now, and more. So I'm pretty sure I have no unfinished business with you or the sheriff's department. I've been clean."

"Well, not really," Mario said as he tugged on the leash that he was holding and pulled out from behind him while saying, "I believe I have something that belongs to you." And Donald looked down and saw Freeway at the other end of the leash. Donald filled up with tears.

"Oh my god! Freeway, is it really you?" Freeway slowly approached Donald who was holding his hand straight out for him to sniff. "Freeway, you're alive!" Freeway slowly approached him and sniffed his hand, and in moments he realized who Donald was, who was getting down on his knees with his tear-filled eyes and grabbed Freeway's head with both his hands and looked him directly in his eyes and could see his reflection in Freeway's glossy brown eyes. "It's really you! I have been searching for months for you and all this amazing stuff has happened to me and you wouldn't believe how much a better person I have become from being so mean to you that night after losing my job. There hasn't been a day gone by that I haven't thought about you and wondered where you are, if you were safe and taken care of. I prayed that you would eventually come back so I can make up to you for that awful night and we could start out over with a fresh start by me making it up to you. You were the one who I could come home to after having a bad day and be there greeting me with your toys and unconditional love, just sitting by me watching television and cuddling up at my feet at the end of the bed after our nightly walk and your doggy breath in my face waking me up to let me know it was time to get up for another new day. I am so sorry for treating you the way I did that night and it will never ever happen again. I'm just so happy to know you're safe and okay. Will you ever forgive me?" he asked.

With that, Freeway gave him a lick on his face and then another and another as he licked away Donald's tears that were streaming down his face. "I guess you forgive me then," he said, and then Freeway let out a loud bark. "I guess that means yes!" As Donald looked up at Officer Mario, he could see that he was touched by the reunion of the both of them because he was rubbing his eyes, and they were red. Was he touched by this tearful reunion? Or was it an allergy to all the dander in the air flying throughout the shelter today?

Mario then gave the leash he was holding to Donald and said, "Take care of him. He is a special dog. He has grown on me. If it's okay with you, I'd like to come by and visit him from time to time if that'd be okay."

Freeway looked up at Donald, and Donald could see that he wanted him to say yes. Who could turn down that sweet face? And with that, Donald said, "Of course you can. Anytime you like or if you happen to be in the area, just stop in." And with that, Freeway let out a few more loud barks as if to say YES!

Mario patted him on the head and said to him, "You be a good boy and I'll see you soon. Now I have to go take care of some unexpected business while I still have the nerve to do it."

"Before you leave, Officer Mario, could I ask you a question?"

"Sure, what is it?"

"How did you know he belonged to me and where did you find him?"

"Well, after putting a few pieces of a puzzle together of something I have been working on recently and then being here today, it all fell into place. See, I found Freeway just outside this shelter a while back, roaming out there on the access road. Then seeing you walk all those dogs through earlier on leashes and overhearing some of the volunteers saying numerous dogs were found in the restrooms abandoned. I have a clue that they came from here and had escaped. You might want to check out your files on those dogs you took to the boarding area and those abandoned. You will find out who they really belong to. I vaguely recall the dog on the expressway when I arrested you that night. But my gut instincts said it was a Border collie."

"Thanks for bringing Freeway home!" Donald said.

"I think he's been home all this time right here at this shelter and it took me today to see it," Mario said.

"Donald! Donald!" He looked over Officer Mario's shoulder to see who was calling him and noticed Ms. Kitty approaching them. "Excuse me for interrupting you," she said, "but we have another situation in the restroom with several more abandoned dogs I found."

"Bring them to the boarding area and bring Martin and Jessie along with you. I would like to have a meeting with the both of them afterward with you present. After the charity event we can all sit down, say around five o'clock. We'll meet in my office," Donald said.

"We'll be there."

"Oh, by the way, I'd like you to meet Freeway!"

"Freeway the dog you been searching for and did all this for?" she asked as she raised her arms to say the shelter.

"Yep, he's home and thanks to this officer right here." Donald introduced them both to each other.

"Nice! Really nice!" She shook his hands and would not let go.

"I must run. I have something I must take care of. Nice to have met you," Mario said.

"Likewise," she said. "Will we be seeing you around here at the shelter again?" she asked.

"I'm pretty sure of it," he said as he looked down at Freeway and turned to walk away.

"Ms. Kitty! Ms. Kitty!"

"Yes?" she said as she watched Officer Mario walk away, being in awe over him.

"I'll just put Freeway in my office and then we'll find Martin and Jessie and get those other dogs out of the restroom and get to the bottom of this."

"That will be just fine," she said. She had a smile on her face as she noticed Mario looking back at her as he walked away.

The moment Donald opened his office door, he found Sheba lying in his chair, and she looked up and saw Donald and then looked down to see Freeway on a leash. She flew out of his chair as fast as Freeway, practically knocking Donald down to come nose to nose to her as they started sniffing one another. "Oh! I guess you both know each other from the looks of it. Stay here. I will be back a little later," he said as he left the two of them together to be reunited, finally settling down side by side under Donald's desk.

Mario was determined to get to the truth, so he was on the prowl throughout the shelter, looking for LaVonda, when he came across Ms. Honeycutt heading toward the hot dog stand. He stopped her and asked, "Have you seen LaVonda?"

"I just passed her over by the grooming area where she was watching a poodle get her hair dyed pink."

"Why would someone dye a dog pink?" Mario asked her.

"I have no clue but it reminded me that it was time for a touch-up of my roots. I was intrigued with the color."

"You would," he said to her.

"I'd look hip."

"No you'd look more like a troll doll. "Go for it!" He walked away, mumbling, "Crazy old bitch."

"One hot dog please with the works," she placed her order with the vendor.

Mario found LaVonda who was talking to the groomer of the pink poodle and interrupted her by grabbing her by her arm and saying, "I think it's time that we head out as the charity event seems to be going well."

"Where is the dog?" she asked him.

"He's with a friend and going to be fine. I'll check on him later," he told her.

"Let me find Ms. Honeycutt and tell her we're leaving and that I'll see her later back at the Dixie Arms when she gets home for work."

"Oh, there she is," Mario said, looking around, "sitting over there on that bench eating a hot dog,"

"I see you found her okay," Ms. Honeycutt told Mario.

"Yeah, she was where you told me she was. We're getting ready to leave and I just wanted to let you know that and if you see the rest of the gang that you came with that I'm planning on barbequing tonight for everyone."

"Sounds good to me. I'll pass the information on when I see them. Now that you mentioned it, I haven't seen any of them since we got off the shuttle bus from work to come here." Mario just received another piece of the puzzle as he stood there listening to Ms. Honeycutt talking with her mouth full.

"See you later," LaVonda said as they walked away.

"Yeah, yeah, yeah," she replied as she was enjoying her hot dog. After putting down two hot dogs, she decided to look for the rest of the gang and came across Martin who drove them here and asked if he had seen anyone else from the shuttle bus, and he said not since he dropped them off.

"It's been crazy here today with the charity event and a bunch of dogs we found abandoned in the restrooms and our manager coming back from a trip from New Orleans waiting to have a meeting with me at five o'clock."

"Would you see if it'll be okay to take me back to Weston? Maybe they left and are playing a joke on me and left me behind. People can be so cruel."

"Come with me. I'll tell Ms. Kitty, my boss, that I'll be taking you back to Weston."

"Thank you! You are such a nice young man," she said as he blushed, and they searched for Ms. Kitty.

Mario and LaVonda were on the way back to the Dixie when he told her he had to stop by the sheriff's department to check on his schedule for the coming days that would be posted today and asked if she minded.

"No, it wouldn't be a problem. It'd be nice to see where you work anyways," she said. They said too few words en route to the station. They talked about the charity event, the people they spoke to, and how well it had turned out for the cause even though she was a bit disappointed in not being able to do any networking for the Dixie Arms.

"You will have plenty of time to network later and no doubt meet many interesting people in the future," he said as they pulled into the compound of the sheriff's office.

Mario, being the gentleman that he was, got out of the driver's seat and walked around to the passenger's side of LaVonda's car and opened it for her. As he escorted her into the station, he ran into his buddy, the one he had the conversation with this very morning about doing the right thing if he knew something was wrong and going on illegally with someone he knew. He introduced them and said to his fellow officer as he grabbed her by the arm, "This is LaVonda, the person we were talking about this morning."

"Nice to meet you," the other officer said.

"Now she is all yours," Mario said as he turned her over to him. "Sorry to do this but I took a sworn oath to protect and serve this community and knowing how fond I have become of you, it kills me to do this. But you're under arrest." He handcuffed her and read her the Miranda rights for committing fraud, tampering with governmental records through the Internet—in other words, hacking into the IRS database—and the list goes on as she stood there with tears running down her face.

"You did the right thing," his fellow officer said as he turned away to take LaVonda in for booking.

Mario walked out with tears in his eyes for he was fond of her; he trusted her as a friend and enjoyed spending time with her, but he had to do what he was sworn to do, to protect and serve.

Months had passed by, and LaVonda was sentenced to five to ten years in prison and did a lot of networking with fellow inmates at the women's correctional prison in Jacksonville.

Ms. Kitty started dating Mario as he spent a lot of time at the shelter visiting Freeway and Sheba who now has free roam of the shelter.

Martin and Jessie were able to keep their jobs but had to return all dogs that escaped from the shelter and get them back to their rightful owners at their expense with them paying for the airfares to get them home.

The Dixie Arms eventually closed its doors, but the charm of the old Victorian was now being renovated into a bed-and-breakfast, which was under construction, since it was in a prime location downtown. The new owner was none other than Donald who had plenty of finances who decided to venture out into the hospitality industry on top of keeping the shelter that was as successful as ever, and he needed a bigger place to live for Freeway and Sheba. He leased his town house over to Ms. Kitty who was looking for a bigger place to live.

The Everything Canine Inc. in Weston and all of its entire inventory was also facing some new changes. Most of the employees never returned back to work after the charity event, and it was operating only on a skeleton crew. Sales were down, and it needed to branch out to survive the wholesale business with more products other than items that only catered to canines and was now going to become a wholesaler for both canine and cattery.

A huge banner read out in front of the building with a new sign saying, "The Feline in Some of Us. Coming Soon," owned and operated by no other than Ms. Honeycutt who had come into a large windfall of cash while playing at the casinos over the past several months. She held on to her winning streak every time she played and was the only employee who returned back to work at the Everything Canine Inc. after the charity event. While trying to survive an eviction from the Dixie Arms while renovation was going on, she struck a deal with Donald to give him a cut of the profit from the Feline in Some of Us in exchange to be able to stay on at the bed-and-breakfast to keep a roof over her head. She now became a top dog. Who knew being crazy could be so fun!

BOOK SUMMARY

A single man from a small New England town decides to relocate South where he held a good job, and over a week's time, his life would change forever. He rescued a Border collie name Freeway, and a friendship began, until he lost his job. Then lady luck changed everything with the help of his assistant, Ms. Kitty, and Officer Mario who worked part-time at a homeless shelter owned by a Southern belle named LaVonda with a past that would come back to haunt her. And an environmental disaster from the everglades changes everyone as their worlds soon collide.

Edwards Brothers,Inc!
Thorofare, NJ 08086
20 September, 2010
BA2010263